Pirates

of

"The Senate"

George H. Whatley

I dedicate this book to all those that have "stood and were counted" to what has seemed to be impossible odds at that moment in time in their lives and won.

For Evil to exist in this world, all it takes is for good men and women to do nothing.

With thanks to Spencer Whatley for his ideas for the cover of this book.

Books: - by the same author

"SAY NO"	
"The Big Boys don't win all the time"	1st in the series
"A code to live or die by"	2nd in the series
"The Pirate of the *Senate*"	3rd in the series

The devastating scenario's portrayed in these books have happened or could easily happen in today's society, the frightening part is the Establishment are aware of it.

The author has become a successful seasoned environmental campaigner, helped lead 4 successful environmental fights against impossible odds, stopping two Oil Refineries, a Bio-Diesel plant, and a Liquid Natural Gas plant from being built within his community.

He has given evidence at 7 Public Inquiries, 2 Scrutiny Panels, and has represented his community in a great number of meetings with the Establishment, including a Prime Minister, a number of Government Ministers, Members of Parliament, the Health and Safety Executive, County and local officials, and the Emergency services.

The Canadian Ambassador, Thomas Waites, was a well known political figure. He rose to prominence from obscurity amid the global oil crisis and seemed to have the backing of new energy and mineral companies and the power they wield.

The finding of new deposits in the Canadian wilderness became an environmental battleground, it was between the local Environmentalists and the Energy Companies.

The Environmentalists wanted the area to stay as natural as it was, but, if in the National economic interest, the Canadian Government decided it was going to be developed, then the Environmental Group wanted to be consulted how the area was developed with ecology in mind, also because they wanted the best way to protect the Environment from unscrupulous developers who would strip it bare.

The new energy companies only wanted the cheapest way to extract the oil and minerals to maximise their profit, no matter what the cost to the local environment, or the community, with false promises of jobs that did not exist, and false statements that they would use the safest methods and there would be no harm to the wildlife, but they were cutting corners and bending the regulations to suit themselves. They were using their political standing with the Canadian Government to open new sites for exploration and development.

The battlegrounds were drawn between the developers on one side and the Environmentalists on the other side and big money was talking and it seemed no one was listening to the environmentalists.

When the local people complained to the authorities, they were faced with a wall of excuses and sloping shoulder attitudes, of it's not me, it's him over there, they seemed to be getting nowhere, they were bogged down in the three-ringed circuses of bureaucracy.

The suspicion that corruption was rife was hard to prove, but there seemed an underlining trend that pointed to big business being involved and was manipulating the Authority.

At the Centre of this Authority was Ambassador Thomas Waites who was also linked to a group that owned a number of gambling nightclubs which on the surface seemed very well and honestly run. But had a dark past.

The men employed by Waites were encouraged to use his gambling houses that had a number of girls employed to entertain the men.

Thomas Waites was on the surface, a man that seemed to be a well-known benefactor and was a collector of 2nd World War trophies and militaria. He had quite a vast collection, which he displayed at his museum in Toronto, Canada.

The underlying factors were that Waites was involved, not only as a lynch-pin with Energy Barons by opening doors for them. He also managed to help get licences for experimental fracking to be carried out in a conservation area.

The granting of licences that allowed Experimental Fracking within a conservation area was a major bone of contention between the Environmentalists and the Oil Barons.

Secretly in the background, Waites was instrumental in getting the sites for fracking opened up for drilling.

At his gambling clubs, Waites was also instrumental in getting under-aged girls to escort the winners at the tables back to their rooms where they were entertained.

It was hard trying to prove there was human trafficking, for as soon as there was too much interest shown in his gambling clubs by the establishment, the young girls disappeared.

The fact that the girls were later found as hostesses in nightclubs across America was suspicious.

How they had got across the American border with what seemed genuine passports was also a mystery.

Laurence Jones was married with two children. He was a high-ranking officer of The Royal Canadian Mounted Police (R.C.M.P.) He had asked his great friend Paul to lunch who was also married but with no children yet but they were hopeful.

Paul was in the Canadian Secret Intelligence Service (C.S.I.S.). Laurence had asked him to check up on Thomas Waites and see what he could find, as there seemed to be a lot more going on in the background than seemed to be going on at the surface.

Laurence also mentioned to Paul that he had heard the F.B.I. were interested in Waites as well.

Laurence mentioned to Paul he had contacts in the F.B.I. These contacts were getting concerned about Ambassador Waites and what seemed on the surface, of him being involved in people trafficking and other unsavoury business issues.

The F.B.I. was also concerned about opening the diplomatic can of worms too soon without some sort of concrete proof.

At the dinner with Paul, which was at the men's club that Laurence used for business, they also met there on a regular basis, sometimes the cases they were involved in overlapped, plus it was a good way both friends could catch up with each other and find out how each other's family was getting on. Paul let Laurence know his wife was now pregnant with their first child which was due in the spring.

Laurence was so pleased for his friend. He wanted to set up a get together with the wives and celebrate.

In the conversation, Thomas Waites' name kept cropping up, when mysterious incidents happened lately, that all seemed either loosely connected or directly connected with Thomas Waites' nightclub or his museum.

Laurence said, “I recently heard a friend of my wife was worried over her man. She had not heard from him since he went for a well-paid job. Apparently, he was going to be working for Waites, what was strange he apparently got the job, but a highly skilled Submarine engineer working in a museum seemed odd but if you need work anything you do is just to tide you over.”

“Well, he phoned his wife from somewhere upcountry, saying it was the first opportunity he had of letting her know he got the job, telling her about the job, she thought he said he was working on an old World War 2 Submarine when the phone call was cut suddenly short and she hasn’t heard from him since.

Also, there has been recently a number of sailors gravitating towards Waites’ gambling establishments. It was noted that the sailors were all submariners.

Those men that did not get a Job went away with large winnings from the tables, but they were later found dead, either by what seemed accidents, or they just disappeared under suspicious circumstances.

Those that Thomas Waites employed, soon went to his other establishment, that the authorities thought was further up the coast, but they were unaware exactly where it was and what went on there.”

What Paul, of the Canadian Secret Intelligence Service (C.S.I.S.) did not know was, Thomas Waites, in secret location had much larger pieces of working German Armament, such as Tanks, half-tracks, grenades and guns, and that was where he illegally kept and held this secret collection. This collection also included a now fully armed and refurbished working German U-boat.

Laurence's friend Paul was getting very suspicious of Thomas Waites' activities as he was investigating the Museum, as a lot of the activities did not seem right. Either way there seemed to be a lot of smuggling into Canada, of either drug or armaments, even both.

Whilst undercover Paul was entertaining one of Thomas Waites' girls in Waites' nightclub. He overheard a conversation that mentioned a secret heavily armed Submarine pen in a remote location further up the coast, by one of the drunk sailors, that was when he asked the girl about the secret Submarine pen and where it was.

The girl suddenly became very frightened.

"I know nothing about a secret Submarine pen", she said, "and don't ask me again."

Paul did not press it. The girl had a phone call and said she had to leave, and they parted company. Paul went back to the Hotel.

In the morning the girl was found dead by some of Laurence's Men. When they were called to the girl's apartment, apparently, she had fallen in her bathroom and hit her head and died instantly.

Paul was suspicious it was not an accident, but he could not prove it.

He phoned Laurence to inform him of his plans to search for this secret Submarine pen if it existed. If it did, to try and find out what was the mystery behind it all.

As to whether there was any link between it and the number of unexplained deaths that seem to be occurring lately, also whether Thomas Waites was involved in any way with human trafficking.

As Paul held a pilot's licence, the Agent hired a small, light aircraft to search remote inlets for signs of any illegal activities.

At the small airport, he was told it was standard safety procedure to log the area he was flying over in case of bad weather or accident, so they had an idea where to search.

A member of the flight club notified Thomas Waites of the flight and told him the area the flight would be covering, and that it was a C.S.I.S. Agent who was taking that flight.

In an inlet off Nova Scotia, Thomas Waites had moored in a heavily guarded secret submarine pen, a refurbished Submarine, it was a working World War 2 U-boat.

It had taken him years to slowly acquire the equipment to refurbish the Sub, to bring it back to a fully working U Boat, including a full arsenal of working torpedos.

The Ambassador had furbished the Submarine slowly, so as not to raise any suspicions with the authorities as to the real reason for having a private fully operational Submarine.

Getting the right engineers to build and refurbish his U boat, plus the right sailors and the training of the crew for the operation required total secrecy.

Whilst it was done in the total secrecy, there was a time limit for them to be operationally ready, and it was vital there was no room for a delay for what was planned.

This was just a small, but a very important part of a puzzle of a much larger plan, that would have the possibility of bringing America to its knees.

The U-boat had been out at sea and was just returning from her last set of sea trials and was entering the Submarine Pen area when Paul flew over the area.

Paul spotted a U-boat heading for what looked like a Submarine pen. He was puzzled as he knew there were no naval operations anywhere near here. He swung the light aircraft round and flew a lot lower to have a much closer look.

He was flying at treetop level and was approaching the area. He saw the activity and what he thought was a World War 2 Submarine. He was puzzled as to why a World War 2 Submarine was entering this inlet and was heading to what looked like a well-camouflaged underground submarine pen cut out into the hillside.

He called Laurence who picked up instantly, he said "Laurence, its Paul, we were right!", that's all he heard as the line went dead.

It was then that an anti-aircraft missile hit him, he had no time to radio his position, the light aircraft hit the ground hard and disintegrated over a large area, killing the agent and Laurence's friend Paul outright.

On the ground, Thomas Waites was very angry. "Who fired that missile?" he said, "it will expose everything we are doing!"

"It was one of our security people", Captain von Dutch said, "They were under orders to not let anyone know we are here let alone what we are doing."

"Bring that man here now", Thomas Waites ordered.

The hapless man was brought before him, and he was shaking with fear, the Captain said, "do you realise your stupidity could wreck years of planning? We are supposed to be hiding away here, not drawing attention to ourselves by bringing down that light aircraft. What if that pilot got a radio message off before you hit him? It would bring the R.C.M.P. down on us like a ton of bricks. I will have to go back to the Museum immediately to cover our tracks and find out if there are any investigations going on."

"Because of you", Captain von Dutch said to the hapless man, "we will have to launch early and lay off the coastline until the whole plan is ready, there is only one cure for stupidity", he pulled out a German Luger pistol and shot the man in the head, His body slumped on the floor, "get this rubbish out of my sight," he said to some operatives close by who took the body out and threw it into the inlet to let the tide take it out to sea.

"Operation clear-up, to be implemented with immediate effect", Waites said as he left for the Museum.

They swung into action, a vast plan that changed the area back into the little inlet it was and disguise there was ever a submarine pen and a working submarine there.

The Submarine and its crew were made ready with no delay, it was to be launched early and to lay-off the coast unseen until it was required to carry out its deadly mission, the mission was to be a vital link in the puzzle that was going to come together with deadly accuracy.

On the high seas, the different elements in the puzzle would be slotted together, there would be a weaving of a web of lies, of politics and deceit, that would be felt across many countries, all this would be exposed on the high seas in the notorious area of the Atlantic known as the Graveyard of Ships.

The Submarine was going to play a key part of this major operation that was going to be a hazardous nightmare, it will require split-second timing to pull it off, and Captain von Dutch was the Captain of the U-Boat and was the man who would play this vital part in the plans of the deadly global organisation.

All crew members had to sign up and be members of this deadly global organisation. Once in, there was no way out, except by elimination, you either died for the organisation doing what it wanted you to do, or you died if you betrayed the organisation.

The Organisation was called, "The *Senate*".

After his interrupted phone call from Paul, Laurence waited in vain to hear back from Paul, so he traced his movements which took him to a light aircraft hangar where the light aircraft was hired from.

After strongly questioning the ground staff, all he could go by was a flight plan that Paul had set out, it pointed to the area that he was suspicious about, and he knew that area was owned by Thomas Waites.

Laurence knew that Paul's flight was overdue, and by now would have run out of fuel, he feared the worse had happened to his friend, and the baby he so desperately wanted would grow up without a father.

He ordered a helicopter to reconnoitre the area to see if anything could be found of his friend.

The report came back, that near an inlet on the coast, some wreckage of a light aircraft could be seen, how that wreckage came to be where it was, would turn out to be a subject of an official investigation, but it was in an area that would be hard to get to, and it would take a little time to arrange.

Laurence made an appointment to see Thomas Waites to ask him if he knew anything about the crashing of a light aircraft near the site he owned.

Thomas Waites was very defensive and said, “It was a private area and no aircraft was allowed in that area but I will get my people to take a look, but it could take some time.”

Laurence felt he was being given the run-around and was very suspicious of Waites, but he could not prove anything against him or that he was involved.

Laurence warned Waites, saying “If anything has happened to my friend and I find you were involved in any way.”

“Are you threatening me?”, Waites said.

Then added, “let me remind you, I am a Canadian Ambassador”, Waites said, “and above your jurisdiction.”

Laurence said, “I am the Royal Canadian Mounted Police, and we have a reputation of always getting our man, no matter who they are or how powerful they are.”

Waites said, “you can’t touch me.”

Laurence replied, “I will find who is responsible for the death of my friend, and I will hunt them to extinction, I will make it a personal vendetta, do I make myself clear?”

Laurence gave Waites a dead look and said, "if you are involved your days are numbered, and I am counting your numbers down, and I will put a way for life who ever it is, no matter how powerful they think they are, is that clear enough for you?"

Laurence turned away and went back to his office. He knew Waites was up to something but he could not prove what it was, he was going to get every available man he had, to curry comb anything involving Waites.

He knew that Waites had very powerful friends, but he felt very strongly that Waites was involved in killing his friend, so that would not stop him, He would get his man no matter what the cost.

It was at 10 Downing Street London, in the Cabinet Office Briefing Room "A (COBRA) meeting was held, the main item on the agenda was the latest report of what was referred to as the "night of the political long knives" when known and suspected members of the deadly group "The *Senate*" had been eliminated or sacked from the political position they held, and the new political Cabinet reshuffled.

Also on the agenda was an item to discuss what to do about the foreign policy with regards to the actions of "The *Senate*" as it looked like there was a powerful organisation at work that was undermining the political balance globally.

It was recently exposed that a highly organized globally energy-based organisation that had called itself "The *Senate*" had shown itself and come to the forefront of the political scene. It was proved to be responsible for an attempted coup that nearly brought the country to its knees during the "Estuary Crisis".

The "Estuary Crisis" was exposed when an industrial accident of biblical proportions that devastated the Estuary and the surrounding area, was at the local Methane Terminal during a ship-to-shore operation. A major spill of Liquid Natural Gas had happened, in doing so the Domino Effect of this conflagration was so great, it was said to have put the area back into the dark ages, the loss of life was numbered in thousands.

A local Environmentalist called Jeff Baker was accused by Sir William Waites (the owner of this and other global energy sites) of being the terrorist leader who instigated a terrorist attack that caused the explosion.

Jeff Baker and a few survivors who had lived in the Estuary area exposed the plot by "The *Senate*" to overthrow the government and replace it with a Dictatorship. Sir William Waites was to be at its head.

Jeff found the evidence he needed to not only prove his innocence but also the plot by "The *Senate*" to create the coup and make the country into a dictatorship.

In the ruins of the aftermath of the deadly explosion, Jeff was hunted by Wilson, who was Sir William's head of security. Wilson was a dangerous killer. It was he and his henchmen, who hunted Jeff across the devastated ruined area known as "The Estuary."

Sir William was arrested but died much later in a secure unit in prison just before he could be taken to a long-awaited trial. There was still an ongoing internal investigation into how Sir William died, and who killed him.

At the Press Conference held a little while after the incident, Sir William's head of security "Wilson" had attacked and wounded Jeff Baker in his attempt to kill Jeff for exposing the plot.

Wilson had nearly succeeded, but John Stone, the Prime Minister's bodyguard, shot Wilson dead during this incident, which was also in front of the world's press.

The concern of "The *Senate*'s" infiltration into the Whitehall departments was the subject of the meeting.

John Stone was outside meeting room "A", waiting patiently for instructions from the Prime Minister.

The COBRA meeting was with the Prime Minister and some other Cabinet Ministers. As the meeting finished and they were going out of the door, John overheard one of the Ministers talking to the P.M. about the Estuary Incident.

"A bit fortunate that Wilson exposed himself when he did at that Press Conference, otherwise you could have been diving out of his way for years to come, knowing how good a reputation that man had for being a professional killer. It was a good job your man here was better", he said tapping John on the shoulder, then the Cabinet Minister left the meeting.

When all the other Cabinet Ministers had gone, John started mulling these comments over in his mind and a few things did not add up. So he confronted the P.M., "how come Wilson knew of and was prepared for that press conference in advance? Wilson couldn't have got a camera gun at that short notice without alarm bells ringing somewhere?"

It was then the realization hit him like a sledgehammer, he turned to the P.M. and said, "you were the one to call that press conference, and you chose the venue." With unbelievable comprehension dawning inside his head, John said, "it was you that let Wilson know about that press conference, so you could bring him out of hiding, hoping I would kill him in a shoot out."

"Well, you did, didn't you?" The P.M. replied.

"What would have happened if I had missed?" John said, astounded. "And what about the other papers that were found by Jeff Baker in Councillor Randle's safe?"

"Well, instead of being beholden to Jeff Baker", the P.M. added, "I would have been beholden to Wilson".

The P.M. continued, "Do you know how they used to trap and kill tigers in India years ago?"

"What's that got to do with the situation?" John asked. Puzzled at the turn of the conversation.

'Well", said the P.M. "when they trap tigers, they leave a goat tethered to a tree and lie in wait for the tiger to attack the goat and then they kill the tiger if they can." Then he added, "sometimes the tiger wins and gets the goat, and sometimes he doesn't and gets shot dead."

"How could you do something like that?" John asked the P.M. disgusted.

"Wilson forgot the basic rules in your profession," the P.M. stated, "don't get emotionally involved with your target, so I counted on Wilson's hate of Jeff Baker to override his professionalism and go for the kill with such a passion that he would expose himself enough so you could take him down".

"What about Jeff and the others? Did they know you had set them up?" John asked.

"They don't have to know. It would spoil their sense of adventure in the life of politics", the P.M. replied.

The Prime Minister then changed the subject and said, "I understand from my sources Jeff is planning to go on a cruise. I am giving you a Prime Minister's commission, where you will only answer directly to me. I want you to try to be on the same cruise with your wife Rose, make it look as though it's a coincidence, you can even tell him you are there as his personal bodyguard, also he trusts you, so whilst you're with him try to find out the where-a-bouts of any more papers from Councillor Randle's safe that Jeff might have found and squirrelled away."

John walked away disgusted and said, "Thank Christ, I am not a politician!"

Jeff Baker had decided to make it up to his wife Karen for all the time he had spent away from home and in the office recently. He had been appointed head of an independent department to implement a "Safe Siting Policy" for "Top Tier" C.O.M.A.H. sites.

Jeff would take her on the holiday he had said she would always have and deserved. They would go on an extended luxury cruise so they could spend some quality time together now that he had got his Department in some semblance of order and running as he wanted it.

Jeff was big built, he stood just over 6-foot-tall, very stubborn, he had very strong principles, Karen had always said he would die by his principles, as he believed with every fibre of his being, that people came before profit or politics. He had a code of ethics he would live or die by, he did not expect others to have his code of ethics, he accepted people for what they were, all he asked was for those same people to accept that his word was his bond, and cast in granite, and he had the code that he would live or die by.

Karen, Jeff's wife was a Brunette very shapely she was about 5'6, she loved Jeff for what he was, and the principles he stood for.

Jeff had seen Cyril and Jen recently, they were a couple he had met and he and his wife had grown very fond of during the incident in the Estuary. Cyril was a wirily built man and he was very intelligent, he was also one of the best jewellery thieves Jeff had known. Jen was a nicely proportioned lady who did not suffer fools lightly. Jen and Cyril had settled down to recently married life and were very happy.

At the same time, Jeff had met up with Derek and Sandra who also recently came back from their extended honeymoon.

Sandra was a slightly built brunette who had been a military nurse and had nursed Derek through his injuries which he also sustained during the same Estuary incident.

Derek was a mild-mannered, gentle giant of a man, big built and very powerful. Sandra had insisted Derek healed from his injuries received during the "Estuary" incident before he took on anything else.

The double wedding of Jen and Cyril and Sandra and Derek was a wonderful occasion.

Jeff gave both brides away, and Karen was the matron of honour.

With all the publicity created from the Estuary incident, Cyril said he was so well known now he would have to give up being a tea leaf. Jen said she could think of another thing he could do with a saucy look in her eye.

Jeff had suggested that if he was bored doing nothing, he could consider specialising in security of buildings such as galleries or museums as he thought it took a thief to catch a thief and with his knowledge, he would be the ideal candidate to prevent theft.

He mentioned the cruise to Cyril and Jen and asked them if they wanted to join them as Karen and Jen got on like a house on fire plus it would be a way of getting some peace away from the media for a while.

"I have never been on a posh holiday," Jen said, "I'd be out of place."

"Don't be silly," Karen said, "you can hold your head up with the rest of them, anyway most of the people that go on cruises have a Champagne lifestyle but lemonade money, which does not apply to you two.

It would be nice to be posh every night and dress for dinner", Jen said then added, "I'd need a new wardrobe", looking at Cyril.

Cyril melted and said, "anything for you" and smiled.

"Do you mean it?" Jen said excitedly, then hugged him.

"I suppose we better do some shopping" Karen said looking at Jen.

"Don't forget Cyril will want a dress suit and a tuxedo for formal nights", she added.

"I'm not dressing up in a penguin suit," Cyril said.

"How about just for me," Jen said looking at him lovingly then added, "I am sure you will look very handsome and I'll make it up to you!" She said saucily.

"Oh alright! I can't refuse you anything", he said smiling.

"It was lovely to see them together" Karen had said, "it made her heart soar."

"Is John married, or does he have a lady in his life?" Jen asked, "I've never heard him mention anyone."

Jeff had also met John during the Estuary incident, he was a personal agent to the Prime Minister.

Jeff said, "I believe he has someone, but he keeps to himself, he said that his latest orders were to keep me safe, are from the Prime Minister, but I always feel there is always something else on the agenda, but I can't put my finger on it."

"Meanwhile", Jeff said to Cyril, "how about contacting Michael?"

"I know Michael is visiting his cousin in America who I believe is someone quite high up in the American naval intelligence", Cyril said. Michael was a retired professional boxer, and he was slightly built but very fast he had been a friend of Jen's for years, Jeff met him and got to like the man a lot during the "Estuary" incident.

It was then that Cyril mentioned, "I believe he's also going to see his relatives in Canada, they are very well-to-do and pretty high up in the Canadian Mounted Police

I believe", then he added, "I think Michael is a bit of a dark horse, I did not know he knew so many influential people, by the way, he did leave me a contact number in case of emergency."

"Do you want me to ask Derek and Sandra", Cyril said, "I know he is away at the moment on holiday he has been at a loose end and bored with nothing constructive to do, he said he wanted to get back into wrestling but with the injuries he got and he really is too old to put in all the training required, mind you, I would not tell him that to his face!"

"With all his experience he had in the ring I would have thought he would set up a wrestling school for youngsters", Jeff said;

"Do you know he could have been a contender for the Olympics if it hadn't been for that bad fall he took?" Cyril said, "and I reckon he could have been a medal winner."

"He never said, what a dark horse, you would not believe it of such a big man" Jeff added.

"So, it could be four couples for the cruise?" Jen said looking expectantly at Karen then added "with lots of clothes shopping beforehand that's going to be wonderful, when do we start going to the shops? I feel like I could do with some retail therapy."

Both Jen and Karen went into a huddle discussing which stores they were going to visit and what days they were going together to shop.

"When are we going to decide where we are going on this cruise?" Jen asked, "as that determines what clothes we need to get."

“Whenever you want”, Jeff added “all we have to decide is which cruise and where we want to go to, we had better get together and decide, so if you come to us this Sunday for dinner, we can discuss it then, I will pull some strings and get my office to book 4 adjoining cabins now, also I will be able to tie up all loose end in 3 months, let’s plan it for then, I’ve always wanted to go round the world if that’s alright with everyone we can start with America and pick up Michael on the way, in the meanwhile we can get some brochures and see what’s out there.

“Oh! No! What a terrible pun”, Jen said, “I hope we don’t have to put up with them on this cruise.”

“What?” said Jeff, “what do you mean, what terrible pun?”

“Look he doesn’t even know he’s doing it, how do you put up with him?” Jen said to Karen.

“With great difficulty” she retorted then they both laughed as they shared their excitement about the shopping they were going to be doing together.

“What pun?” Jeff said, confused.

“Going on a cruise and see what’s out there?” Jen said, “see as in looking, or sea as in sailing?”

They all laughed.

“You have spent too long in business meetings, you are losing your sense of humour the best cure for that is to go on a long cruise with friends and have a good time.” Cyril said, “you need to recharge your batteries.”

When Michael had landed in New York, he was met by his cousin Valerie at the airport, she insisted that he stayed with her at her apartment whilst he was visiting.

She had time owing to her and had decided to escort him around when he wanted to see the sites. Valerie had always had a very soft spot for Michael and secretly hoped they could be an item, but distance and the work she loved, always seemed to get in the way.

The three bedrooms apartment was in a gated community with a security guard at the door and its own parking place for the residents. The rooms were quite large, with a lounge, a kitchen and an office area. It was ideal for holding cocktail parties, not that Valerie was in the habit of entertaining very often.

Valerie liked her creature comforts when she relaxed, but quite often her job in Naval Intelligence kept her very busy, and sometimes she had to work away.

She had worked her way up the promotion ladder and was a very respected member of American Naval Intelligence. She was head of her section that dealt with the safety of the Atlantic border and what happened within the Atlantic Territorial Waters, she worked very closely with the Immigration Department and the F.B.I.

Valerie was very stunning and had always had a lot of admirers, but she had a soft spot for cousin Michael, technically, they were third cousins, and she had taken time out to be with him even though she was on call at all times.

When Michael had settled into one of the spare rooms, they were having a coffee together in the lounge, Valerie wanted to catch up on all that Michael had been doing.

But firstly, Michael wanted to know what Valerie had been doing since they last met, she told him as much as she dared as a lot of what she did was hush-hush, but that was a side of her job she liked.

She asked Michael what had been going on in his life, such as was there anyone else in his life.

He said, "No, to be honest, even after we got notoriety after the Estuary Incident, I got a lot of offers, but I could not get you out of my mind, and the real reason I am on this trip, is to find out if there is still that spark between us, that we had before."

Michael changed the subject quickly before she could reply, he told her about his involvement in the Estuary Incident, and all about "The *Senate*" and how it had nearly brought the English political system to its knees, plus the massive loss of life, how they tried to blame it onto terrorism, just to cover-up their own incompetence, the power struggle, the exposer of the Government ministers involved, plus Sir William Waites, he spoke of how they were hunted by Wilson and his henchmen throughout the Estuary.

Valerie was extremely interested to hear about Jeff, Cyril and Jen, Derek, and John, and their involvement, she added, "when their cruise ship calls in here, we can meet them and have lunch together, I would like to meet them, you seemed to have become brothers in arms during the Estuary incident, I can clear it with my people."

Michael said, "won't that be a problem?"

She laughed, she had a twinkle in her lovely blue eyes, as she laughed, Michael felt her face lit the room up, "not for me," she added, "you don't know the strings I can pull, there are a lot of people in high places that owe me a few favors."

Michael was impressed, then said, "I left Cyril my Mobil number for emergencies, I have his number so I can call him in a few days' time and set it up, once you have had a word with your people."

"In the meanwhile", he said saucily, "you can show me all the sites you want me to see."

Her retort was, with a twinkle in her eye. "You might not want to see all I can show you."

He replied just as saucily, "I would love to see everything, but I am sure it won't be as beautiful as you are, as I don't think you realize how stunning you are, cousin", as he looked hopefully into her blue eyes.

It had been quite a long time since Valerie had entertained a man she was very fond of, and she wondered how much she could safely flirt with Michael, and if he felt the same way about her as she did about him, he seemed to respond to her jokes and her sense of humour, the friendly banter they had with one another was infectious, and they were getting on together like a house on fire.

She felt that old flame being rekindled, a flame that time and distance had taken away, she also could see he felt the same way about her, by the way, he looked adoringly at her and wanted to say so, but she felt his English reserve was holding him back.

Michael was smitten like a dumbstruck schoolboy with Valerie and loved every moment they were together, but he was frightened to make the first move in case he read the signs wrong and it spoilt the special bond they had with one another.

The step between very close friends and lovers is a big step, but a narrow one and there would be no going back to being friends again, once that step had been taken, he was frightened of losing the close friendship they had, for Michael it was like treading on eggshells, wanting desperately to sweep her into his arms, hugging her, and gently kissing her until she was his forever, and the gut-wrenching rejection he might get if he overplayed his hand, if he read the signs wrong.

Just as it did every fortnight during the previous two years the "NATGAS 2" a Giant 200,000 tonnes Gas ship gently slipped its moorings at the port of Rabat in Morocco it was fully loaded with 180,000 cubic meter cargo of Liquid Natural Gas (LNG) stored in its 6 giant double skinned tanks, its departure was assisted by Tugs and led safely out of the port by an experienced Pilot on board.

As the "NATGAS 2" cleared the harbour and got underway the pilot transferred to the pilot boat and watched as she cleared the port, her gargantuan size dominated the evening skyline with its 6 giant double skin sphere-shaped storage tanks, another leviathan of the sea had set sail with a valuable but deadly cargo of cryogenically cold liquid natural gas, the cargo was intended for sale to various industries, power plants and domestic fuel.

The cargo of LNG the "NATGAS 2" carried was sometimes sold on the open stock market whilst ships were in transit, sometimes even the gas ship itself change ownership before it reached its destination, but that was the nature of the energy world and its markets.

Some energy companies were a law unto themselves. They were so powerful that they controlled whole countries and the owners and top directors were powerful enough to be above the law and were able to have a major influence on world governments as they controlled the world's markets in energy and the distribution of oil and gas.

For Captain Don Williams, this was going to be his last trip for a while as he wanted to have some time at home with his wife and his daughter before his daughter went to university.

He had become so familiar with this particular voyage and was looking forward to a break. He was of course under no illusion as to the hazardous cargo contained in his vessel, he did not have any concerns regarding his crew, it was nothing unusual for gas ships to be crewed by seamen from many different nationalities.

Captain Williams had sailed with Abdul as his first mate on his last three trips and he had come to value and rely on Abdul's experience as a seaman, even though he felt Abdul had a much darker side to his life.

But he knew better than most Captains it did not pay to delve too deeply into another sailor's life, as they all had a reason to be where they were and doing this job.

Under cover of darkness at the port of Agadir in southern Morocco a very large powerful ocean-going luxury speedboat called "Fast Lady" was stolen.

An original crew member had helped disarm the tracking device on-board the "Fast Lady", he was handsomely rewarded for his treachery to his employer by Parvis, the leader of the Hijackers.

The crew member that helped Parvis came from the same village as he did and they were close friends.

He had notified Parvis, the leader of the hijackers when the crew would be on shore leave, also that she was being refueled with a full tank of fuel, ready for a scheduled sea voyage.

Parvis and his band of terrorists were carrying out the first phase of their intricate plan when they loaded up the "Fast Lady" with the specialist equipment and armament they had in their truck, they had trained for almost a year for this operation.

For Parvis and his crew of terrorists, it was going to be payback time in a big way, and he was looking forward to being able to strike back at the heart of the infidels.

The very powerful beauty of the sea, the "Fast Lady" was headed fast out into the Atlantic Ocean with a crew of heavily armed and determined terrorists under the leadership of Parvis, who was wanted in many countries.

Parvis and his crew of handpicked men checked over the equipment they had loaded on board the "Fast Lady". It was an arsenal of special hand-held rocket launchers, guns, mortars, explosives, detonators and fuses. They also put on board specialist climbing equipment for the hand-held rocket launchers.

Parvis was a well-known terrorist and was wanted for many acts of terrorism, also for running terrorist cells. He was also wanted for terrorist bombings in nine countries. Over the last few months, he and his fellow terrorists had enhanced their evil skills at the training camps in the foothills of Afghanistan.

The team of terrorists that Parvis led had also learned their latest skills from the Somalia pirates off the Horn of Africa, they would need those skills they learned as the crew prepared their weapons for the assault they were going to carry out. They spoke of their determination to strike at the heart of the west once and for all, as they headed towards their goal to strike nightmare of terror in the western world.

After two days at sea the "NATGAS 2" was a hundred miles North West off the Islands of Madeira it was there that under the cover of darkness of the early hours of the morning the hijacked "Fast Lady" approached the stern of the leviathan of the sea and was totally unseen by the crew of the "NATGAS 2".

As the early morning twilight dawned, the "Fast Lady" was maneuvered very close to the stern of the Liquid Natural Gas Tanker unseen where she sat under the Lee of "NATGAS2" bouncing around in the wash of the giant tanker with its cargo of Liquid Natural Gas. It was then Parvis ordered four of is men to board the gas tanker they had been trained to do by the Somalia Pirates.

The four men fired 2 grappling hooks with specially adapted lines on them out of hand-held rocket launchers situated at the bow of the "Fast Lady." The rockets they fired went up and over the railings on the lowest deck as they pulled on the lines to make the grappling hooks grip, the wire lines opened up to make a wire ladder.

Two of the men lifted themselves gently off the speedboat and swung out gripping onto the wire ladders, then they scrambled up the ladders just above the boiling wash of the giant tanker and tried to board the ship via the stern.

As one of the men was halfway up the ladder he slipped and fell and disappeared into the boiling sea, the hook on the other man's ladder slipped from its anchor point, the man was left flaying around in the air as the ladder tangled around him as he fell away from them and was dropped to certain death into the wash of the leviathan of the sea and both men were seen no more.

The rest of the pirates aboard the "Fast Lady" looked on in horror, Parvis said angrily, "now we have fewer men to work with", and then ordered another three men take their place.

Parvis fired another two rocket launchers with grappling hooks over the stern rail and set another two ladders in a place overlooking the stern of the gas tanker making three ladders in all bouncing in the boiling cauldron of deadly foam of the stern of the giant tanker.

Parvis ordered three more men to board the vessel, the man allocated to the third ladder said, "man, you have ice in your veins, he was your friend", Parvis gave the man an evil look and said, "be careful you don't join him", Parvis added threateningly, "now move!"

All three men knew the evil reputation Parvis had. They also knew he would kill them without compunction, they also knew if they slipped off the wire ladders like their comrades they would fall to certain death in the tumbling cauldron of foam, but this is what they had trained for with the Somalia Pirates off the horn of Africa for months.

So with trepidation, they swung out one at a time swinging into the boiling wash of the giant tanker "NATGAS2" and climbed slowly up the wire ladders out of the cauldron of foam from the wash of the ship, like emerging dragonflies.

They climbed up to the lower deck where they left the ladders dangling from the lower deck with the end of the ladders bouncing around in the wash of the leviathan of the sea.

All three slipped safely over the railing onto the lower deck, one of the men said, "you got to give it to those Somali Pirates they do that using bamboo poles", then all three rushed quietly to get to the radio room to stop the alarm being sounded.

The "Fast Lady" swung around and stood off at the lee side of the giant tanker and waited for full daylight whilst the three heavily armed pirates that had boarded the tanker made their way first to the radio room to stop any alarm being raised.

Once they secured the radio room, they left one pirate there whilst the other two pirates firstly lowered the gangway ladders at the side of the giant tanker to where the "Fast Lady" was bouncing around in the wash of the bow wave caused by the Tanker ploughing through the waves.

The two pirates then stormed their way to the engine room where they took it over by gunpoint, they left one pirate there then the other pirate made his way to the bridge where he burst in at gunpoint taking the bridge by surprise as well.

Abdul the first mate was at the wheel, he was pushed to one side as the terrorist took over control of the ship at gunpoint.

"Prepare to be boarded", the pirate said to Abdul, "or be blown out of the water."

"With this cargo, you will die as well," Abdul said.

"Then we will all see Allah together," the pirate said, with a mad look in his eyes, then added "there is a speedboat out there with hand-held missiles leveled at this ship ready to blow us all to kingdom come, it is up to you if you are ready to meet your maker now", then the pirate screamed fanatically, "stop this ship now, or you all die."

With the pirate pointing the gun threateningly at Abdul and screaming stop this ship now, Abdul took over the wheel and slowed the leviathan of the sea down and was forced to heave to as the powerful speedboat "Fast Lady" came alongside and men aboard rushed up the gangway ladder and boarded the "NATGAS 2."

Captain Don Williams had been in his cabin asleep when the high-jack took place, so Abdul was on the bridge when the armed pirate that had burst into the bridge and was holding the bridge crew at gunpoint, one pirate was left on board the "Fast Lady" Parvis and the other pirates boarded the tanker then made their way to the bridge.

The tension on the bridge could be cut with a knife as Parvis entered the bridge welcome aboard. Abdul said sarcastically to Parvis as he greeted the leader of the pirates,

"That was like taking candy from a baby", Parvis said to Abdul as he entered the bridge.

"May the fleas of a thousand camels infest your armpits," Abdul said venomously.

"Very expensive candy", Parvis said looking around, the tension mounted as he ignored Abdul who treated his remark with contempt, then he approached Abdul pointed his gun at Abdul's head menacingly.

"You could cut the air with a knife." It was then Parvis broke into a huge grin, hugged Abdul kissed him on both cheeks, and said; "well done my friend how are you? This has been a long time in the planning; now the fun and games really begin."

Parvis added, "we have a lot to do in a short while before the world wakes up to what we are doing, this is better than playing with toy boats by the river where we dreamt of taking over the world when we were children."

"That was a long time ago," Abdul said to Parvis, then added, "what are we going to do with the crew? We can't trust any of them."

"What do pirates do to unwanted guests aboard their ship?", Parvis said, then answered his own question, "they make them walk the plank," he said, with an evil look in his eye, "first of all, get them to put the "Fast Lady" on board we might need her later, besides I could become accustomed to the pirates share of having my own sea-going luxury speedboat."

Abdul added, “If I remember you sank the last boat I had with a well-aimed rock.”

“That was after you pushed me into the river if you remember, and I nearly drowned”, Abdul said.

“I got you out didn’t I?”, Parvis added, “besides we both got a good hiding from our parents for getting our best clothes muddy and wet.”

“If you remember it was two days after that when you and I were at school our village was bombed by the Americans, both our parents were killed in that raid, they said they were sorry it was a case of accidental friendly fire.”

They hugged one another in friendship, “now it’s payback time”, Parvis said.

Parvis made the crew of the *NAT GAS 2* haul the “Fast Lady” onto the deck of the Tanker at gunpoint by using the ships Derek, they positioned the speedboat so it could be launched quite easily in the case of an emergency.

After they had secured the “Fast Lady”, Parvis said to Abdul, “now we need to get rid of the excess baggage before they become troublesome.”

Captain Williams and the crew of the tanker were then herded at gunpoint by the pirates to the stern of the tanker where a long plank had been lashed to the stern of the tanker overhanging the wash of the stern of the ship.

Below them, unseen and forgotten were the three ladders still attached to the ship by the grappling hooks, the end of the ladders was still bouncing around in the wash of the leviathan of the sea hidden by the overhang of the upper deck they were on.

Captain Don Williams protested about the way he and his crew were being treated, "oh you do, do you?" Parvis replied, "send a strongly worded letter like we were told to when they killed our parents", then he shot the Captain out of hand and wounded him.

Parvis then pushed the wounded man screaming over the side, three other crew members tried to rush the pirates, they were also shot down in a hail of bullets by the pirates.

Abdul rushed up screaming "stop firing do you want to blow us all to kingdom come, don't you realize we are sitting on a time bomb? If you puncture anyone of those gas tanks we will be freeze-dried by the cryogenically cold liquid gas then blown sky high if that escaping gas finds an ignition source."

The Pirates picked up the bodies of the three crew members and they were slung unceremoniously overboard like sacks of meat whilst the rest of the crew huddled together not knowing what was going to happen next.

Parvis appeared holding a steam hose line, the rest of the frightened crew that had been rounded up were forced to the end of the plank by Parvis using the steam hose.

Parvis was laughing sickly as he sprayed scolding steam at them until they either fell screaming into the sea after being scolded or jumped into the sea to avoid the scalding steam, He commented, "this way is safer and it saves bullets."

"Now that's the first phase completed.", Parvis turned to Abdul and said with a sick grin and a mad look in his eyes as he shut off the steam hose.

Parvis said, "Now we prepare for the next phase, so we need to set a course to rendezvous with our friends, that's when the real fun begins."

Then Abdul said, "lay on a course so we should be able to catch up with them by dawn tomorrow, then it's payback time."

Parvis said, "we can then take our little trip to New York together and hit the Americans where it hurts", then added with a wickedly sick grin "it's a pity we can't fly the "Jolly Roger" I fancy myself as Blackbeard the pirate."

Three months after booking their cruise which was due to sail on the same day that the "NATGAS 2" had set sail, Jeff, Karen, Cyril and Jen arrived at Harwich Port.

The beautiful magnificent white cruise liner *Baroness of the Sea* dwarfed the harbour. It looked like a huge majestic lady ready to welcome them into her bosom then whisk them off to the luxurious holiday they so badly needed.

They were met in the car park by staff who unloaded their luggage from their car, put it into large cages and whisked it off to their cabin. All they had was their light hand luggage to carry.

They were met at reception where they registered their credit card where everything brought on board would be registered to. In return they were issued with a boarding pass with their details on which was to be used for everything required as there was no cash needed on board, from reception they were escorted to the boarding area.

When they boarded the "Baroness of the Sea", they were given a champagne and canape's reception in the opulent VIP lounge, the Captain gave a welcomed aboard address and introduced some of his senior officers and staff.

They were escorted to the dining room where a magnificent buffet lunch was served.

At Lunch, they spotted Derek and Sandra, across the dining room and joined them, "how come you are on this cruise?" Jeff asked Sandra explained it was a surprise for Jeff that Cyril, Jen and Karen had put together. Sandra explained that Derek was getting bored so she talked Derek into it.

Jeff was so pleased to see the couple, he asked Karen if she knew about it, and she admitted Jen and her had started planning it when they were at the shops having retail therapy.

"By the way", Sandra said, "did you know John and his wife Rose is on the same cruise? I saw him at the boarding gate he was in a deep conversation with the chief security officer."

"I wonder why he is on the same cruise?" Jeff said, "but it would be nice for us all to be together."

After lunch, they were to be shown to their individual cabins, "what a civilized way to holiday" Jen said to Cyril, "no queuing like at the airport and because we are travelling from an English port we can take as much luggage as we want, I was able to bring all my new clothes with no weight restrictions."

"What you mean," Cyril said, "whilst we had a weight limit of 200 pounds each, you had 350 pounds and I had 50 pounds."

"You want me to look lovely for you", Jen said rising above Cyril's banter.

"You look lovely to me with no clothes on", Cyril said. "Cyril! Don't make me blush", Jen retorted shyly. They all laughed with her.

As the staff escorted them to their cabins, they were told that their luggage was already in their cabins ready for them to unpack.

Jen whispered to Cyril, "wait till I get you in there", and then she said to the others, "shall we see you for drinks before dinner?"

"We will make a phone call to your cabin and set up a time for cocktails", Jeff said as they entered their cabins, which would be their little nest for the rest of the cruise.

Their cabins were identical with a balcony, on-suite, in the cabin was a large queen-size bed, a table and chairs, and a dressing table, also there were two large wardrobes, there was even a fridge with a minibar attached, and all the cabins were next to one another on the Port side of the ship.

Karen said to Jeff, "Darling, I think I am going to like this very much", exploring the layout of the cabin.

A young man and young lady knocked on Jeff's cabin door, they introduced themselves as their cabin staff and told them either one of them would be on duty at any time.

They explained there were other staff, such as someone to clean the cabin every day and put out new towels and if they wanted anything like tea or the minibar refreshed or even wanted a meal served in their cabin. If they wanted anything such as tea every morning let her know what time they wanted it and it would be brought to their cabin.

As the cabin staff left to see John and Rose in the next cabin, Karen said, to Jeff what a civilized way to travel, I could get used to this, then she hugged him, he kissed her very passionately

She wriggled out of his arms and said, "let me unpack first, then you can finish what you just started."

"If you want you, you can pour me a nice gin and tonic, do yourself a brandy whilst you're at it, then we can find a way to celebrate the start of our holiday", she said saucily.

Jeff went out onto the balcony out of her way as she liked to be organized, with his brandy in his hand he watched the other passengers board, there was a brass band playing the song "sailing" also there was a Scottish pipe band that played a reel when the brass band had a rest.

"This is the civilized way to have a holiday and travel at the same time", he called to Karen. She replied what a lovely cabin it was. When Karen had finished unpacking, she told him where she had put everything.

Then Karen joined him on the balcony and said, "where's my drink?"

He handed the drink he made her and said, "just as you like it with ice."

They watched the last people board the liner, and then the harbour crew prepared loaded the last of the required supplies and the ship was ready for their holiday of a lifetime.

The ship's horn sounded announcing their departure and as the cruise liner slowly left the harbour jetty you could hear the sound of the brass band and the bagpipes playing together to the tune "we are sailing".

He had made them two more drinks to say "bon voyage."

Karen took the drink from him, had a couple of sips then kissed him very passionately then said to him, "that big bed looks inviting? I hope I don't get lost in it", she said.

"I'll always find you and hold you safe", he said.

They both giggled like a couple of school children and fell on the bed wrapped in each other's arms. The sounds of the Scottish pipes playing a lament drifted into the cabin as he looked lovingly into Karen's eyes, he kissed her passionately.

Later in the cocktail bar, all eight of them met up and were drinking cocktails that had been made especially by the cocktail waiter to celebrate the start of the cruise.

John introduced Rose to them all. Rose was slim built and very pretty and she seemed used to John introducing her to new people. She said John had wanted to give her a good holiday to make up for all the long hours his job kept him away from home.

The Captain and his staff were circulating with the other guests and introducing themselves and also encouraging the guests to meet one another.

It was then that the Captain introduced himself to them and to a Middle Eastern gentleman and his wife.

The man said his name was Mustafa Ali and his wife's name was Asar. He said he would not join them in the cocktails but he would drink orange juice with them as he was a Muslim and drinking alcohol was against his religion. He explained that he was the ambassador for a very rich Sheikh who had joined the cruise with his entourage.

Mustafa seemed a very intelligent and a gentle caring man willing to hear the other man's side of the issue at hand before expressing his own very distinctly and in a pleasant way. Mustafa was eager to talk to Jeff about the Estuary incident but it was not the time or the place.

The conversation was polite, small talk as others joined them. Most of the conversation was with the officers and senior crew members asking them about different aspects of the "Baroness of the sea".

The head waiter came into the reception and announced dinner was being served, they finished their cocktails and made their way to the dining area.

As they made their way to dinner, they parted, Mustafa said, he would hope to see more of Jeff but added, he would be very busy looking after the Sheikh and his entourage.

Jeff's party was escorted to their table by the Head Waiter, he explained that this would be their table allocated to them for the duration of the cruise. He also stated that John and Rose also would be on the same table, he introduced the staff that would be looking after them. The head waiter introduced himself as William, the second waiter introduced himself as Michael, and the Semillon was a lovely young lady called Shirley.

Jen said to Sandra and Karen, "we could get used to being pampered like this, couldn't we ladies?" They all said "yes, and we deserve to be", Rose interjected just as she and John arrived to join them for dinner. The ladies looked at one another and burst out laughing together.

"Shall I choose which red and also white wine?" Cyril said they all looked at him and nodded, so he went into a huddle with the wine Semillon, she nodded, then said she would get the wine.

"What have you ordered?" Sandra said.

"You will enjoy the wine, which I guarantee", said Cyril, "I used to run an Off Licence for years in my miss-spent youth and I picked up a bit of knowledge on wines."

They then all enjoyed a lovely 7-course evening meal which was cooked by the ship's chef, between courses they chatted, catching up with what everyone had been doing lately. The ladies mainly were chatting about the clothes they had brought and where they had got them.

They finished dinner with coffee and liquors for the ladies and brandies for the men.

They then made their way to the theatre and went onto see the evening show.

After the show, Jeff and Karen went up to the main deck and had a romantic stroll around the ship before retiring to their cabin to settle down for the night.

The following day at breakfast, Karen, Jen, Sandra, and Rose decided they would like to have a manicure and pedicure before lunch so they booked the salon for 11o/c. They decided all the ladies would meet there just before 11o/c then meet the men for lunch in the snack bar afterwards.

Jeff and Karen decided to look around the shopping area of the ship as they had a few presents they wanted to buy in the vast shopping mall on board.

Jeff and Karen explored the different ship's decks getting the feel of the ship and the lay-out of what was on each deck.

Jeff left Karen outside the beauty salon at 11o/c, just as the rest of the girls turned up to excitedly ready to get their pampering. Jeff went onto the sports deck to find his friends.

Cyril and Derek had gone swimming. Jeff said he would watch them from the upper lounge area, whilst John was in the gym keeping fit as usual.

Jeff was sitting in the lounge overlooking the pool watching Derek and Cyril mess about in the pool when Mustafa joined him with two coffees.

"I took the liberty of getting you a coffee if you want one", Mustafa said, "as I wanted to talk to you alone about the Estuary incident if you don't mind, I did take the liberty of asking the Captain to introduce us as the Sheikh and I had heard of you and we wanted to meet you."

"The people that you met at the Captain's reception that I am travelling with, were there as well", Jeff said, "they can tell you as much as I can, they were the unsung heroes of that incident."

"Yes, they can", Mustafa said, "but they cannot tell me of your ideals, or tell me what makes a man like you tick, and why you bucked the system, and how you won through in the end."

"You won through over impossible odds and you are admired for that throughout the world, there are not many men like you around that will follow an impossible dream and win, the Sheikh and I wanted to understand the principles that you live by."

Jeff's mind flooded back to what was now known as the Estuary Incident, the memory of that incident was still very painful, and he had only just got over the injuries he received at the hands of the professional killer Wilson.

"Look Mustafa", Jeff said as he quickly came out of his reverie, "I just have a code of principles that I am prepared to live by and die for, it's that simple", and turning towards Mustafa said, "I don't expect other people to adhere to my code of ethics, just accept that I have them, as I accept the type of person they are.

"I believe if something is fundamentally wrong", he paused, then said, "there comes a time in life when you have to stand and be counted, whatever the issues that are involved, all a person has is the principles that they are prepared to live and die by."

Jeff had said these words so many times recently, little did he know that these words were going to haunt him over the next few days when the deadly arm of "The *Senate*" would reach out again and try to snare him in a deadly cat and mouse game set in the middle of the Atlantic that would be a political nightmare with biblical disaster consequences.

"Even if standing by your principles would lead to your death?" Mustafa said with incredulity

"Even then", Jeff said, "I happen to believe that all a man has in this world is his word of honour, no matter how rich or poor he is, that is all there is", Jeff added, "I happen to be a man of my word and I will not break my word for anyone or anything, and that is the code that I live by, and will probably die by."

"Anyway", he said with a wry smile, "when I die there will only be two pallbearers carrying my coffin, as there are only two handles on a dustbin", Jeff laughed at his own joke.

"You English have a strange sense of humour," Mustafa said, "you joke about your death, and you do not take life seriously, even though I know you have been close to death a few times, I saw the news bulletin that showed how you were injured when you were attacked by a man called Wilson I believe?"

Then Mustafa added, "Yet you still maintain your sense of humour", then he added, "you English have always laughed in the face of adversity, I find that strange and have never understood it", Mustafa added, "we have men in my country that have said they are men of their word, but they change when they get into a position of power."

Jeff said, "I also believe and understand that power corrupts and that is normally through greed", then added, "but absolute power absolutely corrupts that's what happens when fanatics try to take control through fanaticism and lead normally peaceful people to do unspeakable atrocities, in the name of their fanatics ideals, and I believe that is wrong and that is when you have to stand against them."

"What do you mean by that statement?", Mustafa said.

"I have always understood," Jeff said, "that if we look back in history it tells us of lessons we should have learned, but we never do learn them, it also tells us of atrocities that we should not have let happen, but did, and we still do let them happen today, generally through apathy which I happen to believe is the biggest killer of freedom and truth in peaceful people."

"Can you expand on that", Mustafa said looking puzzled but fascinated by the insight into the mind of a man he and apparently the Sheikh also very much admired.

Jeff said, "for example, if you consider what happened in Communist Russia which comprised of Russians who wanted to live in peace yet Russian Communism was responsible for the murder of about 20 million people, so it would seem the peaceful majority were irrelevant."

Jeff added, "Chinese Communists managed to kill a staggering 70 million but China's population is and was at the time very peaceful as well."

He also mentioned, "In Germany only very few people were Nazis, but before the peaceful people knew it the majority sat back and let it happen and we were plunged into World War II."

Then said, "you have the same in the Middle East where the silent majority of peace-loving people are being plunged into a holy war by fanatics, the victims in any war are the ordinary peaceful loving people very few are the politicians or religious zealots."

Then looking at the scene around him, Jeff said, "I have said before and will probably be saying it till the day that I die I believe Politics is in the word, POLI is many, and TICS are parasites so I translate POLITICS as many parasites and when you look at the different countries and their religious leaders and their leaders in political fields they are many parasites with no consideration for the peaceful people they are representing who want to live in peace. There are fanatics in the Western part of the world, the far Eastern part of the world and also in the Middle Eastern part of the world, it is the fanatics that are the enemy of peace-loving people. It is not class, creed, nationality or religion that divides people", he added, "as they are all acceptable to one another, but it is because some people believe it's nice to be important, but they forget it's more important to be nice, nice people like nice people, no matter what part of the world you come from, or what religion you follow, and it will make no difference whether you are rich or poor."

Jeff was on his soapbox now and bantered on, "I have come to believe that Religion is man-made as it is like a mountain, your view of the mountain is your view of religion, every religion has a higher being, which can be translated as the top of a mountain so your view of religion is the view you see at the time of looking at the mountain, it is the same mountain but you don't see the whole mountain."

Jeff checked himself and said he was sorry to Mustafa for getting on his soapbox and boring Mustafa with his philosophy of life.

"On the contrary, I find what you have to say very deep and thought-provoking, and is worth thinking deeper on", Mustafa said, "I must say I was not expecting that from a political member of the British Government."

"I am not a Political member of the British Government", Jeff said, "I am only a loose cannon that the Government want to tie down. I have no interest in the politics of politicians as I said before many parasites, it's people I care about."

"There are very well-meaning people, that can and do a lot for their community, but it seems when they themselves get bogged down in politics they can very easily lose their way and quite often march to the much larger sound of the fanatics drum instead of the beat of the drum they started with", Jeff added, "do you understand the analogy I am trying very badly to express?"

"I have heard that you have a saying in your country?" Mustafa said, "empty vessels make the most noise, so the fanatics drum might not be making a good noise but it is making a loud noise and that what gets attention, but a drum you're playing has a lovely tune is not always heard."

"Something similar to that, but that's enough of philosophy for one day", Jeff said, "we are on holiday, so let's relax and enjoy ourselves with each other's good company."

"Thank you for your time, Mustafa said, with a slight bow, then added, "the Sheikh would like you and your party to join him at a reception before dinner tonight if you have nothing better to do."

Then Mustafa added, "I hope we meet again soon, so we can carry on our little talk, I was fascinated by your views and I find them very interesting, you have left me with a lot to think about, I hope I did not disturb you too much", and then slightly bowed then he left.

Jeff had a feeling it was not the last he would see of Mustafa.

John joined him and said, "was that Mustafa you were talking too just then as I came on deck?"

"Yes, why?" Jeff replied, "we were talking about Philosophy and politics. He seemed a nice guy", then looked puzzled at John and said, "don't tell me you find that sinister?"

John said, "there's something about him I can't put my finger on, and until I do find out I suggest you avoid him."

"You're telling me I can't speak to someone because you think they are suspicious?" Jeff said very angrily.

"My job is to keep you alive even when we are on holiday", John said.

"Is that your orders from the P.M.? Jeff asked very surly.

John said nothing.

Quickly calming down, "I know you mean well", Jeff added, "but you also know I will not be put in a cage, so don't start now, let's enjoy the cruise, and the good company of friends and I do include you and Rose in that statement," Jeff said to John.

"You make it so difficult for me as your bodyguard to do my job," John said, "one of the first rules is don't get emotionally involved with your client or his family."

"I won't tell if you don't tell", Jeff said jokingly and smiled at John.

They were soon joined by Derek and Cyril who were laughing together.

Derek said, "you should have had a swim with us, Jeff, I managed to duck Cyril a few times."

"What do you mean?" Cyril said, "the pool emptied when you jumped in you big galumph?"

"You might be fast", Derek said, "but even a big man like me can catch you, you must be slowing down in your old age", he added jokingly.

Cyril said to Jeff, "I think I could get used to holidays like this, Cruising certainly spoils you for other holidays and I know Jen is having a marvellous time, by the way when are the girls going to be finished getting pampered?"

"About now I think, perhaps we should join them for lunch before they go into the Duty-Free shops and spend a fortune, by the way," Jeff added, "we have all been invited to a reception to meet the Sheikh tonight before dinner."

"What! We are rubbing shoulders with a Sheikh?" Cyril said, "how come?"

"Mustafa just invited us all to the reception with the Sheikh tonight", Jeff explained to them all.

"Jen will want to wear a posh frock," Cyril said, "as will all the girls."

"I suppose we will have to dress posh as well to make them feel proud of us," Derek said.

"Full bib and tucker", John said, "we can't let the girls down, can we?"

All four of them went off together to find their wives and get some lunch in the snack bar, and tell them about the surprise invite to the Sheikh's reception.

It seemed the Sheikh and his party had taken up a quarter of a deck of cabins of the "Baroness of the Sea".

There was a hive of activity that seemed to be fussing around the Sheikh like bees around a honey pot.

The suite of cabins had been dressed with drapes so as to look like a palatial tent, it seemed it was very rich and ornate.

Their party was met by Mustafa. He was very pleased to see them and chatted to them for a little while the Sheikh circulating with his other guests, Mustafa waited for the right moment and introduced them to the Sheikh saying, "Ladies and Gentlemen may I present Sheikh Ali Mustafa."

Standing in front of them was a young man dressed in robes of pure white, he had a vivid red sash in which was tucked a very ornate jewel-encrusted dagger. The pin that clipped his robe together was also encrusted with diamonds, the Sheikh looked a very strikingly handsome man.

"Welcome to my humble abode Mr Jeff", the Sheikh said in perfect English.

Jeff raised his eyebrows at the Sheikh's command of English.

"I see that you are surprised by my command of English Mr Jeff", the Sheikh said, "then let me enlighten you, I was educated at an Oxford University."

"You speak English better than I do", Jeff complimented.

"That is a very nice compliment coming from a man whose views I very much respect and admire," the Sheikh said. "I understand now when you explained to Mustafa the saying 'whilst it is nice to be important, it's more important to be nice."

Jeff realized instantly that he must have been a subject of their conversations before tonight, then said to the Sheikh "I have always believed it is harder for a poor man to be generous than a rich one so when a poor man gives, he will always give more than a rich man."

"Your thinking interests me," the Sheikh said, "you do not think like most westerners, there is depth in your thoughts and I find that fascinating."

"Let us not bore our other guests with the philosophy and ways of different cultures," the Sheikh said, "you are here to be entertained as my guest."

The Captain and his First Officers had also been invited as were a few important passengers.

The food that was served was delicious, half of which they did not know what they were eating, but it tasted lovely.

The Reception was a resounding success for the Sheikh, and he was pleased that his guests enjoyed themselves. The officers had duties they had to attend to and gradually made their way from the Reception.

Jeff and his party thanked the Sheikh for such a lovely reception and a little while later that they made their way back to their table for the evening meal, they then went onto another evening show.

Jeff asked them all to join him and Karen for a nightcap in his cabin. Derek said "if you don't mind, I will take a rain check on that if I may" and said he had had enough for one night but maybe tomorrow night.

Cyril, Jen, John and Rose came back to Jeff and Karen's cabin for a nightcap.

As soon as they were in the cabin and the door was closed, Cyril said, "if he's a rich Sheikh, then I'm a Dutchman."

"What do you mean by that remark?" John said, "he appeared to be all that he said he was, it was a very nice Reception."

"I know quality when I see it," Cyril said "and he did not have quality, everything about him was false, oh! He spun a good yarn about his father and his Uncles owning oil wells and how rich they were but he himself was false, he might have gone to university in England but he is not who he says he is."

"How can you tell?" Jeff said.

"That robe was not silk as he inferred, the jewels in the pin that held it together and in the dagger were false, they were paste."

"Paste? they looked real to me," John said.

"Believe me, I know jewellery! I've lifted enough to know the difference between paste and the real thing, what puzzles me is why the entire charade" Cyril said, "what does he gain from it, he must have some money because he paid for the top cabins for all his staff as well as all the elaborate entertainment."

"I am very curious, perhaps if you get this Mustafa on his own you might be able to find out", Cyril mentioned to Jeff, "he seems to like your company", and then retorted with a laugh, "I don't know why."

"I don't know what it is but it doesn't hang together quite right", Cyril added, "and the Sheikh seems to have a lot of bodyguards, but they always seemed to be taking their orders from someone else."

Mustafa was so busy with the Sheikh. Jeff saw very little of him over the next day, though he kept an eye out for him.

They had only been at sea a couple of days when their dream holiday cruise turned into the worst kind of a horrific nightmare.

It all started when he looked out of the cabin window early in the morning. Dawn was just breaking, and he could see a very large vessel heading towards them. It looked like it was overtaking them very closely, then it started veering so it would fall in very close to and behind the cruise liner so Jeff went out onto the balcony for a closer look. The nightmare started to unfold as Jeff realized the ship that had headed for them was a very large gas container. He could just make out the name on the bow of the giant gas ship, it was the "NATGAS 2".

At first Jeff thought the *NAT GAS 2* had a problem and the "Baroness of the sea" was on a mercy mission perhaps a crew member on the *NAT GAS 2* had been taken ill and the "Baroness of the sea" was offering assistance.

As the giant gas tanker pulled up close behind the *Baroness of the Sea*, Jeff went to the balcony to get a better view of what was going on, only to see crew members of the *NAT GAS 2* had put fenders all the way along the front and side of the *NAT GAS 2*.

It was then that a crew of the NAT GAS 2 cast a number of lines to the "Baroness of the sea" by rockets, but instead of the crew from the "Baroness of the sea" catching and winding in the tow lines so larger and stronger ropes can be pulled aboard, it was members of the Sheikh's bodyguard.

On the securing of the ropes, the *Baroness of the Sea* and its passengers and crew were now going to be a human shield for the terrorist.

Both ships were keeping the same pace with one another until the tow ropes tightened and the *NAT GAS 2* swung in closely behind the *Baroness of the Sea* secured by the many tow ropes.

The *Baroness of the Sea* with thousands of passengers was to be the human shield for Parvis and the rest of the terrorists, their demands on the United States was for the revenge of the killing of his family all those years ago.

"You're up early, what's going on?" Karen said sleepily from the bed.

"I don't know yet but I don't think I like it", Jeff replied looking worried, then as things started to slip into place in his mind an announcement was heard over the cruise ship's PA system, telling all passengers to stay in their cabins until further notice and they would come to no harm.

Jeff did not like the suspicions that were forming in his mind and the realization he was coming to, his fears that the *NAT GAS 2* had been high-jacked and the pirates were also at the same time high-jacking the *Baroness of the Sea* which meant an estimated 3,000 plus passengers and 1800 crews all would be held to ransom by the terrorists

"I think we are being high-jacked by pirates and I believe we are going to be used as a human shield", Jeff said, "I believe they are attempting to tow a gas tanker behind us and threaten to blow it up if there is a rescue attempt".

"What? How can they do that?" Karen said coming awake instantly then added, "this is a British cruise ship", Karen said, "They can't rob a ship on the high seas. Passengers don't carry large amounts of cash it's all booked to your debit or your credit card and you pay at the end, people will only have travelling cash", then she added jokingly, "and no one is going to pay a ransom for you, you're not that popular!"

"Thanks!" He said.

Just then someone called his name from the adjoining balcony. Jeff went to see who it was. It was John. He said he had just been ushered back to his cabin from the gym at gunpoint it seems they were Middle Eastern extremists.

"Do you know what they want?" Jeff asked.

"From what I can gather, they want to take their fight to America", John said, "by sailing both ships tied together to an American port and blow both ships up in the port killing everybody for miles around the area plus nearly 5,000 passengers and crews from both ships."

"You and I know the Americans won't stand for that", Jeff said, "they will blow us out of the water long before that happens."

"Surely", John added, "it would take a massive number of explosives to blow up a ship of this size. How did they get it aboard the *NAT GAS 2*, or come to that, aboard the "Baroness of the sea"?

Jeff said, "they don't have to have a large number of explosives. The Gas aboard the *NAT GAS 2* gas ship will do the job for them. So we need to find out what is the manifest of the *NAT GAS 2*.

"A gas ship is a gas ship," John said, "the gas ignites when you set light to it".

"It's not that simple," Jeff said, "if it's LPG (Liquid Petroleum Gas) it is stored under pressure so as to reduce the Gas to a liquid state for easier transportation and storage, it is very nasty stuff in a fire as it often explodes."

"If it's Liquid Natural Gas LNG (known as Methane Gas) it is reduced down 620 times its size from a gas to a liquid and transported and stored at cryogenically low temperatures of below minus 280 degrees Fahrenheit, if that is released it will expand 620 times from liquid to gas, everything in its path will be freeze-dried, then it burns at a temperature three hundred degrees hotter than burning petrol."

Jeff added, "don't you remember the massive disaster in the Estuary? That started with a leak of L.N.G., and I can't see the Americans letting that happen within their borders."

"The Americans won't let it get into their territorial waters. They will bomb both ships to the bottom of the sea first", John agreed then added, "if they do that, they kill all the passengers and crew on both ships, and then the Americans do the terrorist job for them."

"The terrorist doesn't care if they die, they have said their goodbyes to the world long ago", Jeff said then added, "if they can force the Americans hand, they would have scored points and this has an advantage in their political game of chess."

Then he said, "we have just become the pawns in that game and we will be the ones sacrificed unless we do something about it before we hit landfall."

John retorted, "don't tell me you want to do something about it?" Then with a dawning realization said, "What! You want to take on a bunch of highly trained armed terrorists, take back two ships that are lashed together with ropes, all with pampered civilians that have a job doing up their shoelaces, who know nothing about sailing Cruise ships or tankers, all before the Americans decide to blow us out of the water, you're off your trolley, we will be slaughtered."

"We are dead if we don't do anything anyway," Jeff said, "so why not go down fighting for what you believe in!" Then added, "I won't go silently into the night to suit some political ideal of a fanatic, or just being the pawn in his world-wide game of chess."

"May I remind you" Jeff added, "pawns may be small but if they co-ordinate their moves together they are a powerful force and can take down a queen, so we need to do something to change this game of chess to our advantage.

"We already have four in our little army", Jeff said, "there's Cyril, Derek, you and myself, that's four people I would not upset, especially now they have ruined our wives holiday cruise, Derek's wife Sandra was in the army until recently, and even I would not upset Jen, she can be quite a formidable force and believe me when you piss off a woman big time you have a tiger by the tail," Then he added, "all we have to do is to find like-minded passengers and crew members."

"You make it sound like something out of "Roy of the Rovers" comic book, you can't create an army out of strangers who have just met, it takes time and training", John said.

"No, it doesn't", Jeff said, "all it takes is enough people to stand and be counted, Bind them together, and then think of ways of stopping these maniacs, as soon as the passengers on board realize nobody is going to rescue us, the authorities will not send in the SAS or the SEALS as we are politically expendable, it is up to us to survive and if it means taking on the terrorists then that's what needs to be done, I don't know about you but I do not intend to go quietly."

John realized what Jeff was saying was true about the situation then said, "if we are to get organized, that means we need to be talking to the other passengers and get their support and we can't do that cooped up in our cabins, I can use my laptop to communicate with number 10 via satellite link so we can use that as a link to the P.M. direct, we must inform him of what's going on, by the way, I can get our location via the same satellite."

"What else can you do with your box of tricks and when were you going to tell me about it?" Jeff said suspiciously, "before or after you reported to the Prime Minister? and how did you get that box of tricks through the security check when we boarded?"

"Let's say the officer in charge of security and I go way back", John said.

"Your coat buttons up over more areas than I like to imagine", Jeff said, "is that more from your cloak and dagger background that you are not going to tell me about?"

John ignored the terse remark, and said, "we need to use all the tools we have in the box, this one gives us an advantage, so whoever is responsible for this high-jack must not know we have a link to the outside world."

As they were speaking there was an announcement over the ships PA system telling everybody that they would be able to leave their cabins soon but they would not be allowed on the outside decks, any attempt to go outside on the rear of deck five by any passenger where the Gas ship was lashed to would be shot.

"What do you make of that?" Cyril said as he came out onto the adjoining balcony of the next cabin, on the other side Cyril's cabin Derek also came out on his balcony, "Jen wants to rip someone's heads off for trying to ruin her holiday."

"Calm her down and tell her we are going to make plans to rectify the situation," Jeff said.

He added, "we have to wait until we can get more passengers involved and we can't do that ensconced in our cabins."

The PA system burst into life again telling passengers they were to make their way to the restaurant deck where they will be fed and there will be an announcement all passengers are to be on that deck by 0800 hrs those passengers that do not comply will be forced to walk the plank.

"Walk the plank? That went out with Blackbeard the pirate", Cyril said.

"Well it looks like we now have his great-grandson to deal with", Cyril said, "I heard what you were saying to John. I'm in! so is Derek, He and Sandra are in the next cabin to ours."

"I suggest we all get up to that deck as soon as possible to see what's going on", John said, "it's 0715 now, see you outside your cabins at 0745 then we can go in numbers, we stand a better chance that way by sticking together."

"Right!" They said, "together."

They all hurriedly got washed and dressed and met outside their cabins and made their way to the Restaurant deck with trepidation but solidarity and determination not to be bullied by some jumped up pirate.

The Restaurant deck was filling up, they made their way to the middle of the crowd of passengers and stood together by a pillar waiting to hear what was happening.

There was a general hubbub of people talking as they wondered what was going on, there was no staff or Officers amongst the crowd.

By the doors were men dressed in black uniforms holding guns and looking very mean, Jeff, recognized some of the men as they seemed to be the same men that were serving them at the Sheikh's reception the previous night.

The talking got louder as the people that were inside were herded towards the small stage area that was acting as a platform.

One of the guards fired some shots into the air and the hub-bub stopped immediately.

Mustafa stepped up onto the stage everybody stood silently but very sullen.

Mustafa said, "I introduce our leader Sheikh Ali Mustafa who will tell you what is going to happen"

The Sheikh dressed in the same white robes as he was at his Reception, he stepped up onto the small stage and waved his hands as if he were their saviour and said, "we are here to remove the yoke of the west from your shoulders that have strangled you and my people for decades."

"Do not be frightened my children, we are your fellow passengers in the struggle against oppression, we are here to liberate you, do as my men ask and you will come to no harm, but if you don't do as we ask, you will face the consequences like the men who were told not to go out on the rear of deck five, see for yourself from the viewpoints."

Quite a number of passengers moved to the side of the restaurant floor to look out over the lower deck five, there lined up at the side of the ship were a number of crew and a few passengers, they were being herded towards a plank that had been lashed to and hanging over the side of the Cruise Liner.

The Sheikh stated, "these people are examples to you that we mean business and you are to do as you are told, with that he raised his hand then dropped it."

The hapless people were pushed towards the plank. You could hear their screams. The people that were herded into the restaurant reacted by screaming that they can't do that, it was inhumane. It was then the guards opened fire and put a volley just above everybody's head.

"The next volley will be a lot lower" the Sheikh shouted. He had a mad look in his eyes. "They disobeyed me", pointing to the people on deck five "and will walk the plank or be shot and then tossed over the side they are already dead, it is their time to meet Allah."

The horror of what was about to unfold was unbelievable. The guards were now pushing the people towards the plank, separated two Filipino crew members from the rest and pushed them towards the plank. The others were forced to the side of the plank. Parvis was on the gas tanker watching with a sick eagerness, through his binoculars, he had recently done this to the crew of the gas tanker and enjoyed it.

The first Filipino rushed the guards and tried vainly to get passed them and away from the edge of the ship, he was smashed to the ground with the butt end of a gun and lay there with his head all bloody.

The other one was pushed towards the edge of the plank with a ring of bayonets from the guards, he was screaming, then pleading with the ring of guards to let him live.

A guard stepped forward they were later to know as Abdul, he looked up to where the Sheikh was standing; the Sheikh moved his hand across his throat in a cutting motion.

Abdul, pushed the hapless man to the end of the plank with the point of his bayonet digging the bayonet into the man's stomach.

The man fell off the end of the plank but managed to grab onto the end of the plank in desperation and cling to it.

Abdul moved to the end of the plank and stabbed at the man's hands that were gripping the end of the plank like a vice then with his bayonet he stabbed at the man's fingers, the man let out a piercing scream then fell into the sea with a splash.

The guards grabbed the other Filipino that had been beaten with the butt of the guns as he was unconscious, they threw him over the side like a sack of meat.

The guards then approached the other prisoners and surrounded them. Abdul looked up at the Sheikh, and the Sheikh held up his hand in a stop sign and signaled the guards to bring the prisoners inside.

A passenger in the restaurant shouted "you evil bastard!" another shouted "Bloody Murderer!" the guards moved in on the two men and smashed them to the ground with gun butts.

'Enough", the Sheikh said to the guards, they backed off, then the Sheikh added, "the two crew members that have just left the ship were an example for you to see that I will be obeyed in all things", just then there was a scuffle at the back of the restaurant and guards entered with the Captain under escort.

The Captain shouted at the Sheikh, "you have just murdered two of my crew, the rest of my officers are locked in the forward locker what have you got to say? You bloody pirate."

"You can join them if you want," the Sheikh said, "or better still you can choose which of your crew goes next or you can shut up and sail this ship to where I want you to sail it."

"This ship goes nowhere," the Captain said, "you can't hi-jack a British ship and get away with it, you will hang for piracy."

"We will see," the Sheikh said, "I hold all the cards, and I will hold this ship and its crew for as long as I want to, and you and nobody can stop me."

"Captain!" The Sheikh added, "I can do what I want, I have the *NAT GAS 2* which is a Liquid Natural Gas ship now being towed by the Baroness of the sea, any interference by you or your staff, or any attempt to rescue you, your crew or your passengers from outsiders, will be met by my men on board the *NAT GAS 2* manipulating the valves and releasing the cargo of cryogenically cold Liquid Natural Gas."

The Sheikh then addressed everybody and said, "for those of you who don't know what Liquid Natural Gas is, it is Liquid Methane, I do have to tell you that once my men manipulate the valves on that gas ship there is no going back, we will meet Allah together, everyone will be freeze-dried before they are incinerated, there will be a fireball for at least ten miles across when it ignites, so as you say in your country I hold all the aces in the pack of cards."

It was then the Sheikh addressed the Captain with a maniacal glare in his eyes and said, "You called me a pirate, so I act like a pirate, by putting over the side people I feel are mutineers if they did not do as I say or argue with my orders."

"From now on you will obey my orders, and if I feel you need persuasion, you and I will pick out the next people to walk the plank, so whoever dies will be your choice, do you understand my meaning?"

"You and your passengers know by me setting the latest example I mean what I say"

The Sheikh on seeing Jeff standing there pointed to him and said, "Mr Jeff is known for being a man of his word in his country, so am I a man of my word and I will keep my word and it will be up to you Captain who dies if I am not obeyed instantly, do I make myself very clear?"

The Sheikh seemed to mentally steady himself, to slowly bring himself back under control and started to calm down, then he said in a pleasant voice, "to show you I am not a cruel man Captain, your passengers can enjoy their cruise, and I want everybody to act as normal", but then he spun around and manically glared at everyone in the restaurant and said, "nobody goes onto the outside deck at deck five without my permission is that clear?", and he spun around and he left the platform surrounded by guards.

There was a general hubbub of noise and screaming of shock from some of the women passengers as they realized, they were being held prisoners, even though it might be on the luxury liner, they were still the hostages of a fanatical middle eastern terrorist.

It also slowly dawned on the passengers they were going to be the human shield of the fanatics in their game of political chess, that was being played out on the high seas against one of the most powerful countries in the world that had a policy of not negotiating with terrorists.

The realization that with a policy of no negotiation with terrorists no matter what, the indignation that their lives were forfeit, just like the two crew members that were sacrificed as a lesson to all the passengers if they interfered with anybody on deck five.

It started to dawn on them that deck 5 is off-limits to all passengers due to the tow ropes forming umbilical cords with the NAT GAS2 and the Baroness of the Sea.

Some passengers surrounded the Captain in desperation, as he was flanked by the Sheikh's guards and were asking him to intercede on their behalf.

The Captain told them that his hands were tied, and he could not intercede at this moment as his officers had been locked in the forward locker hold and booby traps had been set on the doors.

It was at that moment that someone pointing to Jeff and said, "why did he refer to you and pick you out as his hero?"

Jeff retorted, "did you see the look in his eyes? The man's got a screw loose."

"He might have, but he admires you", one of the men said, "so you speak for us, tell him to let us go, we have wives and families, we don't want to die and be part of this high-jack", then he added, "I'm an important businessman, I have important friends in the American *Senate*."

Jeff said, "don't let him hear that. He hates America with a vengeance, so your American friends could get you killed just by you knowing them, so I would keep quiet about them if I was you, I suggest you think of ways of resolving the situation as we are on our own here because no-one is going to rescue us.

"You mean, take on these modern-day pirates?" The man said with disbelief, "but they control both ships, it would mean taking control of both ships at the same time, plus stopping them from manipulating the valves on the gas ship just as he said they would, plus taking on armed guards on this ship all at the same time, may I remind you we are unarmed civilian, it can't be done, not even by the SAS."

"So, are you going to lie down and let him kill you and your loved ones?" Jeff said, "without trying or doing a thing about it?"

As they were discussing the situation, the Captain was escorted away by the guards who seemed oblivious of what was being said.

"Well", the man said, "well, of course, I'd like to do something, but I am only one person and I don't know what to do, but I am willing to go down fighting."

"Well!" Jeff said, "First I suggest you find out who else is willing to do something, and then we can work out if we can do something, if so, what to do, and when we do it because if you lie down and accept your fate without doing something about it and you live through it, you will always live to regret it."

"What is needed is to find out who can, and how they can help, we all have our own skills so we need to find out who has any skills, then we have to work with the tools we have in the box."

"But they have guns", the man said, "also they are killers, we don't have any guns and most of us have never used a gun."

"Then it's time to learn or die, or watch your families die", Jeff said.

"You're a cruel bastard", the man said, "you know we can't fight back."

"Yes, you can", Jeff said, "it's either that or you die whimpering", Jeff added, "I will try to have a word with the Captain somehow to find out how many of the crew that's not locked up we can count on."

"You can help by finding out how many men you have met so far on this cruise we can rely on to let them know we will be fighting back at some time in the near future but above all keep it secret from the pirates because if they get wind of it, we will all die, so far it looks like most of the guards don't understand English that's an advantage."

Just then a group of guards came towards them with Mustafa in their middle, "Mr Jeff", he called, "you will come with me to see the Sheikh now.".

Derek stood in front of Jeff, "you aren't going to kill him not while I breathe," he said looking at Mustafa very menacingly.

"He is not going to die yet", Mustafa said, "the Sheikh only wants to talk with him on his own, but if you don't move aside you will be shot dead where you stand."

"I'll break you in half before you do", Derek said.

"Leave it", Jeff said calming Derek down, knowing that they would shoot Derek out of hand also this was appeasing to Mustafa's pride, then whispered to Derek, "if I don't come back then you can kill him."

Derek tried to hide his grin at the thought of tearing these terrorist apart piece by piece if they harmed his friend.

Karen looked worried as he walked off with Mustafa.

Jen put her arm around Karen and was calming her down and said, "He knows what he's doing."

As they were leaving the area Jeff was telling Mustafa that Derek was not very clever and was hot-headed and protective where he was concerned, hoping Mustafa would believe him so as to save Derek from being shot, then added but he was harmless as he only had the mentality of a child, he is totally a gentle giant and could not hurt a fly.

Mustafa and the guards escorted Jeff to the Sheikh's cabin, on the way Mustafa seemed anxious to convince Jeff that the Sheikh was not the megalomaniac he appeared to be and all he wanted was for people to respect and obey him.

"You tell that to the two unfortunate staff he chucked over the side of the ship," Jeff said, "that was plain murder and murderers might be obeyed by fear for a short time but they don't get respect, that you have to earn."

"I have known the Sheikh all my life. We grew up together, my father is his father's personal bodyguard", Mustafa said apologetically, "though I have not seen him for five years our lives went different ways."

"He called me and asked me in our friendship's name, as we are also blood brothers he wants me to help him make a name for himself so he will be respected by his elders back home. He has always been seeking approval of them, I did not know what he had planned and I do not agree with his new found friends, you must believe me", Mustafa said pleadingly.

"You are his hero," Mustafa added, "he admires you for what you did, how in your country you always took on the establishment against impossible odds and won through, never compromising your code of ethics that you live and will die by."

Then quickly added, "he has read every article written about you and wants to emulate you, he wants to be the people's champion like you are, he read how Wilson hunted you and shot you and nearly killed you but you lived, how you stopped a powerful man like Sir William Waits from taking over your country, and in gratitude your country raised you from the ranks of the poor to the position of power you have today."

"I am not a hero!" Jeff said, "I only stood and was counted, I was prepared to fight for what I believe in like many others", and then added, "you have it wrong, I don't have any power as an individual, I have been entrusted to do a job that I believe needs to be done, that's all, now I am on holiday with my wife and friends."

"Do you know", Mustafa said, "the Sheikh and his new found friends have had this high-jack planned for a long time, I did not find out about it until I was on board, so when he found out you were on board as a passenger he went into ecstasy he reread all the articles written about you."

"Some of those articles are total fiction", Jeff said.

"He believes every word written about you is true", Mustafa said, "you are what he wants to be, a people's champion, a modern-day Robin Hood".

"He has got to have a screw loose if he thinks that", Jeff said.

"Please don't say that in front of him, please don't disillusion him", Mustafa said, "a lot of lives on board this ship depend on it. He is not the man I used to know as a boy, he is, how shall I say, changed, he flips mentally at the slightest thing he feels is an affront to his principles, I am sure he is being used to further the ends of political anarchists or by unscrupulous people in my country using his family name for their own ends, at the moment he still trusts me as his blood brother."

The Sheikh was waiting for them as they got to the Sheikh's cabin and he said to Jeff, "welcome my friend. We are the same you and I, we are men of principle and of our word, are we not?" He looked as though he was looking for approval from Jeff.

"Look at him being modest as usual", the Sheikh added then turning to Mustafa he said, "he does not know I have read every article they printed about him."

Then turning back to Jeff, looking expectantly for approval.

Jeff's retort was "don't believe all you read about me", Jeff said then added philosophically, "to read what someone has written is to borrow that persons thought."

The Sheikh looked puzzled at first listening to Jeff's retort, then realizing what Jeff had said replied admiringly, turning to Mustafa said, "see how deep he thinks?" The Sheikh seemed proud that he had met his hero and was not disappointed.

Then turning back to Jeff added, "We must discuss the virtues of life and how you and I think the same, please sit. I am humbled by your presence", he said bowing his head slightly and pointing towards a table and chairs, then asked, "do you require refreshments?"

Jeff nodded, knowing how important it was to accept the hospitality and guest rights of the Sheikh's dwelling, he sat down trying to get his thoughts in order and trying not to alienate this obviously mentally disturbed man, Jeff realized he was mentally walking on eggshells and had to be very careful what he said so as not to antagonize the situation.

"Refreshments for my revered guest", the Sheikh said to a man standing in the corner, the man left the cabin immediately to get refreshments, leaving Mustafa and the Sheikh and Jeff in the cabin.

The Sheikh sat down with him with his eyes looking at some distant object in his mind then said to Jeff in a voice that was hauntingly strange, "I will be a hero of my people just like you are to yours, we are the same, you and I, we are kindred spirits, we are warriors."

Then he looked fervently at Jeff and started blurting out all the plans he had made, how he and his six tactical advisor friends and their aids had secretly arranged the high-jack of the loaded "NATGAS 2" a short while after it left its harbour.

The Sheikh explained how Parvis and his team of men had used a motor launch and boarded the gas tanker from the stern of the ship and high-jacked it at sea, just like they were trained to do by the Somali pirates off the Horn of Africa.

How Parvis, after meeting up with his life-long friend Abdul who was on the bridge of the Gas Tanker *NAT GAS 2* they had high-jacked, they headed to intercept the "Baroness of the Sea".

As they drew near to the "Baroness of the sea", they arranged for a distress "May-Day" to be sent to the "Baroness of the sea" whilst it was the nearest ship and knowing it would respond straight away to a "May Day" then how they rendezvoused with the "Baroness of the Sea".

"By the time the Captain of the "Baroness of the sea" realized it was a hoax May Day, it was too late, my men had captured the "Baroness of the sea" by taking over the bridge, the Engine room, and the radio room in one very smooth operation."

"Whilst we put the *NAT GAS 2* on tow the Officers and ratings were locked in the forward locker and the Captain is now confined to his cabin under guard. This vessel and all the passengers are our prisoners and our human shield and our key that will open the gates to the American "New York Harbour" where we will make the Americans listen to our demands."

The Sheikh with his eyes glassing overstated, "I will be a hero to my people just like you are a hero to your people."

"The Americans will not attack us or try to recapture this ship as I will give a message to my men on board the *NAT GAS 2* to open the valves and release the cargo in the hold, you know what happens when that is done."

"Yes!" Jeff said, totally horror-struck, "I know what happens, everyone within a ten to twenty miles radius dies, they will be freeze-dried, then, if there is an ignition source, incinerated when the gas ignites."

"Exactly!" The Sheikh said, "and I have made plans that it will happen if they do not do what we want", He then added, "they will not try to bomb us or sink us as we get to New York as that will mean the death of all the passengers and crew and that they will have on their political conscience forever."

"So, as you see I hold all the aces in the deck of cards, and the Americans will do as I say, I am on a winning formula and I can't lose."

As he was talking, the Sheikh then seemed to withdraw into himself, then said, "they will know I will do it as I am a man of my word", then looking at Jeff said, "as they came to know you are, It is fate that had brought us together, two brothers in arms standing together, it is Kismet, I will be a hero of my people, as you are a hero to yours."

Tempting the Sheikh's lucidness, Jeff asked, "what happens if the Americans refuse you entry into America?"

"Then I will get as close as I can to America and release the cargo then we all die martyred to a cause of freedom from oppression", then he stated looking very resigned, "we have already made our peace with Allah."

Jeff realized, he needed to be walking on eggshells as he was dealing with a very dangerous megalomaniac, and the trouble was this maniac seemed to hero-worship him, and that worried him.

Jeff was also worried about the people that were apparently backing the Sheikh that was hidden in the background.

Someone would have had to finance an operation as big as this, plus it must have been planned in detail for a very long time, in fact, to bring all the parties together at the right time needed planning on a global scale.

The booking of the suite of cabins required for the Sheikh's entourage would have to have been booked 2 years in advance, the High-jacking of the "NAT GAS2" must have been years in the planning, the training of how to board the gas ship by the Somalian pirates off the Horn of Africa must have taken some time, plus knowing the "Fast Lady" would be where they could steal her, and also the arsenal of weapons required for such a big operation must have taken some organization.

What was worrying Jeff was it had all the hallmarks of The *Senate*'s involvement, but he understood that organization had been eradicated worldwide after the Estuary Incident.

It was now becoming more obvious from what Cyril had said about the jewels in the dagger being fakes, as he felt the Sheikh was not as rich as he gave the impression he was, but he looked as though he was being used by other parties for their own ends, who by? Jeff would have to find out.

Mustafa broke the silence and said, "my father was the Sheikh's father's bodyguard as was his father before him, Mustafa's family had guarded the Sheikh's family for generations."

A thought passed through Jeff's mind, perhaps the Sheikh's father was still alive so he might only be a Sheikh in title and not in wealth yet, and therefore was being taken advantage of and manipulated by more powerful people with a hidden agenda.

The *Senate* had been behind the incident in the Estuary until he knew more about the Sheikh and his friends, he had to play along with the Sheikh to find out who was pulling the strings as he hoped The *Senate* had not raised its ugly head again.

Jeff needed to know what forces they were up against and how many men did it take to overpower the two ships so he blatantly asked the Sheikh.

"What do you want to know for?" The Sheikh said suspiciously.

Trying to avert suspicion Jeff lied hoping he was convincing and said, "I was only admiring what you did, and how simple you made it sound, I was impressed with what you have achieved in such a short time."

The Sheikh puffed out his chest and said, "you were impressed? That is praise indeed coming from you, the one person I have admired for years."

He looked cunningly at Jeff and said, "I used the men from my household bodyguard that are sworn to me, there are six munitions advisors from a friend of mine, Mustafa his wife, myself and four of my wives, as you can see, we do not need many to hold the west to ransom, are you really impressed?"

"Very!" Jeff said, "you seem to have thought of everything", then he added trying to appease him, "when this is over you will be renowned and respected throughout your country."

The Sheikh stood up the audience was obviously over and he said, "we will chat again soon, I so enjoy your company, men like you and I who are men of their word and should meet more often."

So Jeff left under escort with Mustafa.

On the way back Mustafa was talking to him, telling him how sorry he was for the men that had died so horridly.

"Don't say sorry to me," Jeff said, "be sorry for their families, you killed them in cold blood."

"I did not kill them, or condone their killing," Mustafa said horror-struck.

"The Sheikh's advisors wanted to set an example to make sure everybody obeyed the Sheikh, he had them killed, he let loose that maniac Abdul to carry out that execution."

Then Mustafa added, "Abdul and Parvis who is on the *NAT GAS 2* are a matching pair, Parvis also did the same to the crew of the *NAT GAS 2* and he enjoyed it like Abdul, they are both nasty sick-minded animals."

"You did nothing to stop your friend from killing them so in my eyes you're as guilty as he is," Jeff said, "he set an example alright, by killing those men in that way he proved to everyone on board he will stop at nothing to further his cause", then Jeff added, "he is a dangerous ally to have as a friend and I believe he is seriously mentally sick if he were my friend I would either disown him or try to change what he is trying to do."

"You do not understand," Mustafa said, "our families go back generations, my ancestors have always been bodyguards to his family, I am the first eldest son in my family not to be a bodyguard to his family, I disappointed my father very much when I said I did not want to carry on the tradition.

"How can you protect him when you see what he is doing?" Jeff said.

"He does not keep me as informed as he used to", Mustafa admitted, "he spends more time with Abdul who is one of the six Advisors he spoke of, as I said he is a cruel man and I don't like the influence he seems to have over the Sheikh, it is as if he is being led by him," he mused.

Mustafa added, "when I told him this yesterday, he dismissed me out of hand, he told me I had been out of touch and did not know what the real situation was with the western world."

He added, "he never used to be like that when we were boys, yes, he always wanted to be the Knight in shining armor, and I was his faithful trusted servant, but he has changed and not like he used to be.

I have known him all my life, but he frightens me now, and I don't know what to do for the best." Mustafa added, "please don't tell him we have spoken like this he might not understand, the guards don't speak English so they can't repeat what we have said, the only ones that speak English apart from the Sheikh and I are the six advisors."

Then Mustafa said, "I have loved him as a brother all my life but I am worried that he is out of his depth and has gone too far and can't find his way back, I tell you this because I respect you and you're principles, and I hope you will understand that he is not a bad person, he is only misguided and I believe being led by Abdul and the other five advisors he surrounds himself with at all times."

They parted company and Mustafa said as a farewell, "we will talk again", and left Jeff to find Karen and the others.

He found Karen in their cabin with Jen and Cyril, when Karen saw him she rushed over hugged him and started crying with relief, "you had us worried, we thought he would hold you hostage or something," she said.

"Derek wanted to rip some heads off, but we calmed him down," Cyril said, "the Guards treated the big man as though he was a five-year-old wayward child."

"We did not know why, not until I realized what you had said to that Mustafa about him being a gentle giant, so when Mustafa spoke to the guards in what sounded like Arabic and it was then they treated him very gently."

Jeff said, “if they ever realize how powerful and intelligent he is they will fear him, and quite rightly so, that means he becomes their first target, by him playing weak-minded he lulls them into a false sense of security, I understand they treat the less fortunate with reverence because they believe they are closer to Allah.”

“Very clever, remind me never to play chess with you,” Cyril said.

“Where are the others?”, Jeff asked.

“They should be here any minute,” Jen said, “they went to see the guards to find out if they could get the first Officer or if someone was available to see us, I flooded your bathroom as an excuse to get them here so act indignant about the mess when they get here.”

Karen said, “we have to use it as a cover to talk to a member of the crew. John suspected you had been given guest rights by the Sheikh so the guards would not want you upset otherwise it would reflect badly on the Sheikh’s integrity.”

“It seems John had judged it right”, Jeff said as they were waiting, then added, “it was an interesting meeting, and I had learned a lot from my encounter with the Sheikh and Mustafa, for a start only the advisors speak any English. The guards don’t speak English at all so that might be worth knowing, but I am concerned that the Sheikh’s mind could be unstable.”

As they were talking about what the Sheikh had said, John and Derek arrived with the First Officer and two members of the crew.

Jeff stepped in straight away and said in English "I am speaking to you as if I am very annoyed over the flooding of the bathroom it is only a cover so we make contact," then he pointed at the bathroom and gesturing throwing his hands in the air in mock horror.

It seemed to work as the two-armed guards at the end of the corridor looked at one another and laughed at the embarrassing situation the Officer was being put in.

Quickly Jeff said to the Officer, "we are prepared to go down fighting, we know they intend to blow up the gas ship with us alongside it and they want to do it in an American harbour if they can, we also know there will be no rescue attempt as America will not be held to ransom, so if anything is done we have to do it ourselves or die in the attempt."

"I am afraid what you say is true," the Officer said gesturing with his arms so the guards would not know it was a cover-up and to hide what they were talking about.

The Officer added, "the Captain would like to do something, but they hold the passengers and the crew as a human shield, plus he is very concerned about his crew members that are locked away in the forward hold."

"We can organize passengers, can you organize any of the crew that's left?" Jeff said.

"They are watching the few remaining Officers closely," the Officer said, "they only let us come to you because that bloke Mustafa said to let us come to you as you had some sort of guest rights, Mustafa seems to hold you in high regard and seems quite decent, the others are fanatics."

"How about the catering staff?" Jeff said.

“The other terrorists treat them with contempt,” the officer said, “and the catering staff don’t like it.

“What if we use the catering and cleaning staff as couriers?” Jeff said, “would they help us get organized?”

“It was their friends and colleagues that were made to walk the plank they will not forget that. It was horrible. I believe they would love a chance to strike back in some way.”

Good said Jeff, “at least we can communicate, can you find out how long it will take us to get Seventy-five miles off the American coastline?”

“Why Seventy-five miles?” The Officer said.

“After that, the Americans will not let that gas ship get any closer to their coastline because of the damage it can do when it blows up and they will have no choice but to blow us out of the water before then, so that is the deadline we have in which to do something.”

“Having the *NAT GAS 2* strapped to us on a tow line will slow us down as we lose a lot of trim and have to keep matching speed with it, I will get the navigator to work it out and let you know via your table waiter.

Now let’s put on a show for those bright monkeys watching us, otherwise, they might get suspicious”, Jeff said as he stood by the door and started to rant and rave and gesturing at the bathroom. The guards started laughing again at the officer’s predicament.

The officer shook his hand and said very sincerely, “good luck! We are going to need it,” and left with one of the people he brought leaving the other one to clear up the mess Cyril had made.

Whilst the crew member cleared up the water in the bathroom which had been caused by Jen stuffing a towel down the waste outlet, once that was removed everything was alright and it just had to dry out.

Cyril said, "a good idea using the catering staff as they can mingle with everybody without raising suspicion, as long as the Sheikh does not find out."

"Don't forget that the Sheikh's advisors are the real problem in this poisonous brew," Jeff said.

Jeff then added, "Apparently, he really is the son of a Sheikh, that makes him a royal prince, but he is a royal prince with a very serious mental problem, and I believe he is being used."

"And there's me thinking it might be something simple like we had been high-jacked by some Middle Eastern terrorist organization that wants to pay back the Americans for some insult," Cyril said wryly.

"But if I read between the lines what you are saying," Cyril continued, "we are being held hostage by some spoiled brat of a boy prince who has lost his marbles, on top of that he wants to prove himself in the eyes of his elders."

He added, "he is also being helped by some right-wing advisors of a political wing of some Muslim organization, why does that sound familiar?"

"I believe behind this could be a splinter group of the same fascist organization we ran into that was involved in the Estuary Incident called The *Senate*."

Jeff said, "if it is The *Senate* that has raised its head again, we have a bigger problem than we first thought, there was no reasoning with them at that time, and I don't suppose that has changed now."

"Wasn't Sir William Waits the head of that organization?" Cyril said, "and isn't he still serving 50 life sentences in a maximum-security prison?"

"He was head of the British connection of The *Senate*," Jeff said, "but he died in prison to keep him quiet.

But we always knew there were other splinter groups throughout the world," Jeff added, "even though there was a big manhunt worldwide to eradicate the organization, but it went to ground, so whatever the outcome of these issues that we are involved in now, is only a small part of a much bigger picture."

"It does not come any bigger than the high-jack of a gas tanker and the threat to the passengers on a cruise liner," Cyril said.

"How about the enemy of my enemy is my friend until I get what I want philosophy", Jeff mused. "You talk in riddles," Cyril said, "what do you mean?"

Jeff said, "what if The *Senate* is a bigger and more secret organization than we first thought? What if The *Senate* is playing the Middle East against the West?"

"The two areas have been at each other's throats for years, and you and I know it does not take much to stir up that cauldron?" Cyril mused.

"Keeping on the same train of thought," Jeff said, "what if a very influential Sheikh's over-indulged son is killed by the West in some incident?" Then Jeff added, "it could destabilize the support that comes from the Middle Eastern very powerful Oil Sheikhs and cripples relationship between the West and the Middle East, during this unrest, The *Senate* takes over the destabilized areas as they tried to do in England and very nearly succeeded in the Estuary."

"Jesus Christ! You are a cynical bastard," Cyril said, "where did you think that one up from?"

"from trying to reason out what is happening and why? Because for every action there is a reaction." Jeff said.

Then he added, "there has to be a reason for the action in the first place, I think this is the action that will create the chain reaction that will ricochet throughout the Middle East and destabilize the newly found peace in the Arab States that is held together by the powerful Oil Sheikhs."

"So, all of this high-jacking is nothing to do with an insurgence from a Muslim faction at all," Cyril said, "it is a very unstable sick man being led around by a splinter group of The *Senate* if that is the case how many of The *Senate* are on board?"

"My guess is the six Armoury Advisers," Jeff said, "the rest is just the Sheikh's personal bodyguard, who will be loyal until death to the young prince."

"Where does Mustafa stand in all this?" Cyril said, "I understand those two have been friends from childhood."

"At this moment in time I don't know," Jeff said, "but I will find out, first we have to find out how much time we have till we get near American territorial waters, once there the Americans will bomb us out of the sea before we can get anywhere near their coastline to be able to do any damage."

Jeff continued, "if they are aware of the situation, which by now I am sure they will be, they will tell all shipping to avoid us like the plague, they might shadow us with a sub if they can get one to us in time, but I am sure any sub will have orders to sink us as soon as we near American landfall."

"Can't we signal the sub and ask them to pull alongside and board us, tell them we will help take over the ship?" Cyril said.

"First we have to know if there is a sub out there," Jeff said, "where it is, find out if it is friendly and get a signal to it, then get them to believe we are who we say we are and not luring them into a trap so the pirates then get hold of a nuclear sub as well to add to the party," Jeff said.

Then he added, "no submarine commander would endanger his ship, not even for all the passengers and crew," Jeff remarked. "I think the first you will know when there is a sub out there, is when its torpedoes slam into the side of us or the *NAT GAS 2*."

"I also believe, all the time the *NAT GAS 2* is tied to the *Baroness of the Sea*, we are cannon fodder," Jeff added, "so we have to do what has to be done as we are the only ones that can do anything."

"Until we know how long it's going to take us to get near the American coast," He added, "we can't do anything, because that is the deadline, for once we pass the point of no return, sure as eggs is eggs we will be attacked and we will be destroyed by the American Forces as the *NAT GAS 2* is blown up with us tied to it.

"What about Michael?" Cyril said, "perhaps we can get a message to him, and he can let his cousin in the American Intelligence know what's going on."

Cyril added, "I have a contact number for him, and you could phone him by using John's special phone, or we could use John's lap-top to get in contact with him via the Prime Minister."

"How do you know about John's phone and his laptop?" Jeff said, "and also, he can contact the P.M. direct?"

"You forget I'm a tea-leaf and a good one," Cyril said, "I even know he has a Mobile phone that can get a signal anywhere in the world, and if I was to guess he did not tell you about either of them until he had to.

As I have always said, that John bloke, has more tricks up his sleeve that there are in a clown's pocket and probably always will be a very dark horse."

"Let's meet up with the others over lunch, and we can find out what our options are," Jeff said to Cyril.

Michael and Valerie had done the usual tourist places for the day. They were having a lovely lunch and enjoying one another's company very much when his phone unexpectedly rang, he looked puzzled at Valerie, excused himself and said sorry it might be important.

Valerie was used to having fellow officers having important phone calls in the middle of a meal, but she did not expect Michael to receive a call.

Michael's demeanour changed, he looked serious after listening for some time, "you must be joking," he said, "I thought we cleared out that nest of vipers during the Estuary crisis. I am with my cousin Valerie now. I will have a chat with her now, I will see what I can do," and the call ended.

Valerie said, "what's wrong?" Michael looked about him to see if it was safe to talk, on seeing no one was within earshot, he leaned over to Valerie and started to tell her about the call he had received from Cyril.

"You know I told you about The *Senate* that was involved with the Estuary Incident," she nodded, "well it looks like they have raised their ugly head again, this time its piracy, they have hijacked a Gas Tanker also the Cruise Ship Jeff and the others are on, they are using the cruise ship and its passengers as a human shield, they are going to sail both boats into New York Harbour and blow them up. That's not the worst part. They believe they have an old World War 2 Submarine loaded with torpedoes, ready to put a fish into the Cruise Liner and the Gas Ship if they are interfered with before they can evacuate their fellow terrorists.

He added, "the Passengers are concerned when the American military hear about The *Senate*'s plan they will blow up the gas tanker anyway and sacrifice the passengers on the Cruise Liner just to stop it reaching American territorial waters, the main problem is they don't know where the sub is, but it must be near the two vessels, they want to know if it can be found and if it can be taken out before it puts a torpedo into either ship."

"on board the Cruise liner, my friend Jeff has a plan to take back both ships using the passengers."

"What adventure thriller book did that come out of?" she said.

Michael added, "I have seen that man Jeff fight against impossible odds before, and win, with Cyril, Jen, Derek, John and the others backing him, they are going to be an incredible force, all they need is someone on their side to be in their corner when the going looks tough, they need the right type of help and so far that help is finding that 2nd world war sub."

"Look, if what you say is true," she said, "that's right up my ally, follow me. I can get things into action, and I have the resources to get it done, come with me," Michael paid the waiter, and he followed her into the street where they hailed a taxi.

They did not speak about what Valerie wanted to do inside the taxi.

They arrived at the Naval Intelligence Headquarters, at reception they saluted Valerie but stopped Michael, she said "he is with me, I vouch for him," he was presented a visitors pass and he followed close behind her down corridors turning left and sometimes right, it was like being in a maze.

They came to an operations office where two marines were on guard, she said he is with me to the guards, they allowed him access and he followed the dancing hips of Valerie as she glided into the operations room.

Inside the room was a lot of brass hats who were busy doing their jobs, it was like a very well-oiled machine.

There was a large map of the Atlantic Ocean laid out.

"Ma'am," an officer saluted her, she returned the salute, then announced Michael was her cousin and was under her jurisdiction, they nodded to him.

Valerie said, "heads up ladies and gentlemen, I want you to listen to what my cousin Michael has to say. Listen carefully, gentlemen. This has the makings of a national threat and a big one at that."

Michael addressed the room full of naval personnel, he explained what he had been told of the situation with his friends on board, the *Baroness of the Sea* and the threat of the *NAT GAS 2*, plus the threat of a World War 2 Submarine and concern of finding it before it puts a torpedo into the Gas Tanker and destroying everything for tens of miles away, including the passengers aboard the Cruise liner.

Valerie called all the officers together and explained in detail that she wanted a rescue plan put into operation from what Michael had told her of the threat to the United States, the human shield, how it must not happen. America does not negotiate with Terrorists, but there was the element where with the policy of no negotiation with terrorists.

"If the convoy of those two ships gets anywhere near America to be able to carry out the threat, America could be forced to kill thousands of innocent civilians by eliminating that threat by blowing up the gas ship, then they would have done the job for the terrorists. If this does not pan out, you can put it down to an important exercise and work out a code name for the operation for the politicians, let me know the name you put to the exercise. My cousin has fought these people before and had vital information about The *Senate* that can help us, this information does not leave this room, do I make myself clear?"

They all replied, "Yes ma'am!"

Valerie explained firstly, what she wanted was The *Senate* submarine found at all costs, and destroyed before it made contact with the terrorists on board the Cruise Liner.

She added that all this was to happen before the ships got anywhere near American Territorial waters, she added,

"If they did stand any chance of taking over both ships as the passengers have planned, the most likely area would be off the Canadian border by Sable Island, as you are aware this is the area known as the Atlantic Graveyard of ships. So, ladies and Gentlemen please find me that Sub without any of the fleet being seen and alerting the terrorists aboard the *Baroness of the Sea* or the *NAT GAS 2.* When you find it, let me know instantly no matter where I am, you have my emergency number, use it."

They all sprang into action and got to work immediately, it was a hive of activity as the officers swung a well prepared, plan into action.

"Right," she said calmly, as she turned to Michael, "we can let the boys and girls play whilst we have that coffee in my office, the one we missed when we had lunch."

As they were leaving the operations room an officer said, "ma'am, may we call this new operation or exercise, "Operation Piracy"?

"Sounds good to me," Valerie said with a smile that lit up the room "Operation Piracy it is!"

Michael was surprised and stunned as to the way everyone jumped to obey her commands, and how efficiently she sprang into action.

It started to sink into him how far up the chain of command she was, the marines saluted her as they left and went into her office just a few doors down the corridor to have that cup of coffee.

As they sat down to discuss the plan of action of Operation Piracy, she said, "you can see how much I trust you, I am taking your say so on the situation at the moment, if what you are telling me is right we need to act as soon as possible, but I am sure I will get confirmation soon from a higher authority."

Just then the door opened and in walked the Secretary of State, looking directly at Valerie, said, "what do you know about a High-jacking of a Gas Ship and a Cruise Liner?"

"Apparently, some terrorist wants to sail both ships into New York Harbour and blow them up

I have put a plan in action, as we speak, Sir," Valerie replied, "by the way, this is my cousin Michael I told you about."

Ignoring the introduction, he said, "how come you already know, and I have just been told about it? I came straight to you to tell you to put in a plan of action and use the cover as an exercise."

Valerie said, "on receiving the information from the victims aboard the *Baroness of the Sea* realizing the desperate situation, I took direct action and after coffee, I was coming to your office to report the action, I have taken."

"This comes from the top," the Secretary of State said, "I have just had a phone call direct from non-other than the President, he has had a call from the British Prime Minister, and we have been asked to find a world war 2 Submarine in the Atlantic Ocean, do they realize the size of the Atlantic?"

Then looking at Michael, he then said, "you must be Michael, the British Prime Minister, was talking about, you must know some very powerful people young man because I have been ordered by the President of the United States to give you every available assistance, so we are putting everything we have into finding that Submarine, the

United States does not like being held to ransom, it will not negotiate with terrorists."

"That gas ship will be blown out of the water before it gets anywhere near our territorial waters," the Secretary of State said, "even if it is at the cost of everyone aboard the *Baroness of the Sea* and we are aware of the global political repercussions of that action, that will cause a holy war between the middle east and America, sour our relations with Great Britain and destroy our standing with all the other western nations, it is a political nightmare."

Then turning to Michael, he added, "can you tell me anything you know about this group called The *Senate* that they spoke of, it might help us."

"Not much," Michael said, "We ran into them in the Estuary in England," then he told him all about the disaster caused by The *Senate* when they tried to take over the British Government with William Waites as their leader, also the number of people that were killed in the process, he told him about the killer Wilson and his henchmen that hunted them under orders from William Waites who told him to kill them on sight, "you must have seen that shooting that they put on every television station when the Prime Ministers Agent John gunned down Wilson."

The Secretary of State said, "that was you and your friends that are on board the *Baroness of the Sea* that found out and exposed this group they call The *Senate*?"

"Yes," Michael said, "and my friends are trying to stop it happening again, they are putting their lives on the line to save you a political mess, and stop the killing of thousands of innocent people, they need your help, I for one will leave no rock unturned to find these particular maggots."

Valerie was sitting back in admiration, that Michael was not overawed by the Secretary of State, he said it as it was, not caring if it offended or pleased, no matter who he was talking to, also she liked the fact he was on first name terms with the British Prime Minister, and the links he had with the White House.

Secretly Valerie hoped that he was impressed with her swift actions. She looked at him puzzled by her feelings, no man had got under her skin like Cousin Michael and she was starting to like it a lot.

The Sectary of State turned to Valerie and said, "I presume a plan of action was now being put into operation and the American Atlantic Sea Pack are hunting down their prey, but time was the key, the only hope they had, was depending on how much slower both ships would have to travel, with both ships tied together, it seems finding that submarine in time was key to unlocking this particular can of worms," he said, "I can confirm to the President the dogs of war were now let loose and they were in a hunting mood."

Valerie said "yes I have released the hunting dogs of war, the code name for the operation is Operation Piracy, we must also let the Canadian officials know what was going on," Valerie and Michael looked at one another and said Cousin Laurence's name together, looked at one another and laughed, realizing they had said his named together, Valerie said, "we must apprise him of the situation."

The Secretary of State looked at Valerie and said, "you obviously have contacts in Canada."

"Very good ones," Valerie said, "how about very high up in the Royal Canadian Mounted Policeman that I trust implicitly as he is family."

The Secretary of State raised an eyebrow, and said, "you better get on with it and contact him, but play it close to your chest, also let the American Ambassador there know about the operation, I believe his name is Watson, I have only met him once, I did not get on with him, in my opinion, a bit of a snake, something about him I don't trust, but that's politics for you."

He continued, "Ambassador Watson needs to be told, but no details, I don't want that little snake trying to take all the glory if we get this right, only enough for keeping him in the loop, your Cousin Laurence in the Royal Canadian Mounted Police is safe, he has great integrity and believe it or not, I have met him on a number of occasions, and I trust him too."

The Secretary of State shook both their hands and said, "keep safe and watch your back for any treachery and keep me informed."

Valerie said, "when we know a little more, Michael and I can go and see Cousin Laurence personally and keep him up to speed as to what we know, we can link all three Ambassadors together, the American, English, and Canadian ambassadors. Politically we link our three countries together in an international combined force, that should keep the glory hunting politicians happy."

The Secretary of State smiled, "The politicians will try to get all the glory if this is successful, but they will blame you and hang you out to dry if it goes wrong."

“My people will try to get that submarine chased down,” Valerie said, “but the Atlantic is vast and it will be like looking for a needle in a haystack, we will concentrate on the area near Sable Island, but we need to let the Canadian navy know we are in the area, we don't want to create an international incident with them.”

“Leave that with me,” the Secretary of State said, “I know a few Admirals in the Canadian and American Navy I can trust, I can let them know we are in their area, good luck on your mission,” and he left.

Ambassador Watson got to hear about the interest the Naval intelligence was taking in the Area of the Graveyard of ships, so he phoned the Canadian Ambassador Waites on his private number to warn him.

Waites picked up the phone, listened to what Watson had to say about the Navy having an exercise being operated near Sable Island and did it interfere with the operation they had planned.

Waites said, “I think we are south of them but it looks like we need to keep a lookout, it's too late now, we had to launch the submarine early as the Royal Canadian Mounted Police were sniffing around, she will stay off the air until she contacts our other friends directly or carries out her mission, either way, we will know when that happens.”

Then added, “how was that new bunch of girls I got you panning out? I got all their Visa's cleared, they are being sent to your son-in-law's different gambling clubs as we speak. I can recommend the little blonde one with glasses, I know she is underage and she was frightened at first but she learned fast."

"You sick bastard," Watson said, "if The *Senate* finds out what you are doing and how it could expose them, they will kill you without a thought."

"I'm an Ambassador they can't touch me," Waites said.

"So, am I, but I have to cover my back."

Little did Watson or his brother-in-law know the F.B.I. we're following the girls sent by Waites and where they went to. Raids were being planned to expose the trafficking and shut down the gambling clubs and stop the exploiting of innocent girls.

The F.B.I. had just sent a text to Paul of the C.S.I.S. telling him of their interest in Waites and his link with Watson. They had just heard that there was a bigger agenda than just people trafficking, and could he look into it from his end in Canada, as they needed to know more about them before arrests were made.

Because the F.B.I. would be making multiple raids on the night clubs at the same time, they needed all the information about the link between Waites and Watson as well as the back doorway Waites was getting visas and passports for trafficking the girls, plus there was something bigger, that they heard was going down that involved Waites' and his collections in his museum. They wanted to know whether Paul could look into it for them as it was outside their jurisdiction.

on board the *Baroness of the Sea*, they entered the Restaurant area. The Sheikh's bodyguards were there, searching everybody as they entered the Restaurant, one particular guard was freer with his hands than was necessary and was taking his time and frisking the women intently, this caused a reaction from the women and their partners and a rebuff from the guards.

"This should be interesting," Cyril said.

"Don't you do anything," Jen said to Cyril, "I can deal with it in my way."

As the guard reached to frisk Jen, he put his hand on her chest and took his time feeling her breasts, Jen took hold of his hand, placed her hand over his, then held it on her chest between her breasts, gripping very tightly and holding onto the guard's hand, still holding his hand in place she leaned forward and bowed

The guard could not remove his hand that was flat against Jen's chest because of Jen's vice-like grip, as Jen bowed the guards fingers and wrist were bent backwards even more, as Jen bowed forward, even more, you could hear the guards fingers snap as he went on his knees leaning backwards then onto his knees as he desperately tried to avoid more pain from his trapped hand and hoping his wrist did not snap as well, the leering grin he had had on his face changed to one of surprise and then agony as he tried to remove his hand but Jen would not let go as his fingers and wrist snapped he screamed.

The two other guards that were laughing at first at their friend's predicament now started to react to their friend's screams.

Things happened very quickly, Cyril stepped behind one guard and with his thumbs extended jammed both hands together either side of the guard's head under the earlobes of the guard, then the guard sank to the ground like a sack of spuds.

The other guard was trying to raise his gun to open fire but he found himself held in a vice-like grip by Derek who had put him in a bear hug and was crushing the life out of him.

Mustafa came running up with more guards who opened fire putting a volley over their heads.

Derek dropped the unconscious guards, the other one was also in a heap by Cyril's feet, Jen released the other guard who was screaming in agony and holding his hand.

"What's going on here?" Mustafa shouted.

Jen smiled and said, "he was not treating us, women, as ladies and was pawing all the women when searching them, pointing at the unfortunate guard holding his hand, he wanted to put his hands on my chest so I let him then held his hand there and bowed to him."

Mustafa questioned the guard harshly that was holding his crushed hand.

When he got the answers he wanted, he kicked the crestfallen guard then turned towards Jen trying hard to hide the grin from his face and said, "he will think twice before manhandling the Sheikh's guest."

"The Sheikh will hear of this," he added, "you are shall we say, a guest in his tent, and as such, his staff must accord you guest rights," turning to Jeff said, "you and all your party will be treated with respect at all times. All I can do is apologize for this fool's behaviour and he will be dealt with accordingly."

"The other guards reacted to his pain and were going to attack me," Jen said, "my husband protected me as any man of honour would, as did this poor unfortunate friend of ours," pointing to Derek who immediately adopted the look of an unfortunate idiot.

Mustafa looked at Jen wryly and said, "I will guarantee your safety all the time you have guest rights, and you have my assurance no women will be molested. We are not animals."

Then smiling said, "I don't think any guards will manhandle any more women on board this ship especially after this last demonstration," then added, "he will be taking a lot of stick from his fellow guards, as he deserved what he got, all I can do is to apologize on behalf of the Sheikh."

As he turned, he said with a smile "remind me not to upset you," then he left three guards on guard duty by the door and carried away the unconscious and injured guards.

"I could have told him not to upset Jen," Derek said as Mustafa walked away.

"How did you do that?" Karen said to Jen, admiringly, "all I see you do is lean forward and he was screaming in agony."

Jen said, "I had older brothers that taught me self-defence, I'll teach you what I know it might come in handy."

"How did you do that trick?" Karen repeated.

"When he had his hand on my chest with his fingers pointing upwards," Jen said then she demonstrated, "as I held his hand in place so he could not remove it, I then bow forward trapping his hand. The more I leaned forward, the more I bend his fingers backwards therefore snapping his wrist and fingers."

"We need these to protect us," Derek said, pointing at the girls, "all we have to do is organize them into an army."

As they sat down to lunch Jeff said to John and Cyril, "Derek might have a point there about organizing the girls as a fighting team."

"What!?", Cyril said. "Jen might be capable of handling herself, but not every woman can."

"Whoa back tiger," Jeff said, "think about it. We need to communicate with other passengers freely and co-ordinate any action we will have to take later. What better way than using the women to spread what we are doing to the other passengers in secret."

"That puts the women in danger and no one is going to let that happen, especially me, as far as Jen is concerned," Cyril said very arrogantly.

"You what?" Jen reacted.

"Neutral corners you two," Jeff said, "before we have a domestic in front of all the passengers listen to what I have to say first, then let me have your opinion."

He continued, "have you noticed, women always seem to go to the lady's room in two's and three's, unlike men, they normally go on their own?"

"We taught you, little boys, how to do that when you were very small," Jen joked, "then we let you do it on your own, at least that was something you learned," she said sarcastically.

Ignoring the wind-up, Jeff carried on, "what I am talking about is, as women meet in the toilets more times than men, and in greater numbers, we can let the women be our secret communication system between one another, and as the guards won't disturb the women, not after today's incident, all the guards will do is stand outside the toilets, the women can communicate inside and pass on information without the guards finding out."

"It's not unusual for two women to go to the toilet together where it is unusual for men to do it, and it will allay any suspicion being aroused by the guards."

Just then a waiter came to their table said to them "your tea Sir," and placed a tray of tea in front of Jeff.

"I don't remember ordering tea," Jeff said, as he lifted the napkin there was a plate of small pancakes on the tray. As he looked at the pancakes, he realized there were finely piped wording written on the pancakes "10-00 hrs 7th".

"We have just less than two days before the deadline is reached," Jeff said, handing round the small pancakes showing what was written on them, then they proceeded to eat them.

"I knew you would have to eat your own words someday? Now that's a first," Cyril joked.

"You can eat the next communication," Jeff said to Cyril, "this will create havoc with my figure if I carry on like this."

"What figure?" Cyril bantered and they both laughed.

"Well it seems to be working," Jeff said, "now let's get organized and plan what we can do, and when we can do it."

They settled down into a huddle.

"Somehow, we need to knock out the guards on both ships at the same time. That is going to be very hard to do and will need some organizing."

"We will need to speak to that 1st officer again," John said.

Derek's wife Sandra spoke up and said, "I wonder if they have any Temazepam on board in the medical centre."

"What's temazepam?" Derek said.

"It's a bitter-tasting substance that is misused as a date rape drug," said Sandra, "it can knock a horse out, also it's a medicine that should be carried by all medical centers," Sandra added, "if you can get the guards on both ships to take that, it would put them out for quite some time.

We could get it injected into sweet chocolates by the chef, or sprinkled onto a strong curry." Sandra said, "I understand Middle Eastern people have a very sweet tooth and like spicy food."

"Brilliant," Derek said, "you are not only a pretty face, but you're also intelligent as well," as he turned to her and hugged her.

"There are intelligent women you know," Sandra said from inside his arms.

"Hey big boy," Jen said slapping Derek on the back in a friendly way, "don't think you men have all the brains," she retorted, "it's men thinking that gets us into the problems we have today."

"OK, let's get back to the matter in hand," John said, "what Sandra suggested is a brilliant idea, we need to put that to the First Officer to see if it can be arranged. What we have to work on is a time frame of at least half an hour before the deadline, that's 09-30 hrs the day after tomorrow, after that we are all dead."

Just then Jen spotted a female Entertainment Officer by the door near the ladies toilets, and she said to the others, "Nature calls!" and hurried to the ladies toilet passing one of the guards who followed her towards the toilet where Jen spoke to the Entertainment Officer, and they both went into the toilet together.

Jen looked daggers at the guard he hesitated about following them inside but realizing what Mustafa had said, changed his mind, and stayed outside waiting for them to reappear.

Just as they were discussing ways to administer the drug to the guards Mustafa came into the dining room and approached them.

"You look agitated," he said to Jeff, "what are you up to?" Then turning to Cyril, "is there a problem?"

"My wife has just gone to the lady's room and your guard was going to go in as well," Cyril said, "if he does go in, I don't rate his chances."

"You could not reach him before he put a bullet in you," Mustafa said, "I will go and have a word with him."

Mustafa went over to the guard and spoke to him in what sounded to them as Arabic, Cyril said to the others, "I wasn't worried for myself or Jen, it would be the guard that would have come off worse, and Jen would put his lights out."

They all smiled, Derek said, "she has a fearsome temper."

Mustafa returned and said, "there is no need to worry, I have reminded the guard that you are the Sheikh's guests and as such you are to be treated with the greatest respect as will your women."

Then Mustafa added, "he was concerned that a plot was being hatched by a few Officers to free everybody, but I told him that was impossible as there were not enough of them and they would have to co-ordinate a plan that would mean taking over both ships simultaneously, he also feared the women were part of that plot that is why he was going to follow them into the toilet."

"He would not have come out of there a whole man if he had done that," Cyril said.

"As I said," Mustafa added, "you would not have reached him and unfortunately would have been shot in the process, and we would have breached guest rights as you are under our protection as our guests."

Dismissively Mustafa said, "don't worry your head about your women, I have left instructions that the guards will not molest or follow empty-headed, chattering women into toilets, that would serve no purpose, and it would only unnecessarily inflame the men on board and could cause unrest.

We in our country don't allow women to be part of any decisions," Mustafa added, "as women are put on this earth to please their men."

"But we will discourage any group meetings of any of the men, excluding meal times of course, because that is when you will be under scrutiny by the guards.

I came to tell you the Sheikh would like a word with you after you have had your lunch," Mustafa said, "he would value your opinion on a little matter that affects you all, shall we say 14-00 hours?" He then turned on his heels and walked away.

"What an arrogant person," Rose said, "doesn't he know women stopped being chattels for men over a hundred years ago?"

"It is the way that men think in his country," John said.

"That could be to our advantage," Jeff said, "by leading them into a false sense of security. As you know I led them to believe Derek is a harmless nit-wit, but we know that he is very powerful and very intelligent. If we can make them believe we treat our women as chattels and don't take any heed to anything they say," Jeff said, "they will think that is normal, we can then use that as an advantage, and the women can carry out the vital role of communications right under their noses in secret. It can all be done in all the ladies toilets throughout the ship."

Just then Jen returned, and Cyril told her what happened whilst she was in the lady's room.

"He would have been singing soprano when he left the ladies room," Jen said, "if he had come in there whilst I was in there."

"See, I told you she had a fearsome temper," Derek said, "even I avoid upsetting her, and she would have crucified that guard had he entered the lady's room, wouldn't she?" Turning to look at Cyril.

Cyril said, "and some, when I said to Mustafa, I was concerned over the situation he thought I was going to attack his guard to protect Jen, it would have been the guard who needed protection from Jen."

"Well enough of that," Jen said, "that Female Officer I just met is going to help be a go-between the officers and passengers but it has to be co-ordinated and before 10 o/c tomorrow. That is the deadline, so we have to have a coordinated plan of attack by then.

But according to her, there is still one other major problem," Jen added, "they have placed explosives against the bulkheads of the *Baroness of the Sea* that can be detonated by a plunger placed near the explosives, apparently, we are lucky they are not remotely controlled."

John said, "our biggest problem is the crew on the *NAT GAS 2* tanker. If they get wind of anything amiss, they will manipulate the gas valves on the tanker. We need to silence them first and the only way to get to the *NAT GAS 2* is via deck 5 and that is guarded."

"We need to find and disarm the explosives on board this ship," Cyril said.

"Then we need to cut free the *Baroness of the Sea* from the *NAT GAS 2* and get the two ships at least ten miles apart," Jeff said, "whoever takes on the *NAT GAS 2* will be on a suicide mission."

"At the same time all the guards have to be disabled on board this ship all in 36 hours by ordinary people and a few of the cruise ship's staff," Derek said, "what bright bastard thought that one up for us?"

"We also need to get a message to the Americans, hopefully before they blow us out of the water," Jen said, "and tell them what we are planning to do without the Sheikh or any of his cronies finding out."

"How are we going to coordinate all this if you men aren't allowed to talk to the male members of the crew," Jeff's wife said,

"Then we need to see the Captain and find out if he can get a message out to the Americans from his radio room and help organize his crew."

"There' another complication," Jen said, "according to Mary that female Officer I spoke to, the Captain is kept locked in his cabin with two guards outside when he is not on the bridge."

"Then I will visit him in his cabin," Cyril said, "and have a word with him to find out what can be done."

"How are you going to get to him?" John said, "he is guarded at all times."

"If I know Cyril, he will find a way," Jeff said.

"Is there something I don't know?" John said.

"Let me introduce you to the now-retired squirrel," pointing at Cyril, "and he can get in anywhere if he wants to, he does not have that nickname the squirrel for nothing," Jeff said.

"Your reputation precedes you," John said, "I never knew it was you. I have heard of you under that name, but only by the reputation of being one the best tea-leaf in the world."

"How do you think we got that information about Sir William Waites out of the terminal and to you right from under their noses?" Jeff said.

"I never knew," John said, "what a dark horse you are," John added as he turned to Cyril.

"Never mind that, I will go and have a chat with the Captain," Cyril said.

"Be careful dear," Jen said, "I don't want to lose you now that I found you."

"There's no fear of that you sexy thing," Cyril said.

"Cyril!" Jen said, "you will make me blush."

"I'll be a little while, you keep everything warm till I get back," and kissed her and slipped away.

Jen coloured up embarrassingly, and then lovingly said, "I will sort you out later," as he walked off.

"I will have a wander around to see if I can find where these explosive devices have been put,: John said.

"Before you say anything," he interjected, "I used to be a demolition expert for the army before I worked for the P.M. so I do know what I am doing, and I will know the best places where to put explosive devices. If I can disable any of them without them knowing I will, but I have to find them first and I don't know how many there are," and he wandered off.

"Please take care of yourself," Rose said, he squeezed her hand lovingly as he left.

"I have to go and see the Sheikh," Jeff said, "what about I do not know. How do you talk to a mad man and not go mad yourself is beyond me, but Mustafa said he wants a word with me. Perhaps I can find out what he intends to do, knowing your enemy is half the battle."

"You better be careful as well," Karen said, "I don't trust that Sheikh."

"Neither do I," Jeff said, "but it would help us if we know what he has planned and when he plans to do it. I will see you back in the cabin, Derek will see you are safe."

"No one will harm you while I live," Derek said to her, "you are all safe with me."

Jeff walked away to find the Sheikh, whilst the girls went back to their cabins escorted by Derek who they knew would lay down his life for them as Jeff remembered he had done for him in the past at the Estuary.

That seemed a world away from what was happening now as Jeff was escorted to meet the Sheikh near his suit of cabins. As he approached, he was speaking to Abdul one of the English speaking advisors, and the Sheikh had his usual amount of 4 bodyguards with him who kept their eyes on the Sheikh at all times.

The Sheikh greeted him with a smile saying, "it is my birthday today, and to celebrate it, it is custom in my country to give presents to those who you admire and are friends, and I wanted to give you a present to celebrate my birthday," as he handed Jeff a jewel encrusted dagger.

"This is a very expensive gift you give to a poor and humble man, I am overwhelmed," Jeff said bowing, as he did not want to make the Sheikh suspicious then added, "surely it is for people to give you presents on your birthday? Not for you to give expensive presents to others, if I had known it was your birthday, I would have arranged something for you."

The Sheikh tut tutted, "If you remember, you said if a poor man gives someone a present it is a rich gift, if a rich man gives a rich present, it is not a poor gift but its value is less because it costs the rich man less than it costs the poor man to give the gift."

"You know I respect you, and the wise words you say," Jeff said to the Sheikh, bowing, as he was trying to hide the total confusion as to what the Sheikh meant but wanted to appease him as he had the look of a madman in his eyes.

The Sheikh's eyes changed and lit up when Jeff said that he was wise and he respected him.

"That is praise indeed," the Sheikh said to Jeff, "coming from someone like yourself who I respect greatly, that really is praise indeed," and he seemed to puff his chest out, then he added as he turned to Abdul and said, "see? I knew he and his friends would join me in my struggle to prove I am worthy of respect, I told you so, he just said he admires me and my wise words, I told you Jeff's and my life are linked in the eternal struggle of life."

Jeff's mind was doing overtime, it seemed the Sheikh had flipped over the edge of reasoning and was in a world of his own. He expected him to turn at any moment into the dangerous megalomaniac he knew he was, it was then he had a wild idea.

"Will you permit me to arrange for a small humble celebration for you and your party, just to celebrate your birthday?"

"You would do that for me?" The Sheikh said, looking surprised, then added, "it would have to be tomorrow night as I have to leave to see my father. You can come with me and tell him what you have said, there will be room for Jeff and his party won't there Abdul?"

"My friends and I would arrange a special birthday party for you, if you will allow us access to the officers and catering staff so we can arrange a themed, formal surprise party for you."

Abdul interjected and said, "the Sheikh is very busy and it's not advisable for you to mingle with the staff at this time, I don't condone it."

"The party will be for the Sheikh, not for you," Jeff said to Abdul, testing where he stood with Abdul, then pushing his luck and relying on the Guest Rights he had with the Sheikh, he said to Abdul, "anyway who are you to tell me I can't arrange a party for someone I have come to respect and admire?"

Abdul's eyes flared up, it was clear he was holding back his temper in front of the Sheikh. Jeff thought he was going to leap at him and attack him. He knew by his reaction that he had just made an enemy of someone that was a handful in a fight and looked as though he had a very vicious killer streak about him. It was obvious the man was not used to his opinion being questioned and would find a way to make Jeff soundly aware of it if the opportune moment arose.

It looked like there would be a standoff between Jeff and Abdul. When the Sheikh interjected and said to Abdul in Arabic, "you are my paid advisor in military matters, and I respect your opinion very much, I also have great respect for Jeff and what he has achieved, but I would so like a party, I have not had anyone give me a party for years, and I do so love Birthday cake."

Then the Sheikh looked as though he was looking into the distance and lost himself in another world of his own making, then said in English, "I haven't had a surprise party done just for me in years," and then he snapped back into reality and said to Abdul petulantly, "I can't see why not."

"I still don't advise it," Abdul replied in Arabic, "you don't know what they will get up to?"

"What can they get up to?" The Sheikh said to Abdul, "they are surrounded by armed guards and we have the *NAT GAS 2* in tow ready to manipulate the valves and blow her up, we also have the Baroness of the Sea passengers and crew as a human shield, plus your men ready to make sure no one attacks us by surprise from the sea, and we have explosives in strategic places on board the Baroness of the Sea ready for someone to pull the pin. What more do you want? They can't do anything."

"I still don't trust them," Abdul said.

"You jump at shadows, I don't think you even trust your mother," the Sheikh said to Abdul petulantly, "and anyway I would like a party for my birthday," he said sullenly.

"Well! You better watch them closely," Abdul said, "I still don't trust them," looking at Jeff with hatred.

"You're being paranoid," the Sheikh said to Abdul, then turning to Jeff he said in perfect English, "would you and your friends do a party for me? I would so love it. I am sure it would be a great success," then looking away in the distance said, "I can dress in my best robes, you and I will have matching daggers, we will be brothers in arms celebrating. It will be such fun."

"Leave it to me," Jeff said, "I will give you a late-night party you will never forget, but I will need time to get it done so I better start right away."

"I will get Mustafa to help you, we have been blood brothers from our birth you know? He knows what I like," the Sheikh said, "that way we can appease Abdul here that you are being watched and not planning to kill all of my guards and stop me from blowing up the ship at any time if I wanted to."

The Sheikh had a sly crazy look about him as if he was dreaming and was in his own world óf make-believe, then his eyes cleared and it seemed sanity returned, "I will look forward to it," the Sheikh said. As they parted

Jeff headed back to the cabin with his idea's growing in his head as to what they can do, but the timing has got to be perfect otherwise they are all dead.

When he got back to the cabin, they were all there except John, they were all looking anxious.

He explained to the others what had taken place at the meeting with the Sheikh, as he showed Karen the jewel-encrusted dagger, Karen said, "you could not accept such a gift from someone who is obviously mad,"

Jeff said, "I had no choice, I had to appease his ego, it seems the only way to get through to him at the moment. It's Abdul that is the nasty one," he added, "that one is pure evil and looks as strong as an ox."

"You leave him to me," Derek said, "he won't hurt anymore people after I have finished with him."

Then he told them of his idea of throwing a late-night party, "so we need to get everyone together then we can take back the ship whilst the Sheikh celebrates his birthday."

"They don't drink alcohol, so how are you going to disable every one of the guards?" Rose said.

We have to find out if the Medical Centre on board has a supply of that Temazepam, Sandra spoke about, and how much of it they have."

"We can lace the icing of the cake with enough Temazepam to knock out a horse, as Sandra suggested," Jeff said. "Temazepam has a bitter taste, but if we put it in the icing we can disguise it, also the Middle Eastern people have a very sweet tooth and love things like any icing on cakes or sweets and chocolates."

"The guards are not likely to refuse a piece of the Sheikh's birthday cake," Jen said, "those that do we can hit over the head, either way, they finish up with a headache an aspirin won't cure."

"We then need to get the two ships parted at the same time of disabling the bombs on board this ship that is not going to be easy," Karen said, "but we will need to rely on John for that."

"The only access to the tow ropes that bind the two ships together have to be accessed via deck 5 and that is heavily guarded and those ropes are fastened in quite a few places," Derek said.

"It will take at least ten men to cut those ropes with sharp axes, and the cutting of those ropes have to be co-ordinated, as it has to be done at the same time as the swell of the two boats merge," Jeff said, "otherwise, it will create a shudder through the ship that will alarm the Sheikh, and I don't know if he has a remote detonator that will blow up the *NAT GAS 2* or the explosives on board the *Baroness of the Sea*."

Then he added, "whoever boards the *NAT GAS 2* will be on a suicide mission unless they find a way of getting off the ship before it is either blown out of the water by the Americans or it blows up on its own," then he said, "that gas ship has to be ten miles away from us if we are to survive it blowing up even then it will be a close-run thing."

"We have to have co-ordinated teams to find and disable the explosives on board this ship otherwise we will end up in Davy Jones locker anyway," Jeff said.

"All this whilst coordinating a party for a megalomaniac and his sidekick and it has to be done so he or his advisors are not suspicious," Karen said, "have you got any more rabbits to come out of this hat?" She said turning to Jeff.

As they were discussing the issues Cyril slid silently into the cabin and started to listen to what was being discussed then added, "I got into the Captain's cabin saw the Captain," It gave everyone a start as they did not hear him enter, "I gave him a bit of a start too just like you lot he had not had anybody visit his cabin via the balcony before.

The guard came in during my visit but the Captain hid me in his shower until the guard went back on guard duty."

"How did you find what cabin the Captain was in?" Karen said.

"That's a trade secret," Cyril said to her.

Jen said, "my Cyril is the best tea-leaf in town," then added proudly, "there is no-one he can't find and there is not a locked room he can't get into, I thought Jeff would have told you that."

Karen looked shocked.

Jeff turned to Karen, and said, "I will, and have always kept Cyril's secret," then added, "and so must you dear," then added, "what the Sheikh and Mustafa don't know gives us an advantage".

"Now what did the Captain have to say?" Jeff said.

"The first officer is allowed to see him," Cyril said, "so he communicates to the First officer in secret, right under their noses, and whilst the guards and one of the English speaking advisors are in the room, they do it via the signal flags that are surrounding the edge of a chart he has layed on his desk. Apparently, each flag means a word or letter and they just point to it and they have a conversation in front of everyone without them realizing it. It's brilliant."

"So, what are they planning?" Jeff said.

"Well," Cyril added, "they have a specially equipped radio room that looks like an ordinary crew member's cabin and they are in touch via a special link with the British COBRA incident room and they, in turn, are in touch with the American equivalent.

You were right, the Americans want to blow us out of the water," Cyril said, "but are being held in check for the time being, or until all the options are looked at and a plan of action takes shape, mind you, they don't have many options."

"I told the Captain what we were planning to do, he did not like it, but it was better than he can do with his crew locked in the forward Locker room. I said we would try to find a way to release them, remember this is not a military ship and it is fraught with danger. I also told him that we would muster the male passengers together and would communicate with one another via the women when they use the toilets. He thought that was a good idea. He also said he would communicate via the first officer to let the Medical Officer give us all his supply of Temazepam or any other sleeping draught he might have, so we can put it into the guard's food when we have the Sheikh's party."

Just then, John returned.

"What have you found out?" Jeff said.

"Well," John said, "as far as I can make out there are 3 lots of explosives, one in the stern of the ship in the lower deck just below the waterline, one in the middle of the ship on the port side at the same level and one in the bow of the ship, that one is above the water line but I believe it is next to the bulkhead where the crew are being held, each one has a guard within 20 to 30 feet of the detonating plungers, it will be a job to surprise them."

"Now we have to find out how many guards there are on board the *NAT GAS 2*," Jeff said.

"How do we do that?" Jen asked.

"Well they have to eat," Cyril said, "so, the catering staff might be able to tell us as they send across food by breaches buoy at mealtimes."

"I can't see them putting up with army rations if there is luxury food next door," John said, "troops are the same world-wide they march on their stomach's, so someone is supplying them food, and that has got to come from the kitchens on board this ship, all we have to do is have a word with the catering manager to find out."

"That can be done when we meet up with them to organise the Sheikh's surprise birthday party," Jeff said.

"What surprise birthday party?" John said.

"The one I talked the Sheikh into letting us organise for his birthday," Jeff said.

"If he knows about it, how come it's a surprise?" Derek said.

"If we use this as an opportunity to talk to the officers and willing passengers when we organise the surprise, it will be a birthday he will not forget," Jeff said.

"He let you talk him into doing a surprise birthday party for himself?" John said, "when did this happen?"

"When he sent Mustafa to bring me to his cabin and presented me with this as a present to me on his birthday," he showed John the jewel-encrusted dagger the Sheikh had presented him with.

John whistled, "that's a few pennies," then added. "He must respect you to give you something like that."

"It was then I thought of doing a party for him as a cover to try to take back the ship," Jeff said, "but that advisor, Abdul, he does not leave his side, he is suspicious of my motives so we have to be careful."

"And I thought politicians were devious," John said, "but you take the biscuit, if it works, I will take my hat off to you."

"We have permission to organise a party for the Sheikh, so let's go and organise one," Jen said, "and boy will there be a few surprises," she chuckled.

"Now see what you've started," Cyril said to Jeff, "once she gets the bit between her teeth there will be no stopping her, this is what happens when someone upsets her and she plans retaliation."

"It will be fun," Jen said, slapping Cyril on the back, "I think I might enjoy this, I like a challenge."

"This will be a job for the men," John said.

"Oops," said Cyril, as Jen rounded on John.

"You are not one of these men that think women are chattels and are meek little things that need protection all the time," Jen stormed at him, "let me tell you, we are better adapted in protecting our loved ones than men and don't you forget it."

"I did say not to upset her," Derek said to John.

John started to bluster, "that's not what I meant," he said defensively.

Rose smiled knowingly at Jen, and said to John, "darling when in a deep hole stop digging, you will only make it worse for yourself and you will be up to your neck in it."

It all went quiet for a minute, and then they looked at each other and burst out laughing.

"On a more serious note," John said, trying to recover from his mistake, "what worries me is that we have not had the serious sabre-rattling normally associated with a political high-jack."

"What do you mean?" Cyril said.

"Well," John said, "we have not had the usual call for worldwide media cover to highlight the plight of their cause, also they have not demanded the public killing of hostages in front of the media."

"What were the deaths of the two crew members about then?" Jen said, "that was an execution, making them walk the plank like that, it was horrible."

"That was a demonstration of what would happen if the crew and passengers did not toe the line," John said, "it was a way to keep us all in check until they got within striking distance of America, where they could force America to do the killing as they would kill everyone on board by blowing up the *NAT GAS 2* to stop it from entering American waters."

"But what does the Sheikh get out of this because he will die as well," Jen said.

"Notoriety," John said, "I believe Osama Bin Laden once said, we are in love with death, the west is in love with life, and that is the difference between us."

Then added, "it looks like this Sheikh wants to make a name for himself by taking on the biggest country in the world alone, with only a handful of personal bodyguards in some macabre David and Goliath confrontation, and these 6 so-called advisors are encouraging him for their own political ends."

"I believe there could be some truth in what you say," Jeff said, "as Mustafa hinted that the Sheikh was out of favour with his father over him acting like an over-indulged child and the Sheikh took exception to it."

"That makes him even more of a dangerous nut case, as we don't know what he is going to do next," Cyril said, "he is a ticking time bomb waiting to go off."

"So, all this might not be a Middle Eastern confrontation with the west," Derek said, "just a spoiled brat stamping his royal foot at his daddy.

"If that is the case," Jen said, "how is he going to get off the ship before it blows up so he can tell his daddy I told you so, as I see it any vessel that leaves this ship will be monitored closely and it will be boarded."

John was thinking deeply then said, "what if it was not a surface ship that takes the Sheikh and his men off the *Baroness of the Sea* and the NAT GAS 2, what if it is a fully equipped submarine."

Then John added, "they could either blow holes in the Baroness of the sea with the explosives they have put on board so she sinks, therefore, dragging down the NAT GAS 2."

Jeff interjected by saying, "which in turn when the Liquefied gas comes into contact with the seawater will explode in a rapid phase transition and then boil off into an unconfined vapour cloud which also could explode, or if that did not happen as they wanted it to, they could always put a torpedo into the side of the NAT GAS 2 to make sure."

"That is fiendish," Karen said, "nobody in their right mind would do something like that."

"We are not talking of someone in their right mind," Jeff said, "we are talking of someone who has lost the plot but is also powerful enough to do a lot of damage, he could even wait until there was a rescue attempt as the *Baroness of the Sea* is sinking and then put the fish into the side of the gas ship taking out the rescue crews as well."

"That's horrible," Karen said, "they would murder the thousands of people on board as well."

"That is why it makes it even more imperative that we carry out our takeover of the two ships as soon as possible," Cyril said, "also we need to let the Captain know of our theories so he can contact the authorities so they can put in a co-ordinated plan of operation."

"Won't they sink us out of hand?" Sandra said, "because we are a threat to their territorial waters and coastline."

"I am sure they will wait until we are near their coast, in case there is a chance of a rescue attempt," John said, "but not close enough so as they are threatened, but there will be a point of no return when they will order us to be sunk out of hand and hope there might be a chance of some survivors."

If we can let them find out if there is a submarine out there," Jeff said, "then they might be able to find it and take it out before the Sheikh gets off this ship and onto the Submarine, then we get a small advantage."

"Are there any habited or uninhabited Islands between where we are now and the North American coast?" Karen said, "if there is, we might be able to use the lifeboats to get people off the ship."

"Not in the middle of the Atlantic," Cyril said.

"That's not quite true," John interrupted.

"What do you mean? Not quite true, I know the Atlantic is a vast ocean but I believe we are too far north to be near any of the Madeira Islands," Cyril said.

"But we do go within fifty to a hundred miles or so off Sable Island," John said, "It is an Island which lays about 150 miles of Halifax, Nova Scotia, and about 750 miles from New York, the Island is about 22 miles long and about a mile wide at its widest point it lays off the American, Canadian border, it has a Canadian research station on it, herds of wild horses and is a home for seals and not a lot else. The sea bed rises sharply about 25 miles from its coastline, Oh I believe it is a hunting ground for the great white shark, it is a pretty bleak place, there are I believe half a dozen scientists living there at most."

"I've never heard of it," Cyril said, "but it seems like hells back yard."

"There have been 350 wrecks off Sable Island with the loss of thousands of lives," John said, "it has the reputation of being the Atlantic graveyard of ships."

"Not a popular holiday destination then," Cyril quipped.

"The Canadians are very particular about who actually lands on Sable Island," John added, "also you need special approval from the Canadian Government," then he added, "It has quite often been mistaken for the coast at Nova Scotia because when you first see it from the sea it looks like a large piece of the main coastline as I said it's about 22 miles long and only 1 mile wide but it is surrounded by rocky outcrops and sand bars that's why there have been so many wrecks on it."

"The Island itself is a long narrow slightly curved Island shaped like a long sabre," John added, "and Nova Scotia is just over half a day's sailing away and New York is still about one and a half a day's sailing away from Sable Island, it does have a helicopter station and a small runway for small aircraft on the beach."

"It seems better than nothing or Davey Jones' locker," Cyril said, "at least that could be our point of no return if we are to carry out our plans of taking over this ship."

"Well, if we are talking of doing something to rectify our situation then we better set up teams and get ourselves organized," John said.

"How many teams do you need?" Sandra said.

"Well," John said, "we need one team to liaise with the catering staff then to organise the party, get the cake made with the sleeping draft in it to knock out the guards and those on deck 5 will have to be knocked out first. Then we need another team to find out how to board the Gas ship and disarm the guards on board and be ready to sail that away from us when the ropes are cut. We then need another team to cut the cables between the two ships that will take at least ten men to cut the cables with axes all at the same time. Then we need another team to disarm the explosives on board which will also have to be done at the same time."

"If there is a submarine out there, we need to get the Americans or someone else to find it and knock that out before it can torpedo us, or the *NAT GAS 2*. I doubt that it can be done," Sandra said, "it will be like organising a military operation with civilians, they are not disciplined enough it will be a blood bath."

"What other options do we have, except to put our heads between our legs and kiss our backside goodbye?" Jeff said, "we must be under no illusion these people play for keeps and the Americans will blow us out of the water rather than let us anywhere near their coastline, so we have to do something about the situation or die in the attempt, look at it this way, if we do nothing we are dead, but by doing something we have a slim chance of living through it, and if we don't, at least we can say we said NO and we had a go and did not give up and go quietly into the night with our tails between our legs, we stood and made a difference, that's the important bit."

"Right," Cyril said, "I will pay the Captain a visit and let him know about our suspicions of there being a submarine out there to pick up the Sheikh and his men. Maybe he can use that secret radio to alert the Americans. Also, I will tell him what we intend to do beforehand, he might have a member of his crew that knows about explosives."

"I will also contact our people in Whitehall via my laptop," John said, "and let them in on the act they may be able to get some military support for what we are doing."

"Can I use your Mobil phone to contact Michael?" Cyril said, "he might be able to get some pressure put on from his end via his cousin in the United States Naval Intelligence."

"How did you know about my Mobil phone?", John said looking at Cyril suspiciously.

"You would be surprised what a good tea-leaf knows," Cyril said proudly.

"I know about explosives," John said changing the subject but still looking at Cyril with a surprised look, then added, "but we will need at least two more to help disarm the explosive devices if we are to do it at the same time, perhaps if we can release some of the crew members first from the forward locker, maybe one or two of them might be able to help with the explosives."

"Yes, you can use my phone," John said, still shaking his head in disbelief that Cyril knew about his secret phone.

"Maybe some of the ship's officers or crew might have knowledge of explosives," Cyril interjected, "they would be able to help too."

"Don't forget to mention to the Captain when you see him, we need a volunteer crew to sail the *NAT GAS 2* and that will possibly be a suicide crew," Jeff added.

"If you girls want to use the ladies public toilets and spread the word to the other women on board but make sure they are aware we need at least ten volunteers to cut those cables that tie us to the *NAT GAS 2* and we need women to help co-ordinate this, but above all, it must be kept secret otherwise we are all dead," John said.

"Now we need to organise and dress the main dining room for the Sheikh's surprise party," Jeff said.

"Leave that to us women we are best suited for that job, we can do that without raising any suspicions," Jen said.

"Come on girls we have work to do," Karen said getting into the spirit of the challenge.

The girls left the cabin to spread the word amongst the other passengers via the lady's toilets.

Cyril went to the balcony and just disappeared. Jeff did not see the going of him.

John said, "that was slick I did not see the going of him, no wonder he is a good tea leaf,"

Derek said, "what can I do to help?"

"Be my bodyguard, John is very fit and can look after himself, Cyril is as fit as a butcher's dog but I am still recovering from the injuries I got from Wilson," Jeff said,

"but carry on acting as though you are a can short of a six-pack it will lull them into a false sense of security, anyway I will feel safer with you looking after me than anybody else."

"Aw! Jeff you know I love you like a brother, we will be the dynamic duo again, or if you like beauty and the beast and you will be the ugly beast this time," he joked, "and I will protect you with my life," the big man went all mushy.

"I know you will," Jeff said, "but don't forget to act stupid in front of the Sheikh and his henchmen, then when the time is right, you can show them just how skilled you are."

"I did that in the ring sometimes, it always worked," Derek said, "did you know I was a contender for an Olympics? But I had a bad fall it put me out of wrestling for months, by the time I healed the Olympics were over, after that, I never wrestled in the ring again."

"Cyril mentioned it," Jeff said, "have you ever thought of training young hopefuls in your art so they might be able to get to the Olympics?"

Derek looked as though someone had switched a light on, and then said, "No I never thought I was good enough to train someone, anyway I understand Arabic if it helps."

"What," Jeff said, "how come you can speak Arabic?"

"I can't speak it very well but I understand it, a friend of mine and the man who I trained with was an Arab, he was a lovely man, he taught me some lovely wrestling moves and some of his language, I understand it better than speaking it."

"Well from what Cyril tells me," Jeff said, "you are more than qualified as you have been there and got the tee-shirt."

"If we get out of this alive, I think I might set up my own training school," then changing the subject Derek said, "what are our chances of getting through this?"

"We have the element of surprise on our side, and the Sheikh thinks he has us by the short and curlies, but he has underestimated us and believes we will accept our fate, but he has forgotten the bulldog spirit of the British."

"I believe he wanted to lull me into a false sense of security with the presentation of that jewel-encrusted dagger, but I had a feeling he wanted to take it back after I was dead, I got the impression he was an Indian giver."

"What's an Indian giver?" Derek said.

"It's what the new early American settlers said about the Native American Indians when they traded goods as they always wanted something to their advantage in return if they gave you something, I hope what the Sheikh wants is not going to be too expensive otherwise he is going to be very disappointed, and I get the impression if he gets disappointed he turns very nasty," Jeff changed the subject and added, "Now we need to wait to find out what Cyril finds out from the Captain."

Back in the American Military Headquarters, Michael had a call telling him about the plans the hostages of the *Baroness of the Sea* were going to carry out, he told Valerie what they had planned, "they would try to take back control of the two ships, at the Atlantic Graveyard of Ships off the Canadian Coastline near a place called Sable Island."

"The plans had been confirmed that was sent via a link between a secret radio message sent from the Captain of the *Baroness of the Sea*, it was confirmed by a British Government agent named John who was on board the Cruise Liner with a link to the British Prime Minister who in turn appraised us of the situation.

Valerie said, "we were right to concentrate on the area around Sable Island apparently, this taking back of the two ships is being organized by a man you know called Jeff Baker."

"Jeff?," Michael said, "that does not surprise me, it's the type of thing he would try to do, he does not like bullies, he led the fight in the Estuary in England against Sir William Waites and The *Senate* and he exposed that worldwide terrorist organisation that caused the death of thousands in the Estuary, he will stop at nothing to bring these bastards down."

Valerie said, "also involved with this Jeff is a Jenny, Cyril, Derek, John and their wives, what do you know about these people."

Michael said, "They are my friends who I helped to bring down The *Senate* at the time of the Estuary incident."

Valerie said, "you are a dark horse Michael, I am impressed, you and I must join this fight against The *Senate* together."

Michael looked at Valerie and said saucily, "as much as I would look forward to tumbling with you together in private, on this issue we need help, I have tangled with these bastards before and they play for keeps. "

Valerie reacted to his saucy remark about tumbling together with a smile and a sparkle in her eye, then she concentrated on the issue of stopping an incident that would have world-wide political implications for her country.

Michael added, "we need to let the Canadians know what is planned in case they can help, as Sable Island belongs to them, and if that's where it's all going to kick off that's where we need to be also."

"Perhaps our contact, cousin Laurence," she added, "he is high up in the Canadian Mounted Police, perhaps he can do something his end, I have his number if it helps, I have not seen him for years but we send the usual Christmas card."

Valerie rang the number, and Laurence answered the phone, the voice at the other end said, "Hi Cousin, how are you? Long-time no see, what's kicking off at your end of the Country?"

Valerie told him as much as she dared about the situation, he said, "leave it with me we can be on top of this as soon as we can, also I can make arrangements for you to visit with Michael if you fancy the trip."

Valerie said to Michael, "Laurence, has invited us to stay with him in Canada whilst we sort this out, my people can deal with the details this end, everything we can do is in motion, at the moment all we can do is wait for our navy to find that submarine in time and sink it, the rest is out of our hands and up to your friends until we can put a rescue plan into operation, if or when it is needed."

Then she added, "We will have to deal with this organisation The *Senate* after this incident is over, all we can hope for, is your friends are as good as you say they are and wish them luck."

Then looking at Michael with inviting eyes said, "you never know perhaps we can have that tumble together you suggested on the way."

Valerie let the operations room know where she was going to be, and her contact number, and for her to be kept up-dated, she told them she would be in Canada linking with the Royal Canadian Mounted Police as she had good contacts there and it looked as though that was the area for the showdown.

Valerie said to Michael saucily, "We better get back to my place and get packed for a trip, who knows what will happen on the way, we might have to stay in a motel together on this trip."

They tumbled into her apartment and were laughing together, then as the door closed and shut out the world, they looked lovingly into each other's eyes. They were looking forward to the adventure together, and then there was that moment when time stood still and they kissed, both knowing that was where they both wanted to be for the rest of their lives.

Valerie led him to her bedroom and said, "it's been a long time since I felt safe with a man, I feel safe with you."

Michael said, "it's been a long time for me too," they tumbled onto the large bed and started to explore and learn about each other.

Tomorrow they would be up very early and go to Canada to see Laurence, but now will be their time and they would enjoy the short time they had in harmony.

Valerie literally purred as she melted into his strong arms, "I think I am falling in love with you," she said.

Michael said, "I have always loved you from afar, now I can love you up close, at last, you will fulfil all my dreams," they melted into each other's arms.

Tomorrow will be another day. They would travel to Canada together and face whatever that brings, they will face it together, this moment was their time, and they would cherish every moment and make up for that lost time.

Meanwhile, the Atlantic sea pack had been alerted, the tactics no surface ships to approach within 15 miles of the hijacked ships.

No military aircraft to be within the same distance, in case they were seen and it triggered a devastating response from the High-jacking terrorists, it was to be a modern Submarine hunting an old Submarine, when they found the old terrorist submarine, they were to sink it instantly.

But first, the American Submarine's had to find the Terrorists Sub, it will be like trying to find a needle in a haystack, and the search area will be in the Atlantic Graveyard of Ships.

The dogs of war were released the Atlantic Ocean was its hunting ground, they would find the sub but it was a matter of time before it carried out its murderous orders of killing the thousands of hostages.

When the captains opened their orders of Top Priority of Hunt and destroy the Submarine, it also read under no circumstances are the terrorist holding the hostages as a human shield to be allowed to enter American Territorial waters. Both ships are to be sunk, even if it means a total loss of life. America will not negotiate with Terrorists.

Their first mission was to seek and destroy. Their second mission was the prevention of the Gas ship from being exploded in New York Harbour by any means no matter what the cost and that cost could be the lives aboard the *Baroness of the Sea*.

The hopes and wishes of the best-case scenarios for the Atlantic fleet lay with a few passengers aboard the *Baroness of the Sea*. If they were not successful, then the fleet were committed to killing everyone on board both ships if they attempted to enter American Territorial Waters.

Cyril entered the Captain's cabin via his balcony after making sure he was alone. The Captain was startled but pleased to see him, and he asked him, "How do you do that? Appear from nowhere like that."

"I am not going to divulge my trade secrets," Cyril said to the Captain, "I am here on a mission to let you know what we are doing and also to ask you to let the Americans or whoever you contact that we suspect there is a submarine out there ready to pick up the Sheikh and his henchmen, and we want it found and destroyed before we carry out our plan of attack otherwise it might be able to put a torpedo into us or the *NAT GAS 2* at any time."

He went on to tell him about the plans they had and asked if they could rely on the crew for help as this was going to happen with or without the help of his crew. He asked if there were crew members that knew anything about explosives, and asked if he could get any volunteers to sail the *NAT GAS 2* away from the *Baroness of the Sea* once the tow rope cables were cut that bound the two ships together like an umbilical cord. He also asked if the Medical Officer would let them have the drugs to help knock out the guards by putting it in the cake for the Sheikh's birthday.

The Captain said, "you seem to have a plan that might work," but he said, "there is a deadline that the Americans won't let you go beyond."

It was then Cyril asked him if the two ships would go anywhere near Sable Island as he understood to the layman that looked like the American coastline from a distance. He wanted that to be the point of no return and if the worst happened, they might be able to evacuate some passengers there.

"That's not American, that is Canadian territory though it's quite near to America it is closer to Nova Scotia in Canada but I understand where you are coming from, you do know it has the reputation of being the Atlantic graveyard for shipping, but you can rely on my crew to help where they can and I will get my First Officer to ask if we can get any volunteers from them and let you know."

Just then the door handle rattled and Cyril dived for the balcony and was gone the Captain went to the door to slow down whoever was coming in to give Cyril time to get away, Cyril got back to his cabin unseen.

Meanwhile, the girls had set themselves up in parties of two's and started visiting all the ladies toilets to spread the word as women came into the toilets they were told to keep what they heard a secret as their lives depended on it. Then they could let their men know what was planned and then wanted to know if they could rely on some of the women to help and make a difference.

It was all going as planned until one woman started to get hysterical. She started screaming saying we will all be killed, we should do nothing then perhaps they might let them live, and she went on and on as to the Americans would not kill them as they were British allies. She said she was going to tell the guards what they were doing then the Sheikh would be pleased with her and let her and her family live if she said they were fellow Muslims.

Jen knew the noise the frightened woman was making would attract the guards so she had to react quickly.

Jen stopped her near the door spun her round and swung a right hook which caught the woman on the nose, the woman went down as if she was pole axed, and she was out cold.

"Remind me not to argue with you," Karen said to Jen looking at the unconscious woman.

"That was close," Jen said, "now quickly! get a member of staff. We need to get her to the medical centre and get her sedated. We can tell them she tripped and fell and hit her face on the sink."

Karen got a female member of staff, who in turn got a medical carrying chair and all three took the woman to the Medical centre.

They explained what was going on to the Medical officer, who said he had already been informed of what was coming down the pipeline, and he was there getting the sleeping drafts ready, then said, I hope we don't get too many panicking people otherwise it would jeopardise the whole plan, he said he would keep her under sedation until this was over.

They both went back to spreading the word via the ladies toilets and in general, after a few expletives about the Sheikh, the response was overwhelming in favour of helping in any way they can and above all, they knew secrecy was the watchword otherwise they could all die as the Sheikh would show no mercy.

It would mean putting on a brave face at the party for the Sheikh, but it was the best smokescreen they could come up with, and if it worked, it was their only chance of survival.

Meanwhile back at the cabin as Derek and Jeff were talking, there was a knock on the cabin door. Jeff opened it and there stood Mustafa with two guards.

"You are to come with me," Mustafa said, "the Sheikh has summoned you and wants to see you now," Derek moved forward and went into his role-play of acting stupid then shaking his head and said, "No."

"Easy Derek," Jeff said, taking Derek's lead in the role he was playing, "he probably only wants to talk to me, I will be alright with Mustafa," and then turning to Mustafa said "he gets very clinging sometimes can he come with us? I don't like to upset him."

"Alright, he seems harmless," Mustafa said.

"He is," Jeff said, "he is a gentle giant and would not hurt a fly, and he will be good," then turning to Derek said, "won't you Derek?"

Derek nodded and adopted a very pleased child look about him.

As they made their way towards the Sheikh's suite Mustafa said, "We consider people like your friend Derek children of Allah, as they are amongst the unfortunates of this world but we believe they have been touched by Allah."

Derek kept up the appearance of being a child out on a trip with his friend.

Derek had found out from his experience in the ring that if you let people think you are stupid and harmless they let down their guard and talk as though you don't exist, so that way you can learn more about your enemy by lulling them into a false sense of security, he also knew they had limited resources and needed to find out as much as he could about the opposition. He knew it was a wise man who knew his limitations and played to his strengths and the weakness of his enemy.

When they got to the Sheikhs cabin, Abdul was there as well, the Sheikh greeted them and then asked, "who is this with you?" Then added, "I only sent for you so we can talk."

"This is a travelling companion of mine, he is one of life's unfortunates and he is totally harmless. His wife Sandra went off with my wife Karen to do some shopping in the on board store and I said I would keep an eye open for him whilst she was away. When you summoned me to your cabin, I asked if he could come with me rather than keep you waiting whilst I found the women so they could keep an eye on him."

"Summoned to my cabin?" The Sheikh said defensively, "what gave you the idea I summoned you, I mealy put out the invitation for you to join me to discuss a proposition I have for you."

Derek stood by the table near the other door looking at the bowl of differently coloured wrapped sweets.

"Help yourself," the Sheikh said to Derek.

Derek looked at Jeff pleadingly. Jeff said, "alright but not too many you will spoil your lunch."

Derek sat down gently picked a sweet of the pile and slowly unwrapped it laying the sweet paper out and flattening it gently ate the sweet and did the same with the second sweet making a pattern of the wrappers trying to look totally harmless and in a world of his own.

"He likes the coloured wrappers to play with," Jeff said.

Just then there was a knock on the cabin door and an advisor called Jake entered, looked at Abdul and said "we have a problem," and then suddenly Jake realized the Sheikh had company and shut up.

The Sheikh said to Jeff come with me onto the balcony we can talk there in private, staring angrily at Jake, "your friend looks harmless and happy enough with the sweets I will get him a bowl full to take away with him," and they went onto the balcony.

"What seems to be the problem that you have to burst in here at this time," Abdul said in Arabic to Jake who had just entered.

The man who had disturbed them turned to Abdul and said "sorry but it is urgent," then seeing Derek said, 'what about him?" pointing to Derek.

"Don't worry about him. He's a dummy and has a job understanding English he won't understand what we are talking about but speak in Arabic to be on the safe side just in case the dummy repeats anything."

Derek carried on as if in his own little world and playing with the sweet wrappings and eating more sweets, he also developed a silly grin as if he was in a world of his own, but he was listening intently to everything that was being said.

Abdul insults Derek in Arabic looks at Jake and states "See I told you he was a dummy, now Jake tell me what the problem is. But keep your voice down while our so-called Sheikh is entertaining a guest."

"Well", Jake said, "it's the 6 man crew on the *NAT GAS 2* they have had no sleep for over 48 hours and they are getting tired, and they are making mistakes and at this stage that could be dangerous," Abdul said, "all the men have had virtually had no sleep for 48 hours on board here they are tired too."

It was then Abdul mused, "at first, I was opposed to this party this Jeff bloke is throwing for the Sheikh's birthday, but now I might use it to our advantage."

"By the way," Abdul added, "I must say I admire those Somali pirates they certainly know how to board ships, we did it with steel wire ladders, they do it with long bamboo poles they hook over the railings then shin-up the bamboo pole like a monkey up a tree."

"That reminds me when you go back to the *NAT GAS 2* use one of the port-side lifeboats as a tender, you will be seen by the bridge on the *NAT GAS 2* that way, on the starboard side you are blind to the bridge of the *NAT GAS 2* as they can't be seen from the bridge and you risk being shot as they won't see you coming."

"I nearly got shot the other day because they did not see me coming we did not realise the blind spot from the bridge of the *NAT GAS 2* when I used a lifeboat as a tender from the starboard side of *Baroness of the Sea*, don't forget to leave the lower ladder down for the gang plank, you will have lots of time if you need to pull it up in case you are boarded but we need it down whilst we are on skeleton crew in case we need to support each other in an emergency."

"How about the steel wire ladders hanging over the stern do you want me to pull them up out the way?" Jake said.

"You won't have time," Abdul said "anyway don't worry about them, no one is going to board the tanker using them," Abdul added, "it took us weeks to learn how to do that and we were taught by the best and we still lost two men when we took the tanker."

"The only regret I will have," he also added, "is leaving that lovely fast ocean-going boat the Fast Lady on board the *NAT GAS 2* I would have liked her for myself as a present, mind you the money we make from this deal, I can buy fifty Fast Ladys and still have change."

"What will The *Senate* say if we deviate from the set plan?" Jake said.

"The *Senate* taught us to think on our feet and adapt to the situation to our advantage," Abdul said, and then he replied to Jake in a whisper, "anyway I was thinking of using this party them pilgrims are throwing for our so-called Sheikh, to our advantage."

"How do you mean?" Jake replied.

"Well," Abdul whispered, "We could use the time to try and get our men some much-needed sleep, at the moment I could not spare the men, but with a party going on I can put men on standby use a skeleton crew, so if I let them rest now, then they can take over whilst the others put their heads down," Abdul added, "you know I was not sure about this party but on reflection, it could be to our advantage, and to the advantage of The *Senate*."

"So make up a skeleton crew," Abdul said, "no more than ten men, plus two advisors, use Parvis as one advisor for the *NAT GAS 2*, we can keep that on autopilot, eight for this ship, two on the bridge and two either end of deck five as we can't let anybody onto deck five otherwise they might spot the submarine's signals and we don't want anyone on board knowing about The *Senate*'s Sub just yet, not even our so-called Sheikh, as that is our escape route."

"They will know about the Sub after we are on board it and we put a fish in the side of the *Baroness of the Sea* and the *NAT GAS 2*, they will be so busy trying an impossible rescue of the passengers of the *Baroness of the Sea*, it will be then that we make a clean getaway."

"Let's get down to details," Abdul added, "we can then have one armed guard each end of the main dining room with you and I and two of the advisors as a backup."

"That will leave one advisor to guard the explosives on this ship also it will give the illusion there are more guards, we can get that ten and the advisors to put their heads down now, tell the rest of the men to hang on for a few more hours until early evening."

"Whilst our so-called Sheikh is celebrating his surprise birthday party, under cover of darkness, we can put the gas ship on autopilot and we can match that with this cruise ship, tell the men they can get some sleep then, we need them fresh for when we transfer to the submarine The *Senate* has supplied at dawn."

"What is going to happen about the Sheikh and his friend Mustafa?" Jake said, "how do we get them to co-operate with the change in plans?"

"We don't tell them. They have been useful tools in The *Senate*'s plan they are expendable as is the rest of these pilgrims on board."

"By the way don't forget to tell them to switch over to the remote on the timers set on the explosives that are set in-between the inner and outer hull of the *NAT GAS 2*, we don't want our men to be asleep and on board when it goes up and we don't want to be aboard this ship when those other explosives go off either."

Whilst this conversation was going on Derek was forcing himself to act as though he was mentally challenged and focused on making pretty patterns with the sweet wrappings and eating sweets

"Are you sure about him?" Jake said.

"Yes, don't worry," Abdul said, in Arabic, "he ran through the stupid forest and kissed every tree," then turning to Derek smiled and said loudly, "Thick as two planks end on, aren't you?"

Derek smiled at Abdul in a very harmless and friendly way.

"See, I told you he was not all there, so don't worry, and he certainly won't be able to understand Arabic, so you just concentrate on getting the men rested so they are fit for tomorrow. "

With that, Jake hugged Abdul and left the cabin.

In the meanwhile out on the balcony, the Sheikh was talking to Jeff.

"You know how much I admire you and what you do," the Sheikh said, "you and I have so much in common and I believe you and your talents are totally wasted and not appreciated by your people, so why not come with me and I can make you very powerful and a very rich man, that invitation does include you, your wife and your friends. We will be leaving this ship soon." the Sheikh said, as his eyes glassed over and he went into his own little world, then developing a mad look in his eyes, he said, "I have shown my father I am a man not to be messed with, as I now hold that so-called great nation America to ransom and I have brought them to their knees.

The Sheikh came out of his revelry and he returned to some normality and said, "what do you think?" And then suddenly he flipped back into his own little world again, "we can rule the world you and I."

Jeff realized the Sheikh had a major problem mentally and it seemed to be getting worse and he would need delicate handling, he had to keep him sweet otherwise he could flip at any moment and order everyone killed out of hand.

"This is a great honour and major surprise," Jeff replied, "and I would have to talk it over with my wife and my friends."

"You will have to let me know before tomorrow morning," the Sheikh said, "after that, it will be too late," and gave Jeff a look as though he would not be pressed on the matter.

Jeff said, "I will give you my decision at your surprise birthday party tonight then we can celebrate together."

"Does that mean that you accept my proposal," the Sheikh said looking excited.

"You will have to wait until your surprise party tonight," Jeff said.

"I want to know now," the Sheikh said petulantly.

"All in good time," Jeff said, "so don't spoil the surprise, you have been very generous to me, let me be generous to you, so you will have to wait until tonight, then we can all celebrate."

The Sheikh looked like a cat that had been given the cream jug, and he was excited and said, "I am really looking forward to tonight. I will wear my best robes in celebration," he said as he escorted Jeff from the balcony and they joined Derek who was still playing with the sweet wrappings.

"Till tonight," the Sheikh said, then he turned to Derek and added, "Allah has blessed you," as he handed Derek a large bowl of sweets for him to take away.

Derek looked at Jeff expectantly as though he was a child that had been given a Christmas present.

Jeff nodded and said, "don't forget to say thank you to the Sheikh."

Derek said "thank you very much!", and hugged the bowl of sweets like an excited child. They left the Sheikh's cabin and they returned to Jeff's Cabin.

When they got back to Jeff's cabin, the women were there having a drink together. When the cabin door was closed, Jen explained about the woman who nearly let the cat out of the bag, then Karen said how Jen can pack a good right hook and how the woman will be sleeping off the rest of the trip.

"Don't you feel sorry for me," Cyril said as he came in from the balcony, "see what I have to put up with, she beats me terribly, you don't want to see the bruises," he mocked.

"I wish you wouldn't do that," Jen said "spring out from no-where like that, you made me jump, if you like I'll give you a smack you might like later if you behave yourself," Jen said saucily, "so let's find out what you know."

Cyril told them about the conversation with the Captain, then said to Jeff, "I understand you got summoned to the Sheikh, and I gather you took Derek with you, now that was sensible, he is a good man to have at your side in a tight corner."

Jeff told them about the conversation with Sheikh and all about his offer.

"I hope you told him to put it where the monkey puts his nuts," Cyril said.

"I told him he would have to wait until tonight's party where we were planning a surprise for him on his birthday, but I don't think he is going to like the surprise and I think it will be then we might have a few problems with his army of guards. The trouble is we don't know how many he has and where they are?"

"There's only going to be ten guards and four advisors on duty including Abdul and Jake," Derek said to Cyril, "they were discussing it in front of me in Arabic in the Sheikh's cabin."

"How do you know Arabic?" Cyril said, looking astounded.

"I learned a bit of Arabic from my wrestling trainer," Derek continued, "he was an Arab, lovely man he was, that was when I was first in training for the Olympics, so I was able to understand most of what was said by Abdul and that man that burst in the Sheikh's cabin, I believe his name was Jake."

Derek continued, pleased with himself that he had a very attentive audience that was waiting on his words, "Apparently the guards have been without sleep for over 48 hours and they are making mistakes because they are so tired, so Abdul wants to use the party as a way of getting his men some sleep before tomorrow when they need to be very alert for when the submarine arrives to take them all off."

"John guessed right about that Submarine then," Cyril interjected.

Derek continued, "He is going to install a skeleton crew of ten men whilst the party is on, then he has ordered the others to rest, I even know where he is going to put the ten guards."

"That's brilliant!", John said as he was sitting quietly in the corner, "where?"

"But there is a downside to this," Derek said, "The *Senate* is involved and it's them that is sending the submarine."

"What?" John said, "I thought we had eradicated them, after what they did in the estuary area and when they tried to destroy the British Government."

"Apparently not," Derek said, "according to Abdul, The *Senate* are behind this."

"There had to be a reason why the Sheikh seems frightened of Abdul and also seems to take his orders from Abdul," Jeff said.

"What else did you find out?" Cyril said.

"There will only be two guards on the bridge of the *NAT GAS 2* plus that evil swine Parvis," Derek said, "the *NAT GAS 2* is going to be put on autopilot which will be set on the same course as the *Baroness of the Sea*, which will also be put on a matching course and set on autopilot with two guards on the bridge of this ship."

"There will be two guards either end of deck five to stop people going out onto that deck he added, and there will be one guard either end of the dining room, the Sheikh will be at the party, the only other thing is we don't know where this Abdul or this Jake will be and those two I don't trust as far as I can throw them, they both look nasty pieces of work, if the other four advisors are like them two we could have a problem on our hands."

"Also to add to the problem," Derek said, "Abdul has a remote, he can reactivate the timers set on the explosives on board the *Baroness of the Sea* and on board the NAT GAS 2."

John said, "the fact that we now know for certain they have a submarine on standby is important, but that is something we can't do anything about, all we can hope for is the Americans can take it out before it can do any serious damage or it evacuates the Sheikh and his henchmen."

"They might not be evacuating the Sheikh or Mustafa," Derek said, "according to Abdul he is only on board to serve a purpose and then is expendable."

"I bet he and Mustafa don't know that they intend to abandon them, so they take the blame for them and hide the fact that The *Senate* is involved right up to its neck."

Cyril turned to Derek and said, "that was a wonderful idea letting them think you were a dummy who did not know Arabic, which gave them a false sense of security and exposed their plan. We can make good use of that."

"He's no dummy," Sandra said defensively turning to Cyril with her eyes flashing.

"Sorry, if that came out wrong," Cyril said, apologetically to Sandra, "I did not mean he was a dummy I was only saying that by him acting as a dummy he has been very clever."

Then all the girls started laughing at Cyril, as he slowly realized, he was being wound up by Sandra.

"You got me fair and square," Cyril said, holding his hands up.

"Well," Jeff said, "we know who is going to be where, apart from the advisors, now all we have to do is to get ourselves organized when we know that, we can let the Captain know what we plan.

The Captain can get his officers to co-ordinate with us as to what they are going to do."

John said, "the ten men who will be cutting the tow ropes that bind the two ships together will have to have very sharp axes, and don't forget they won't be able to take them into the party as they will be searched on the way in, so how do you suggest we get the axes to them without raising any suspicions."

"How about using the axes by the fire stations set along the deck?

We can use waiters to bring some of the men sharp knives from the kitchens," Jeff said, "no one will suspect a waiter if he is carrying a tray with a cloth draped over it, and he can be circulating the party and handing out the knives to the chosen men."

"That's good I like you're thinking," John said, "but how will the waiter know who to give the knives to amongst the men at the reception?"

Karen spoke up and said, "how about the men who require knives and are cutting the rope with axes, wearing a red carnation in his buttonhole, the carnations can be got from the flower shop, you could even use different coloured carnations for your different teams so as to identify one from the other without raising any suspicions by the Sheikh and his men, and we could use the waiters to arm all the men you need armed."

"That's brilliant," Cyril said, "I wish I had thought of that."

They all nodded in approval.

Jeff said lovingly, "now I know why I married such a beautiful and clever woman."

"You men don't have a monopoly on brains you know," Jen said, "we women can use our grey matter sometimes," as she gave Karen a hug.

"Now how do we find out who our volunteers are without putting them under suspicion?"

Jen said, "Us women will have to go to the toilets again, as we did ask the women, we approached to let us know by mid-day one way or the other?"

John's wife said, "how about getting them to give us their cabin number and we can coordinate what we are doing by using the cabin phones between 2 o/c and 3 o/c then only the people that are directly involved will know what team they are on and who they will need to cooperate with and what coloured carnation to wear and what their task is?"

"How will they know it's us talking to them over the phone and not the Sheikh's men?" Sandra said.

"We can use a password," Rose said.

"Sounds good to me," said Jen, "what will it be?"

"How about British Bulldog," Karen said.

"British Bulldog it is," they all agreed.

"They have got this down to a fine art," John remarked, "thank Christ they are on our side."

"Women are more dangerous than men when it comes to defending their loved ones," Jeff said, "and I am glad I have got these four ladies on my side, I am proud of them."

"Crawler," Cyril remarked jokingly to Jeff.

"I have you know I can get under a snake's belly with a top hat on if need be," Jeff retorted.

They all laughed.

"After a while," Jeff said, "you four be careful out there, we care an awful lot about you."

"Come on girls let's take them on," Jen said, "as the four girls make their way out of the cabin."

Jeff said, "what worries me is that right-wing group The *Senate* is involved in this, they seem to be manipulating everything in the background with their usual cunning but not getting involved directly."

"There is not a lot we can do about The *Senate* at the moment," John said, "we have enough troubles trying to get out of this situation as it is, so let's concentrate on what we can do, then let the governments deal with them afterwards, they will by this latest escapade of theirs piss-off America big time, and they will hunt them down."

"This will be the second time we have run across them," Cyril said, "It seems they want world domination by playing both sides against the middle on a global scale," then he added, "next time I see the Captain I will tell him The *Senate* is involved and they are the one's supplying the Submarine, perhaps this Submarine can be taken out of the equation earlier by the Americans now that they know who is involved."

"By the way, can I use your phone now to call Michael?" Cyril said.

John handed Cyril his Mobil phone, and Cyril dialled the number he had remembered, there was a connection on the other end of the phone and he heard Michael's voice say hello, they exchanged pleasantries then Cyril told Michael what was going on and asked him to intercede for them with his cousin in the American Naval Intelligence.

"Already in hand," Michael said.

Cyril also outlined the plan they were going to adopt and how it all depended on The *Senate*'s submarine being taken out before they took on the pirates on the *Baroness of the Sea*.

Michael let him know the American fleet are hunting for the sub at this very moment but they have not found it yet.

Cyril also told him that if they managed to get off the *Baroness of the Sea* they would try to make it to Sable Island.

Michael said, "we guessed you might try for Sable Island, it's the only area where you stand a chance of saving your passengers and crew if things go wrong.

He added, "I am in touch with my Cousin Laurence, he is a member of the Canadian Royal Mounted Police, he can pull a few strings and get help if you need it."

Cyril said, "we are going for it, wish us luck, I think we are going to need it to pull this off."

"Valerie has got her people working on the situation, and she and I are on our way to Canada to see Laurence and get support for you there, good luck, we are doing all we can."

Whilst this was going on Jeff said, "what we need to discuss is who is heading which team and how we are going to approach the different obstacles we have overcome."

"Firstly, under cover of darkness, we have to have a party of at least eight men to secure deck five, ideally knock out the guards and dress four of them in the guard's uniforms to ally suspicion.

Secondly, we need to get a small party on board the *NAT GAS 2* and take that over. Those men must have some idea how to operate that ship, they take out the two skeleton crew plus Parvis, these men must be volunteers as they might not make it back and if that tanker blows they will go up with it."

"How do we get them on board the *NAT GAS 2* without being seen?" John said.

"The same way they first took over the tanker in the first place," Derek said.

"How was that?" John asked.

"By wire ladders trailing from the lower deck at the stern of the *NAT GAS 2*," Derek added, John looked shocked at Derek

Apparently, they left them there when they first boarded the *NAT GAS 2*, Derek said, "they were taught by Somalia Pirates how to board vessels off Somalia as part of their training."

Then getting into the spirit of all the intrigue said, "if we can get one man on board that way he can get around the side of the *NAT GAS 2* and make sure the lower ladders on the gangplank is down and stop anybody pulling it up, by keeping the lower the steps of the gangplank down, we can get a team on board unseen by the bridge."

Derek said, "we will need to use a starboard lifeboat as a tender, apparently launching a tender from that side of the *Baroness of the Sea* it can't be seen by the bridge of the NAT GAS2 it's because of the angle we are at the moment, well that's what Abdul was saying when he thought I was a dummy."

"By the way," added Derek, "as a matter of information, did you know Somalia Pirates creep up behind a ship and use bamboo poles hooked over the stern of any ship, they hook them over the bottom rail on the lower deck then shin-up the bamboo pole in the dead of night and high-jack any ship they want around the Horn of Africa. We could take a leaf out of their book and board the *NAT GAS 2* the same way they high-jacked it in the first place."

"Then we need a party of at least ten men to sever the tow ropes securing the two ships together," Jeff said.

"We need a party to retake the bridge and get the Captain back on the bridge as he is the best one to sail the *Baroness of the Sea*," John said.

He added, "we need a party to release the rest of the crew of the *Baroness of the Sea* held in the forward hold first as they might have volunteers with skills, we might need. Also, we need another party of volunteers to find and disarm the explosives on board this vessel that has to be done before we take back this ship in case they detonate them first.

Cyril added, "we need another party to take out the guards at tonight's surprise reception and party for the Sheikh, Abdul and that Jake I feel are going to be our biggest problem, they both look as though they can handle themselves."

Then added, "we also need people to distribute the food with the sleeping draft in it, we need to speak to the first officer to find out what help we are going to get from the crew."

"Have we missed anything out so far?" Jeff Said.

"Timing is going to be critical," John said, "and whatever happens, you have to be at that reception otherwise the Sheikh will get suspicious. It would be a good idea to take Derek with you he will be able to handle anybody like Abdul, if they get out of hand."

"Where are you going to be?" Jeff said to John.

"Disarming those explosives on board this ship and making them safe," John said, "before they can be set off remotely."

"Why you?" Cyril said, "you could be blown to bits."

"Because I was in the bomb disposal service at one time," John said, "and I know about timers and explosives and that makes me the best man for the job, and besides I know where they have put the explosives."

Jeff said, "I will need to talk with the First officer to find out if any of his crew will volunteer to sail the gas tanker."

Cyril said, "in that case, I will take charge of the party that takes over deck five and also the rope cutting crew."

"That just leaves the girls to get the other women organized for the surprise party and get the drugged food to the guards," John said.

"That does not leave Derek and me a lot to do," Jeff said.

"You have to do the most dangerous job," John said, "actually being in the lion's den and bullshitting the Sheikh," then he added, "above all Mustafa and the advisors must be made to believe that this surprise party is for real."

"I mean this as a compliment," John continued, "but you are the best bull-shitter I know, I have seen a lot of politicians in action but you take the biscuit for bullshitting and can run rings around most of them."

"We all will be relying on you to be convincing enough to allow us to do our part," then he added, "if they for one minute suspect what we are doing, we are dead in the water, you will need Derek with you because with the Sheikh on the cusp of sanity, and the looks of Abdul and that Jake, you will need instant backup if things turn nasty.

The other two guards on that deck can be taken out by crew members, then all we have to deal with is the sleeping guards and that is the easy bit," then John looked at him slyly and added, "may I remind you it was your idea to throw this surprise party so we could retake this ship with the minimum loss of life, and it might work, therefore you have to be the best host there is to ally their suspicions."

"We will have to give the sleeping guards a chance to go right off to sleep before we get a party to round them up," Derek said, "how about letting them have some drugged food before they bed down, they are bound to be hungry, then all we have to do is go round and pick them and their guns up."

"That's a good idea," John said.

Derek pointed to his head, then to his feet and said, "up here for thinking, down there for dancing."

All four of them smiled.

Cyril said, "we now have to wait until the girls get back, then they can make the phone calls to the different cabins, it's best for them to do it as they have met the wives and they are best at organising a party anyway."

"Cyril is going to see the Captain, don't forget, and I will need to see the First officer," Jeff said.

"When I see the Captain, I will get him to get a message to the first officer to come to see you rather than risk you being caught in the act of something suspicious at this late stage."

"Now comes the hard part waiting until we can put all this into action," Jeff said, "I think it's going to be a long night and I suggest we get some rest."

Jeff had had his lunch and was having a lay down in his cabin trying to catch up on some sleep whilst the women were in Cyril and Jen's cabin organising the different parties into colour-coded operations by what carnation they were wearing, when there was a knock on his cabin door, he slid off the bed and opened the door and there was the first officer standing before him.

"I understand you wish to make a formal complaint," he said loudly, the faint hub-bub from Cyril's cabin stopped instantly, "as the first officer I am here to take your written statement so we are clear as to the nature of your complaint."

Jeff looked up the corridor to see two guards laughing and another guard trying to translate from English into Arabic what the first officer had said.

As the third guard turned around, he could see it was the man who had entered the Sheikh's cabin unannounced by the name of Jake and he was translating what the first officer had said to him.

It was obvious from the show the first officer was using the embarrassment ploy to fool the two guards at the end of the corridor.

"You had better come in so we can get it written down."

The guards continued to laugh and take great delight at the officer's embarrassment.

When Jeff had closed the cabin door the officer said, "We will have to continue that charade when I leave, I have a written false claim in my pocket, the captain tells me you wanted to talk to me urgently."

Jeff explained what they had planned and when it was all going to take place and he then explained that they needed a volunteer crew to sail the NAT GAS 2 once it had been cut free from the Baroness of the Sea but it was a suicide mission.

The officer said, "I will find you that crew," he then added, "once the ropes are cut binding us together, if we change the course of the *NAT GAS 2* slightly we can then leave it on automatic pilot for a while, that will probably be long enough to steer it gradually clear of the *Baroness of the Sea*, if we alter course slightly of the *Baroness of the Sea* to veer away from the *NAT GAS 2* for quite some time, it will still appear on radar or Sonar by any following submarine, that we are still connected when they do realise the two ships are parted it will give us a fighting chance to get clear of the *NAT GAS 2* before it explodes.

"Sounds good to me," Jeff said, then added, "how far away are we from Sable Island?"

"We pass within fifty to a hundred miles from it between 5 o/c to 6 o/c in the morning why?" The officer said.

“Well, I understand as a landlubber on a misty morning, it looks like the American coastline,” Jeff said.

“That is true,” the officer said, “but it is Canadian territory and it is not called the Atlantic graveyard for nothing. There have been hundreds of ships lost there on the deadly sandbanks that surround the Island.”

“Well, if things go belly up with what we plan,” Jeff said, “we might need to get any survivors off this ship, we are too far away from America or Canadian mainland for a rescue attempt for this amount of people.”

“Besides, they will sink us if they feel we are a threat to them, and all the time the *NAT GAS 2* is tied up to us we are a definite threat, they will definitely sink us before we get too close either mainland.”

“I can change our course slightly,” the officer said, “without raising any suspicions to get us to veer nearer to Sable Island.”

He added, “by dawn, you will then be able to see Sable Island on the horizon with the naked eye and at the angle you want, but as you say America or Canada won’t let us get much closer to their coastline without reacting in a way we won’t like.”

Jeff said, “if they think they are closer to America than they first thought, it might be enough to fool the terrorists on board for a while.”

“That’s why our timing is crucial,” Jeff said, “we have to act at the end of the surprise party so we can take back this ship before the Americans decide we are too close to their territory and blow it and all the people on board out of the water.”

"We do need the Americans to take out that submarine that is lurking out there somewhere as soon as possible," Jeff added, "or at least before you change course, otherwise the submarine might give the game away to whoever is talking to them aboard this ship, if that happens we could get a torpedo in our side to add to our problems."

"What happens if the Americans can't find and disable that submarine?" The officer said.

"The only thing you need to fear is fear itself," Jeff said, "these people rely on the fear factor to make people do what they want. If you remove the fear factor then their control over you melts away."

"I never would have thought of it that way, but you are right," the officer said.

"By the way," Jeff said, "so our people can recognise and tell which of your crew will be helping us, get the ones that are willing to do something to help to wear a carnation as a sign they can be trusted, now we better get on with the charade of my complaint so as to fool the guards."

The first officer opened the door to the cabin immediately went into a humble stance as he got out of the door, "I will see that your complaint is addressed straight away," he said loud enough for the guards to hear, "I have all the details, all I can do is to humbly apologise for any inconvenience caused.

The guards smiled at the First Officer's predicament as he left.

Jeff lay back on the bed trying to think if there was anything else he could do when Karen walked into the cabin.

"Hi lovely," Jeff said, "how have you girls done today?"

"Jen and Sandra are fantastic at organising," Karen said, "it's all in place, and all we have to do is wait until tonight when it all slips into place just as you planned. By the way, we decided it is a formal dress party to help cover that a lot of people will be wearing carnation buttonholes.

"That won't please Cyril," Jeff said, "he doesn't like dressing up as a penguin as he puts it."

"Can you pour me a drink?" Karen said, "I could do with one before we have to start getting ready for tonight's surprise showdown."

Jeff said very lovingly, as he handed her the drink, he had poured out for her, "I am very proud of you and the way you have supported me in this, even though we might all die."

"I love you not only for you but for what you stand for," Karen said, "and if in my small way I can help and support your principles that you live and die by, then I am content."

"Now I know why I love you so much," Jeff said, as he hugged and kissed her.

"Enough of that," she said, "If I am going to go, then I want to look stunning when I do go, and I don't want you looking scruffy either."

They both laughed.

Aboard the American Submarine Texas Ranger which was one of the American fleet Submarines hunting down the elusive The *Senate* Sub

Echosounder. "Here Captain, there's a faint underwater echo directly ahead."

"Follow that Echo," the Captain said, "full speed and don't lose it."

The First Officer said, "it might be whales."

"Echo room here Sir, begging your pardon, but in my experience, it is too strong for whales."

"Time is not on our side," the Captain said, "we have to take a chance, it's the best echo we have had so far, and I have a hunch about it.

Just then the radio room announced, "screws in the water dead ahead, we found her and she is blowing her ballast tank ready to surface."

The Captain said, "load forward tubes one two and three, ready to surface, blow tank and surface fast, I don't want her to have time to send out any signals."

The Texas Ranger hit the surface first, the crew manned the guns fast.

The much older and slower The *Senate* Submarine surfaced right in front of the Texas Ranger.

The Texas Ranger opened fire, The *Senate* Submarine dived down in an emergency dive to escape the withering fire that was peppering holes in the hull of their submarine.

Like a hunting dog the Texas Ranger followed the submerging The *Senate* Submarine on sonar. The *Senate* sub fired its rear torpedoes at the Texas Ranger who in turn fired two torpedoes at The *Senate* Sub which did an emergency dive for the bottom of the sea.

As The *Senate* Sub dived to try to escape the torpedoes of the Texas Ranger over the sonar, they heard the creaking sound of the hull and then the unmistakable sound of the Submarine imploding and then there was a deathly silence.

The crew of the Texas Ranger took no pleasure in hearing the implosion which meant certain death of fellow Submariners, but they had a job to do, and that was only part one of that Job.

The Captain of the Texas Ranger reported to headquarters they had found and sunk The *Senate* Sub and they were on standby to carry out the second part of their orders.

Now they had to carry out part two, it would mean they would lay in wait ready to deal out death to innocent civilians as dawn broke if the *Baroness of the Sea* and the *NAT GAS 2* passed the invisible point of no return, and entered the American Territorial Waters.

Their orders were specific, sink the *NAT GAS 2.* Under no circumstances was it to be allowed to enter American Waters even if in doing so, all the passengers on the Cruise Liner *Baroness of the Sea* were to be sacrificed.

It was an order that the Captain of the Texas Ranger dreaded carrying out, but he would carry out his orders even though it would stick in his craw.

Jeff, Karen, Cyril and Jen, Derek and Sandra, John and Rose left their cabins together.

As all eight of them made their way to the cocktail lounge for drinks before dinner they were joined by Mustafa and Asar his wife.

"I hope this surprise party tonight is going to be successful?" Mustafa said, "the Sheikh is so looking forward to it, what surprises have you in store for him? He so does like surprises."

Jeff had come to like Mustafa and Asar and felt the man was in deeper than he wanted to be and wanted to get out if he could, but his loyalty to the Sheikh and the Sheikh's family was very strong, his family had always been bodyguards to the Sheikhs family for generations and he was the first one that had broken that tradition.

"It would not be a surprise if I told you what it was, would it?" Jeff said.

Then Jeff added, "the surprise you have to worry about is the surprise Abdul and Jake have in store."

"What do you know about Abdul and Jake?" Mustafa asked quizzically.

"Ask them if they are members of the *Senate*," Jeff said.

"Who and what is the *Senate*?", Mustafa asked.

"Ask them," Jeff said, "and if you get the answer I think you will get," he continued, "come and find me at the party, as you ask them your questions think about the conversation you and I had about the Russian revolution, the Chinese uprising and the German Nazi's and the cost in millions of innocent lives, and all for a political cause."

Mustafa left with his wife to find Abdul and Jake whilst Jeff's party made its way to dinner and surprise party.

"What was that all about?" Cyril said, "you're playing it close to your chest with him."

"Divide and rule," Jeff said, "it is about time we put some dissension in their ranks."

He added, "If Mustafa wants out, as I think he does, but can't because through family loyalty to the Sheikh, then if he thinks the Sheikh is in danger, he becomes the enemy of my enemy that makes him my friend."

Jeff added, "we can tell him all we know but because of his family's loyalty to the Sheikh he won't believe us, and the only way he will find out the truth as to how he and the Sheikh are being manipulated, is by him cross-questioning Abdul and Jake, all I have done is to sow the seed of doubt in his head and now we let it grow."

"Remind me not to play poker with you," Cyril said, "you are too devious for me."

"There is more than one way to skin a rabbit," Jeff said, "now let's go and eat and you can order one of your lovely bottles of wine."

"You must have ice in your veins," Cyril said, "what we are doing does not faze you does it? I believe you are enjoying the challenge of going against impossible odds, with little hope of winning."

"We have nothing to lose and everything to gain," Jeff said, "if we do nothing, we are dead, if we all do something, we might all live, and if we fail and die in the attempt, then we will have chosen the way of our death."

They went into the dining room, and they were impressed by the number of men wearing different coloured carnations, including a vast number of waiters and all of the senior catering staff that were dotted about in what seemed to be strategic positions.

The food was excellent as usual, and if you looked very closely as the plates were cleared you could see the men with carnations being given different sharp knives from the kitchen by the waiters.

Their waiter serving them at their table gave them all a knife including one each for the four women, which they hid for safekeeping in case they were needed.

They had finished their meal and were making their way the reception area which was being used so the catering crew could prepare the dining area for the party, the area had already been dressed up and the final touches were being added.

There was an air of expectancy that you could feel in the room.

As they entered the reception area, they were handed a glass of champagne.

Mustafa spotted Jeff and his party and made his way towards them. He looked very worried and agitated and seemed as though he was having a hard time to control himself, and blurted out, "you were right, how did you know?"

"The *Senate* were behind the Estuary Incident, which very nearly brought down the British Government," Jeff said, "we thought we had rounded them all up, but it looks like they are trying to take over your country as well now by getting the Americans to attack your country in retaliation to holding them to ransom over this high-jack."

Jeff also added, "they are still stirring up bad blood between friends, tribes and nations for their own ends and they don't care who or how many people they have to kill to furnish their own ends."

Then he added, "You, your wife, and the Sheikh, his wives and his personal bodyguards will not be allowed to leave this ship when they transfer to the submarine, as I believe there is only enough room on board the sub for the six advisors and I also believe they are the only members of the *Senate* on board this ship and remember that sub belongs to the *Senate*."

"By them using your lifelong friend and taking advantage of his sickness they are manipulating the situation for their own ends," Jeff said.

"That is a farfetched story," Mustafa said, "I don't believe you. By the way, how did you know about the submarine?"

"Derek overheard Abdul and Jake talking about it in the Sheikhs cabin," Jeff said, "he understands and speaks Arabic and he also heard what they planned and how they intend to dump you and the Sheikh at the first opportunity and leave you two to carry the can."

"But he is a dummy," Mustafa said, pointing to Derek.

"I have always found it is better to let someone think you are stupid than to open your mouth and prove them right, you then have the advantage," Jeff said, "and by the way, Derek is far from stupid because he fooled you and all the others into you letting down your guard."

Derek interjected and obliged him by speaking to Mustafa in Arabic.

Mustafa looked stunned, and said, "I don't believe it!"

"I am good at reading someone's character," Jeff said, "and I believe you don't want thousands or possibly millions of deaths on your conscience, and I also believe you are torn between your loyalty to your friend and his family and the realization of being the instrument of those deaths, and that is tearing you apart. "

"There is nothing I can do," Mustafa said, "my family have always been bodyguards to his family, and the tradition goes back decades, I am the first eldest son in my family who did not follow that tradition."

"You and I know the Sheikh is not well," Jeff said, "he needs protecting from himself and from the *Senate* and you are the best one to do it, you are his life-long friend, he will listen to you when he is more lucid."

"What are you going to do as a surprise for him at this party?", Mustafa said.

"That is a surprise that we will enjoy giving Abdul and Jake also anyone else that stands in our way," Jeff said.

"You can't, they have you surrounded and out gunned," Mustafa said, "besides they have explosive charges placed in strategic places on board both ships any attempt to take back this ship will be met with violence and those explosive charges will be detonated, look around you, all you have is a few unarmed guests dressed up as a dog's dinner waiting for free drinks and free food."

"Look more closely at them," Jeff said, "every one of them is armed and they are not only fighting for their own lives but also the lives of their loved ones, and when that happens don't stand in their way because you will have to either stand with them or behind them, if you get in their way, you will not survive," Jeff added, "have you ever seen a pack of hyenas take down its prey? It is not a pretty sight."

Mustafa looked shocked at what he was realising and he knew that the people he was looking at were not going to roll-over and give up. They would die for what they believe in and that was the survival of their loved ones at any costs.

"You now have a choice," Jeff said, "you are either with us or you are against us."

"What about Asar?", Mustafa said, "she has nothing to do with this."

"If you are with us, I will put her under my protection, if you are not with us then I cannot help you if things get nasty, but one way or another we intend to take back this ship even if we die in the attempt, if that happens we will take a lot of them with us including the Sheikh, so if you want to save him now's the time because here he comes with Abdul and he has Jake with him as well."

The Sheikh was dressed in white robes. He looked stunningly handsome and proud. He had a very large jewelled broach pinned to his chest, he also had a matching dagger to the one he had given to Jeff tucked in his waistband.

"I am looking forward to my surprise party," the Sheikh said, "when do I get my surprise? I can't wait."

"You would not like me to spoil the evening by giving you my surprise too early, would you?", Jeff said, "we need to get everything ready, in the meanwhile, we can have the dancing girls on for your entertainment."

Jeff lifted his hand, signalled the entertainment officer who was at the side on the staging and a troop of dancing girls appeared from the side staging and started dancing.

As the guests mingled, it was slowly getting obvious, they were getting nervous and agitated the longer the evening went on.

"What about my surprise?", The Sheikh reminded Jeff. "I have not had it yet, and you have not yet given me your answer if you are going to join me."

"Firstly, let me present your birthday cake," Jeff said.

Rolled in on a trolley was the most gorgeous cake you have ever seen shaped into the image of the cruise ship.

Jeff produced the ornate dagger the Sheikh had given him and said to the Sheikh "shall we cut it together?", pointing to the Sheikh's dagger.

The Sheikh smiled and produced his dagger and cut the cake with him, "let everyone on board eat cake," the Sheikh said, "we must share it out with everyone."

Jeff's heart sank, he was relying on the drugged cake knocking out all the guards and with them asleep taking over the ship but if they ate the drugged cake, they would be knocked out also and their plans would go up in smoke.

The Sheikh waited for Jeff as he hesitated to eat the piece of cake, he had given him.

Karen said to Jeff, "You will love it. It's your favourite cake and it was made especially for the Sheikh, the other identical cakes are being cut up and circulated to everyone on board in honour of the Sheikh's birthday."

Karen knew Jeff was not a lover of cake, but what she was telling him this cake did not have any sleeping draught in it and was safe to eat.

The Sheikh's birthday celebrations carried on.

After an hour the Sheikh came up to Jeff as he stood with his wife, Derek, Sandra Jen, and Asar.

Before the Sheikh could get to Jeff's party of people, Abdul and Jake joined him and they both looked angry and concerned.

"When am I going to get my surprise you promised me?", The Sheikh said.

"Now if you like," Jeff said.

"See I told you he had a nice surprise for my birthday," the Sheikh said turning to Abdul and Jake.

"It's not your birthday surprise we are concerned about. It's the fact we have not heard from the sub," Jake blurted out, "they're supposed to have called us as we got near to the American coast," Abdul said.

"Check your radio again," the Sheikh said, "we have already been through this, and it's probably a delay in the signal or something," then turning to Jeff said, "I have been very patient all evening now where is my birthday surprise."

"It will certainly be a surprise to you," Jeff said to the Sheikh.

"Are you are going to join us," the Sheikh said expectantly, then he seemed to go into a world of his own, then added, "we can take on the world you and I, we will be unstoppable."

"No, I want you and Abdul and Jake to surrender me now," Jeff said

"What?", The Sheikh said coming out of his reverie and looked shocked.

Abdul interceded and said, "you must be joking, we outgun you, outnumber you, plus you have a torpedo aimed at you right now." Abdul said, "All I have to do is snap my finger and we all die."

"Now we know who is pulling the strings," Jeff stated, "it's you and the *Senate*," Jeff said, looking at Abdul.

Abdul looked at Jeff with astonishment and blustered, "what do you know about the *Senate*?".

"It was the *Senate*," Jeff said, "that caused the mass murder in the estuary, killing thousands on and around the Estuary area, they tried to destabilise the British Government so they could take over the country and change it into a right-wing state."

"They failed as this attempt is going to fail," then Jeff added, "your submarine has been taken out of the equation by the Americans that is why you can't get a signal from it."

Abdul looked suspiciously at Jeff, and said, "how did you know its location."

"We didn't," Jeff said, "the Americans hunted for it and found it."

"How did they know there was a submarine out there?", Abdul said.

"We told them after you let our friend Derek know."

"He's a stupid dummy," Abdul said, "how would he find out?".

"You told him, when I was talking to the Sheikh on the balcony and Jake came in the room Derek was sitting down pretending to play with the sweet wrappers as he was listening to your conversation."

"But we spoke in Arabic Abdul said, he could not have understood."

"You overlooked one thing. You underestimated Derek," Jeff said, "you treated him as a stupid backward foolish idiot, in fact, he is quite intelligent, and he understands Arabic."

The realization suddenly dawned on Abdul that he had been suckered, Abdul said, "you will die for that," as he approached Jeff pushing the Sheikh out of the way and grabbing for the dagger in the Sheikh's belt and slashing it at Jeff.

Derek moved with lightning speed he swung a punch at Abdul catching him square on the jaw, Abdul went down like a sack of spuds, but Jake jumped on Derek's back and held him in a wrestler's stranglehold.

Jeff held his dagger to the Sheikhs throat, and he said, "let him go or the Sheikh die's right now."

Jake scoffed, "we don't care what happens to him, kill him if you want to, he means nothing to us, he never did, he is only a means to an end, and we used him to get what the *Senate* wants."

As Jeff was distracting Jake, Derek suddenly spun around releasing the hold Jake had on him, at the same time Derek turned and put Jake into a spine lock, as Jake struggled in Derek's vice-like grip then you heard a clear snap and Jake went loose and he saw his eye's glass over.

There was a look of horror on the Sheikh's face, the Sheikh then blurted out, "he was one of our countries Olympic wrestlers and you snapped his neck just like that."

"I told you not to underestimate him," Jeff said, as Derek dropped the body of Jake and left it lying in a heap at his feet.

"Now where is that other toe-rag?", Derek Said.

Abdul was no-where to be seen, in the confusion he had made his escape.

Whilst the scuffle was going on between Jake and Derek the guards on the door had been taken out by the people near the door.

Whilst this was going on, on deck five, three guards had been taken out by the party headed by Cyril, but the fourth guard had got himself in a position that controlled the deck area and nobody could get to him without being killed.

Mustafa approached Cyril, "I can get to him and take him out, give me one of the guns from the guards."

Cyril looked at him and said, "I am not that stupid."

"It's the only way," Mustafa said.

"You can have the gun but it won't be loaded," Cyril said.

"Right, fire a few shots in the air," Mustafa said, "and do a bit of dying or moaning if you get my drift."

Cyril fired a few shots in the air and Mustafa called out in Arabic to the guard that he had shot the insurgents and he was coming out to him as everything was alright now.

Mustafa slowly made his way toward the Guard.

The guard looked relieved to see Mustafa.

"It's all right now," Mustafa said in Arabic, "a few of them decided to make a fight of it, we just killed the last of them."

The guard looked relieved and as he relaxed and stepped in front of Mustafa, Mustafa hit him on the back of the neck with the butt of the gun Cyril had given him, and he collapsed in a heap.

Mustafa waved to Cyril to come out on the deck.

"Well done," Cyril said, "now all we have to do is get our volunteers on board the *NAT GAS 2*."

"I will have to go with them," Mustafa said.

"What, that is suicidal," Cyril said.

"No one speaks Arabic," Mustafa said, "and the sound of those shots might have alerted those two guards and Parvis the advisor on board the *NAT GAS 2*, I don't need to remind you they are armed and they can set off the charges at any time."

He added, "I would not put that pass Parvis, he is a nasty bit of work, you need someone who can speak Arabic to talk them out of setting off those charges, also you need to concentrate in getting those ropes cut and part these two ships, otherwise if that gas ship is not clear of this cruise liner by dawn America will sink both ships."

"Because by then we are past the point of no return, it will be false dawn in about two and half hours time, dawn will be a short time after that it's then the Americans will be all over us like a rash."

"You can't do that on your own," Cyril said, "handing Mustafa a loaded gun and a spare clip of ammunition showing him he trusted him.

"Look I admire what you are standing for, and I realise I was on the wrong path, and Jeff trusts me now, otherwise he would not have suggested I help."

Mustafa said, "also he has guaranteed the safety of Asar who is with him now, we both know the Sheikh is not a well man and he has been taken advantage of by the *Senate*, Jeff has said, he will try to keep him out of harm's way until he can get some medical help for his condition."

Cyril could see Mustafa was having a job to come to terms that whilst he had been away pursuing his own way in life, his lifelong family friend the Sheikh had become mentally ill and desperately needed help.

Mustafa seemed to check himself and said, "now let's get down to business, time is running out, out of the ten volunteers we have chosen five and that includes me, I understand there is a fast motorboat on board the gas ship, they used it to hi-jack the *NAT GAS 2* in the first place, if we can launch that, we might get a chance of getting away before it blows up if things go wrong."

"You know your chances are slim or none," Cyril said, "so why are you doing this?"

"I don't expect you to understand," Mustafa said, "but my family have been responsible and looked after the Sheikh's family for decades, my father and his father and his father before him, to be a personal bodyguard to the Sheikh was to be my role in life, but I wanted a different way and left to find a different path."

"The sadness and disappointment I caused in my family," Mustafa added, "I was not aware of until tonight, I now know I was wrong, and even though I know the Sheikh is not a well man, I will follow in my father's footsteps and try to prevent him coming to any harm, even though it might cost me my life, that is what it is to be a personal bodyguard."

Resolutely Mustafa turned to the four waiting men and waved them forward, then said to Cyril, "now let me get on board that tanker with my four volunteers, by the way we took our guns from the rest of the sleeping guards, whatever you gave them knocked them out for the count, their sleeping like babies."

"Give me a bit of time before you start cutting the tow rope, I will try to give you a blast on the horn when It will be the best time for you to cut the tow rope," with that parting remark he disappeared into the gloom as he made his way to get over to the *NAT GAS 2* with his volunteers.

Mustafa and the picked crew launched one of the rearmost starboard lifeboats with the help of some of the crew, two of whom stayed with the lifeboat to help handle the lifeboat, and bring it back to the *Baroness of the Sea*, the lifeboat swung out and circled round to come up behind the giant tanker *NAT GAS 2* Cyril was relieved when he saw they had all made it to the launch without incident he also knew once Mustafa disappeared into the darkness he was on his own creeping up behind the *NAT GAS 2* unseen.

Now would be the hard part, waiting to give Mustafa time to get to the bridge of the *NAT GAS 2* undetected before his crew cut all the tow rope, at the same time he knew when that happened, he would be leaving Mustafa and his six volunteers stranded.

Cyril gave the signal for all the men to stand by, they had allocated two men to each of the five tow ropes and they waited for the signal and were ready to cut franticly at his command, Cyril said, "pass the word along for them to lay down flat when you cut the rope because if the rope is under strain when they are cut, the ropes will act like a bullwhip and kill anybody the rope hits."

Mustafa asked the coxswain to switch off all the lifeboat lights then circle as wide as he could so the lifeboat would not be seen from the bridge of the *NAT GAS 2* then he asked him to get as close to the stern of this Leviathan of the sea as he could.

The coxswain eased the lifeboat into the wash of the *NAT GAS 2* and the closer they got to the giant tanker the more they were bouncing about in the tumbling cauldron of the wash, they could see the ends of the steel ladders that were hanging from the lower deck and bouncing around in the wake of the tanker. The closer they got to the swinging steel ladders the more the lifeboat was bouncing around as they got closer and the bottom rungs of one of the ladders was bashing against the lifeboat one of the crew members grabbed the ladder and swung out over the boiling water his lower legs and feet were dragging in the sea, slowly he climbed up the steel ladder hand over hand knowing that if he lost his grip he would plunge to certain death.

As he gradually made it to the lower deck and swung himself over the guard rail the crewman then made his way to gangway ladders and lowered the lower steps of the gangway to sea level

As Mustafa saw the crewman disappear over the lower deck railing, he ordered the other crewman to bring the lifeboat round to the side of the tanker hugging the side so as not to be seen from the bridge of the NAT GAS 2.

They got to where the gangway steps were and as the lower steps were lowered he and the other five chosen men sprang aboard the *NAT GAS 2* and made their way to the bridge leaving the coxswain and the lifeboat to fall back behind the *NAT GAS 2* then make its way back to the *Baroness of the Sea* as best as it could.

Mustafa and his small band of followers managed to get onto the lower deck of the NAT GAS 2 without being seen, he knew that it was at that point that he and his volunteers would be at their most vulnerable, if they were spotted then they could be picked off like clay pipes in a fairground shooting gallery.

They made their way carefully to the gangway that would lead them to the bridge, he knew there were three heavily armed men on board the gas tanker and he had to either capture or kill them, apart from his surprise attack the only other advantage he had was he knew the pirates were tired from lack of sleep.

He split his small attack force into two to approach the bridge from both sides.

As he got halfway up the gangway steps that led to the bridge, he saw a shadow at the top of the gangway steps, he was caught out cold and expected bullets to rain down on him.

He decided he would try to bluff his way out of the situation he found himself in, so he called out in Arabic, "it's Mustafa, and the Sheikh sent me across to tell you we have put down their little rebellion so there is no need to worry."

"Come up here where I can see you," the voice said warily.

Mustafa raised one hand and used the other hand to hold onto the gangway railing as he mounted the steps to the top of the gangway, he stepped out on deck as he cleared the gangway steps an evil looking Parvis stood facing him, he looked alert and ready for action, we had better tell the others as Parvis waved his gun at Mustafa and pointing towards the door that led to the bridge.

"How did you get on board?" Parvis said,

"Up the gangway ladder," Mustafa said, "why?"

Whilst this was going on, the other volunteers had made their way around to the other side of the bridge and had entered the bridge from that side.

There was an exchange of gunfire in the wheelhouse as they got to the bridge door and started to open it.

After what Cyril thought was an eternity, he thought he heard small arms fire coming from the bridge of the *NAT GAS 2*, Cyril gave the order to cut the rope instantly, knowing he would be condemning Mustafa to his fate.

The men franticly started chopping at the ropes the held the NAT GAS 2 to the *Baroness of the Sea*.

The last tow ropes was taunt and snapped when they had been cut, and made weak enough for the strain on them made them part with a resounding crack like a giant rifle shot, then the last umbilical cord that had held the two ships together was straining to breaking point it was like a giant tug of war between two leviathans of the sea at last parted and the two ships lurched violently as they parted, then slowly pulled away from each other.

As the two ships got further apart Cyril could just see by the lights on the bridge of the NAT GAS 2, a battle raging for control of the bridge of the NAT GAS 2, after a flurry of shots all went quiet as the two ships drifted further apart, after what seemed a lifetime the horn on the NAT GAS 2 sounded and the NAT GAS 2 sailed towards the false dawn that was rising in the east.

On the skyline, you could just make out land or it might have been low cloud giving the impression it was land, Cyril was relieved, he knew they had cut their timing very fine, he mentally wished Mustafa and his band of volunteers good luck as he knew they would need it.

As the two ships lurched apart when the binding that was holding the two ships together parted with a loud cracking sound Parvis turned around in surprise and Mustafa attacked him, they struggled together then the NAT GAS 2 lurched again this time righting itself, this threw Parvis off balance and Mustafa pushed Parvis at the same time, Parvis hit the railings and toppled over, the man travelled at least two decks before he hit a mooring cleat on the next deck with a sickening thud and did not move his back obviously broken from the angle he lay at.

When Mustafa entered the wheelhouse, there were four people lying in a pool of blood, two volunteers and the last two guards.

Just then one of the injured guards reached for a device that had fallen out of his hands grabbed it and then activated it, he then succumbed to his wounds and died.

"What did he activate?" Mustafa said, "look around and see if you can see anything on the bridge."

"We had better disconnect the autopilot and head us away from the cruise ship and towards that spit of land on the horizon where there is a lighthouse light you can just see in the gloom of the expected dawn."

Mustafa said, "I am going to check on Parvis as he just took flying lessons."

Mustafa went down two decks and approached the man who lay still and twisted on the deck, as he approached him, he moaned, calling out for water.

"What was the device they activated in the wheelhouse?" Mustafa asked the dying man.

"Water," Parvis said.

"What was the device they activated in the wheelhouse?" Mustafa asked more insistently.

"Auto destruct device," the man said weakly, "it's been set in-between the inner and outer hull, between the storage tanks and the ship's hull, it's set with a two-hour delay."

"How do we deactivate it?", Mustafa said.

"You can't. Once activated it stays that way, we were always going to blow the gas ship up no matter how much ransom was paid," Parvis said weakly, "you have time to launch the speedboat and get clear, take me with you," and then he grimaced in pain and then died.

"Great," Mustafa said to the heavens, "we are sitting on a giant time bomb and the time is ticking away."

Mustafa made his way to the bridge to tell the remaining two volunteers the news they did not want to hear, the only way off this floating time bomb was by the speed boat Fast Lady that was used to high-jack the *NAT GAS 2* in the first place but before they could launch it and use it, they had to get the *NAT GAS 2* away from the *Baroness of the Sea* as far as possible, and they would still need time to get clear before the *NAT GAS 2* went up in a ball of flames.

On board the Texas Ranger, the Captain ordered, "make ready tubes 1 through to 6, flood tubes, get ready to fire," they were now tracking and closing in on the *NAT GAS 2* and the unfortunate *Baroness of the Sea* and the victims of human shield.

On the chart, they could see both ships were getting ever nearer to the invisible line that showed the American and Canadian Territorial Waters and the point of no return, when the Captain would order torpedoes to be fired on an unarmed Gas tanker and the devastation that was going to cause when the Gas Ship exploded.

Sonar on board the Texas Ranger was monitoring the two ships very closely, the operator thought he saw a gap appear between the two ships and alerted the Captain.

"Captain, Sonar here, there is a gap developing between the two ships, they are definitely moving apart very slowly."

The Captain ordered the Texas Ranger to be brought up to Periscope depth.

"Keep a close monitor on those two ships and let me know if there is any increase in distance between them," The Captain ordered.

The Captain was relieved and was hoping against hope that the passengers had succeeded in the attempt to take matters into their own hands.

"Sonar room here Captain, the two ships are still veering apart very slowly."

"Torpedo room here Captain, tubes flooded, fish ready for firing."

"Stand down, torpedo room, we will give it a few minutes to see if the Gas ship is getting clear of the Cruise Liner. If so, we will follow that Gas ship. When she is in a safe distance from us, we will put her at the bottom of the sea."

"Sonar room here Sir, the *NAT GAS 2* and the *Baroness of the Sea*, they are definitely parting company and veering apart."

The Captain said, "radio room signal to The Atlantic sea pack, apprise them of the situation and tell them we are following the *NAT GAS 2* and awaiting instructions."

"Radio room here Sir, reply from Atlantic Sea Pack, follow orders blow up and sink the *NAT GAS 2* when the distance is ten miles away from all shipping."

"Rescue ships to monitor Cruise Liner *Baroness of the Sea* to see if she needs assistance, but wait until the *NAT GAS 2* is clear, there will be a tidal wave from an explosion on that ship if she explodes too close to other shipping so be on the safe side and batten down for the severe storm."

As false dawn started to break the NAT GAS 2 headed towards the Atlantic Graveyard of ships off Sable Island, with its many sand bars that surrounded the Island that had caused the death of over 300 ships in the last 300 years,

Mustafa knew there was going to be another ship added to the list, the trouble was, he was on it.

By using the bridge binoculars, Mustafa could just make out the waves breaking over the sand bars at the end of the long narrow spit of land. He had cut the engines of the NAT GAS 2 and using the momentum of the ship headed the NAT GAS 2 towards the sand bars to beach it.

He knew it could take up to two miles before this leviathan of the sea would stop, he could just made out *Baroness of the Sea* in the distance and hoped they had changed course away from the deadly cargo he was sitting on that was about to blow them to kingdom come.

Mustafa and the two remaining volunteers launched the Fast Lady with the on board Derek, but it seemed to take an eternity. The timers were counting down on the explosives between the double-skinned hull of the Gas Ship. The sand bars were getting nearer, it was going to be a close-run thing.

They cleared the on board Derek, and boarded the Fast Lady and gunned the powerful engines into life. They headed away from the *NAT GAS 2* at full throttle. As they got about a mile clear of the gas tanker there was a scraping sound of the Leviathan of the sea running aground on a sand bar.

Mustafa gunned the engine of the high-powered Fast Lady and sped away from the stricken gas tanker and out to sea towards the *Baroness of the Sea* where his wife was waiting for him under Jeff's protection.

As they were getting nearer the Baroness of the Sea, Mustafa could just make out that the cruise liner seemed to be listing slightly to one side.

Just as he was trying to make out why the Baroness of the Sea could be listing, there was a violent explosion emanating from the stricken *NAT GAS 2* behind them.

Mustafa killed the speed of the powerful Fast Lady, swung it round to look in the direction of the *NAT GAS 2* only to see his worst nightmare as the giant gas leviathan of the sea started its death throws.

The auto-destruction device had done its job, the double skinned side of the stricken gas tanker opened up like a tin can, which now started an irreversible chain reaction of events of biblical proportions.

The cryogenically cold cargo of Liquid Natural Gas (Methane) of below minus 160 degrees Centigrade poured out of the damaged hole created by the explosion.

The freezing cold liquid gas reacted with the outer metal hull of the gas ship, fracturing and bursting the brittle metal sections of the hull apart and exposing the liquid gas which in turn at those cold temperatures freeze-dried everything in its path in an ever-expanding boiling off-gas cloud.

The liquid Methane poured into the sea at a temperature of below minus 160 degrees Centigrade. When the liquid gas came in contact with the seawater, it exploded violently in a Rapid Phase Transition (it was like dropping an ice cube into boiling water) as more liquid gas escaped from the stricken gas ship and poured into the sea that too reacted to the seawater and exploded violently.

The molecules of liquid Methane expanded from liquid to gas 620 times its volume into a gas instantly, reacting to the seawater so quickly it exploded, the boiling liquid gas spread into a fast-expanding deadly gas cloud of Methane gas started spreading from the crippled *NAT GAS 2*. When this expanding gas cloud reaches the right mixture of between 80% and 95% air to gas, it can ignite with the slightest spark and burn 3 times hotter than burning Petroleum.

The escaping gas expanded 3 times faster on water than on land, at this alarming rate it spreads out like a white fog of death, freezing and killing everything in its path, anyone unfortunate to be caught in its way could be affected with blindness and asphyxiation. It has no smell or taste, as it rolled over the sea like an ever-expanding deadly fog of methane gas.

It was unbelievable the speed of the ever-expanding boiling off deadly gas cloud if and when it found an ignition source, the heat sear from this burning gas could be felt for many miles further than the exploding gas cloud.

The unstoppable chain reaction had started, the liquid gas was expanding 620 times its size from liquid to gas instantly there were a number of large explosions called "Rapid Phase Transitions" that caused further damage to the ship's hull and the remaining tanks holding the deadly cargo, this released even more liquid gas, from other tanks on board the NAT GAS 2.

Mustafa was witnessing the phenomenon at first hand, and he did not like what was unfolding before his eyes.

He saw the deadly cargo of gas expanding and flowing towards him and then onto the *Baroness of the Sea* where his wife was in Jeff's safe hands. He knew if the unconfined vapour cloud reached the *Baroness of the Sea* then any spark on board the liner would ignite that gas cloud and envelope the *Baroness of the Sea* in a fireball of temperatures hotter than burning petroleum, no one on board the Cruise Liner would survive that scenario.

There were two options, one he could hope the spreading gas cloud dissipated into the air away and be blown away from the *Baroness of the Sea* on the wind, or the gas cloud had to be ignited before it reached the *Baroness of the Sea* where his wife who he loved with all his heart was on board.

He was hoping the first option of the gas dissipating would resolve the problem, but the gas cloud kept expanding at a phenomenal rate and was getting nearer, he gunned the speedboat at its top speed away from the stricken *NAT GAS 2* and towards Asar aboard the Baroness of the Sea.

Even as fast as the Fast Lady was, it seemed to be making heavy weather of the distance between the Fast Lady and the *Baroness of the Sea.*

Mustafa was worried that he had taken too long getting off the *NAT GAS 2* and he had not left himself enough time to make it back to the safety of the *Baroness of the Sea* and the woman he loved.

The gas cloud he was desperately trying to get away from was still getting closer to him. It was expanding at a phenomenal rate and the wind was driving it towards him and the Cruise Ship.

He gradually came to the conclusion of the only desperate option left open to him was to ignite the gas cloud before it got to him and to his wife Asar aboard the *Baroness of the Sea*.

He said to the two men he had left with, "The only way is to ignite that cloud. When we do that our best cover is to go over the side and dive deep to avoid being burned, hand me that vary pistol and get ready to go over the side and dive as deep as you can when that cloud ignites."

Mustafa stopped the Fast Lady and turned her towards the approaching expanding gas cloud. He loaded the vary pistol with the cartridge, then he pointed the vary pistol high in the air towards the expanding gas cloud and fired the pistol.

A red star shell erupted from the vary pistol and arched its way towards the expanding gas cloud, it hung high in the air for what seemed like ages, then as it started to arc downwards and hung in the air, suddenly the edges of the gas cloud ignited, the flames flashed back to the heart of the expanding gas cloud, and the gas cloud erupted into a fireball of impossible comprehension.

As the roaring fireball that was like an exploding sun blotting out the sky and rushed towards them, the three men dived in the sea and swum down as deep as they could, above them the surface of the water sparkled brightly with the detonation of the devastating fireball that seared across the surface of the sea above them.

After what seemed an eternity with bursting lungs, they were forced to the surface to find the speed boat they had abandoned earlier burning.

They swam to what seemed to be the wrecked Fast Lady, the front part was burning from the devastating heat sear of the exploding gas. They got back on board via the stern section, they retrieved the fire extinguisher and proceeded to put out the fire on the bow of the boat.

Mustafa was surprised how soon they got the fire under control, and he breathed a sigh of relief, "see if the engine still works," he said to one of the men.

The man tried to start the engine, the engine struggled but eventually coughed into life, "I didn't expect that," he said to Mustafa, and then added, "perhaps our luck has changed."

Mustafa looked in the direction of the *Baroness of the Sea*. He could see some structural damage on the upper decks from where he was but she was still afloat but seemed to be listing even more than the last time he looked.

Mustafa turned and looked in the direction of the *NAT GAS 2* but he could not see all of it. In the distance where the giant leviathan of the sea had been, there was a hulk of a ship with an increasing fireball like a newborn sun rising out of the sea, the sea was also tilting at a crazy angle.

As he watched the sea, he came to the realization that a giant wave caused by the concussion of the explosion on board the *NAT GAS 2* was heading their way. There was nowhere to go except to hope to ride out the wave.

He shouted to the two men, "Strap yourselves down! That wave is going to hit us shortly and we need to turn into it. Give it full power! It's our only hope."

The wave was climbing in size, getting bigger and bigger as it headed towards them, they could not run for the *Baroness of the Sea* because she was too far away to make it in time. All they could do was to give the powerful engines of the Fast Lady full throttle and hope there was enough power to ride out the giant wave.

The giant wave came crashing towards them, it picked them up like a toy, the world tilted crazily out of kilter as the wave came crashing in. They seemed to be riding on a giant white knuckle ride as the powerful engines of the Fast Lady gave all the power it had as they attacked the wave head-on.

It seemed as though they were climbing a giant hill of water and as they were going to crest the giant wave and they toppled on the brink of the wave, the screws of the propellers were screaming as they were turning in empty air, but the flow of the wave went under them and they drove down into the trough of the giant wave, they crashed into the trough of the wave only to find another wave right on top of them.

Mustafa pushed the straining engines to their limit ready to attack the next wave with the battered Fast Lady, this time they almost got to the top of this wave when it crashed down on top of them and swamped them, burying them in a wall of water.

Water cascaded down on them but the Fast Lady popped to the surface and crashed down into the next trough, only to face another wave heading towards them. All Mustafa could do was to steer the Fast Lady towards the next wave when she started to flounder.

Mustafa felt like a cork in a washing machine being tumble about as the Fast Lady started to disintegrate around him, all he could do was pray that she held together long enough for them to survive.

The next wave was not as powerful, and they rose to the top of the next wave, and then pitched down into the trough of the next one and gradually the sea settled around them.

They were very battered and bruised but miraculously they had survived now they were drifting aimlessly on the ocean and at the mercy of the sea.

As he looked to where the *Baroness of the Sea* was last seen, just as the first of the giant waves that had battered them was breaking over the *Baroness of the Sea*, the cruise liner tilted upward at what seemed an impossible angle with its bow pointing into and buried by the crest of the first giant wave and it looked as if the cruise liner would flounder, but what seemed to be a miracle the *Baroness of the Sea* pushed its way through the crest of the first wave.

As the ship tilted towards the trough of the next wave, he could see the mighty propellers that were the powerhouse of this mighty floating luxury hotel come out of the water, he then lost sight of the vessel as the second wave crashed over it.

Suddenly he realized his own predicament and that the Fast Lady was swamped with water, he looked around for the other two men that had come with him, but they were not to be seen, he was the only survivor. He looked around desperately to see if he could see them but to no avail, he then started bailing out the stricken Fast Lady and prayed that someone would see and help him before the Fast Lady sank. In the meanwhile, he would have a desperate battle against time to survive as the tide was slowly drifting him and the wrecked Fast Lady towards the burning hulk of the NAT GAS 2.

As the Texas Ranger was on the surface following the *NAT GAS 2* waiting for the distance between the Cruise Liner The *Baroness of the Sea* and the *NAT GAS 2* to increase to a safe distance, when they were far enough apart, they could sink the giant gas ship with torpedoes.

Lining up ready to fire her front tubes with six torpedoes into the NAT GAS 2 had run aground, then there was a number of massive explosions from the Giant Gas ship as it exploded before their eyes

"Emergency dive!" the Captain shouted, the crew scramble for the conning tower fast and as the Submarine dived the hatch was closed.

"Periscope depth," the Captain ordered, then said, "batten down for stormy weather we will be riding out a storm."

Looking through the periscope, the Captain saw the fireball of impossible size followed by the tidal wave from that massive explosion.

"Dive, Dive," the Captain ordered, "close all water-tight doors, rig for a severe storm."

In the meanwhile, John had checked and made safe the explosive devices in the stern and the middle of the cruise ship and he was checking the last of the explosive devices by the forward locker and had just made them safe then he was able to release the rest of the crew from the forward locker. An officer who introduced himself as the Chief engineer thanked him. John said, "you better go to the Captain and take back your ship," the Officer shook his hand and said to the men "come on the Captain needs us," the crew were picking up anything they could use as weapons as they rushed to take back their ship.

John was making his way back to the middle of the deck he was on when he heard running footsteps on the grating above where he had finished off making the devices safe. He looked up just in time to see Abdul making his way into a small cargo hold, he did not realise was there.

John followed Abdul to the hold he had gone into, he spotted Abdul over the far side he was bending over with his back to him.

John's foot knocked against a small piece of metal lying on the floor and this made a scrapping sound, Abdul spun around, saw John and said, "you! you are the one that stopped me from detonating the charges I laid, now I know why my remote didn't work."

Then Abdul added, "well you won't stop me this time," he said. He then turned away from John reached down and lit the fuse that was trailing from explosives that were pressed against the outer hull.

John rushed at Abdul, but Abdul was ready for him, they clashed together as they met in the middle of the hold.

Abdul was a highly experienced assassin, he had been picked out by the *Senate* for his skills.

John had been a member of the elite SAS and he had kept up his training and he exercised every day.

As soon as they clashed together each new from experience from the first holds that they had an experienced opponent that would take all their skills to overcome the other one.

They crashed together smashing into stacks of metal racking that was in the hold. This racking started tipping over and as it toppled it, crashed into other stacks of racking that also toppled over like tumbling dominoes, all this metal crashed into the emergency escape hatch blocking it, the only way out of the hold now was the way John and Abdul had come in.

John was trying to get to the explosives to defuse the detonator, and Abdul was going to stop him at any cost, it was a clash of the titans and there seemed no impasse.

As the fight ensued the burning fuse to the explosives was getting shorter and shorter.

John knew he had taken on a killer with a lot more experience than him, and it would only be a matter of time before Abdul got the upper hand, and could feel Abdul knew it, as he looked over Abdul's shoulder and saw the burning fuse to the detonator had got so close to the explosives that it was about to detonate, he gave one last mighty heave and pushed Abdul towards the explosives, turned and made a dash for the inward opening door.

Abdul smiled knowing he had beaten the Englishman and started to stalk him.

John made it to the door and managed to get out of the hold just as Abdul got to the metal door of the hold as John was closing it. Abdul yanked at the closing door trying free it from John's grasp and open it when the explosives detonated blasting the door shut with Abdul inside the hold. The concussion from the explosion killed him outright.

John had the protection of the metal door from the blast but he was still thrown down the gangway with the force of the explosion.

Stunned and with his ears ringing he made his way slowly back through the smoke to the restaurant area where Rose was waiting.

After Cyril's crew had axed through the ropes securing the gas tanker to the cruise ship, Cyril made his way to the bridge of the *Baroness of the Sea*. As he approached the wheelhouse he heard small arms fire coming from that direction and there was obviously a gun battle going on for the control of the bridge.

Cyril went up the gangway on one side of the deck that would take him to the bridge just as bullets were ricocheting off the guard rail of the ship. He could see the first officer leading a team to take back the bridge from the other side of the deck but he was pinned down by a fuselage of gunfire from the bridge. Using the guns taken from the guards they had disabled, Cyril and the men that were with him opened fire from their position catching the guards that were in the wheelhouse in a crossfire, the guns in the wheelhouse went silent.

The two groups approached the wheelhouse from both sides very warily to find three men lying in a pool of blood two seemed dead and one was badly wounded.

"Was I pleased to see you," the First Officer said, "They had us pinned down and there was nothing we could do, they were first alerted by the gunfire on deck five, then by the gun battle on board the *NAT GAS 2*, so when we put our heads above the parapet so to speak they were taking potshots at us and we could not return the compliment."

"Good job you came at them from a different angle and caught them in a crossfire otherwise they would have had us pinned down forever."

"Now," the Officer said, "we need to get this ship off the autopilot and onto a different course away from the *NAT GAS 2* that looks like it is heading for the Atlantic Graveyard of ships off Sable Island and we don't want to be in the same part of that graveyard."

As the first officer took over the controls and took the ship off automatic pilot there was a massive explosion and a black cloud and a massive spray of water emanating from the side of the *Baroness of the Sea*. "Good God! What was that?" the first officer said as the acrid cloud of smoke bloomed from the side of the liner. "We've must have been hit by a torpedo or we have hit a mine?", the officer added.

Smoke was now billowing from the side of the cruise liner, "see what damage there is," The officer said to one of the crews.

The man dashed out of the Bridge to investigate.

The first officer said, "I don't know what damage has been done but she is starting to get sluggish, then ordered another crew member to find the Captain and if he was alive to get him up here quickly.

Just then the crew member he had sent to have a look at the damage to the ship returned and speaking breathlessly said, "I don't think it's a torpedo or a mine, looking at the way the plating is twisted if it had been a mine or a torpedo the plating would have been bent and twisted inwardly, but by the looks of the damage it looks like it was made from inside the ship, the bad news is it looks like a large hole just on the waterline and we seem to be shipping water every time we roll with the swell of the sea."

"It looks like the only option we have now is to try and make it to Nova Scotia before we sink," the first officer said.

"How about this Sable Island you spoke about?", Cyril said, "that's nearer and we can see it on the horizon it looks like a big enough piece of land from here."

"What you can see is what has made a fool of a lot of mariners over the last 300 years," the first officer said, "that land is very long and it is very narrow, it's shaped like a long curved sword blade of land surrounded by treacherous sand-banks, that why it's called the Atlantic graveyard, over 300 ships have been lost there, to beach a ship there has to be a last resort, our best bet is still Nova Scotia."

As all of this was going on at what was a reluctant birthday party reception which had now turned into a survival party, with people congratulating one another and cheering as the *NAT GAS 2* had sailed away,

the body of Jake lay on the floor ignored. Derek had taken the Sheikh back to his cabin for safekeeping before the people turned into an angry mob and wanted revenge against the Sheikh for what they had been through.

As the people calmed down and looked out at the *NAT GAS 2* in the distance they could feel the *Baroness of the Sea* was starting to make heavy weather of the relatively calm seas.

Then from the doorway of the restaurant came a blood-curdling scream, "you betrayed me," people screamed and run away from the entrance.

There in the doorway stood the Sheikh, he was armed with the jewelled dagger, that was dripping in blood. He looked as though he had finally flipped into insanity, he had a crazy look in his eyes, he was drooling, and emanating hatred and revenge.

By the doorway there were wounded people who had got in his way, they were injured from the frenzied knife attack from the Sheikh.

He was staring at Jeff, he said, "Why? Why? I would have given you everything you ever wanted, why did you turn on me? We are men of our word," with a crazy look he said, "We could have ruled the world."

Then looking deadly serious, he aimed his hatred at Jeff, and said, "well, nobody plays me for a fool, you will die for your insult to me," then he started stalking Jeff, slashing out at anybody who got near him but slowly making his way towards Jeff.

"I will cut out your heart," the Sheikh said, "and I will feed it to the fish, I will make you obey me," and the Sheikh was shouting at the crowd of passengers that were trying to avoid him, "I am your ruler, I am your Sheikh and I will be obeyed, or you will suffer, and die, I will show you what I do to treacherous dogs like him," pointing at Jeff.

The Sheikh circled Jeff, slashing out at him with the dagger.

Jeff backed away from the danger of the slashing blade, and then dodged around a pillar still facing the Sheikh. It gave him a little ground in which to manoeuvre, as he gained a little ground he slid his right arm out of his coat, off of his shoulder and wrapped the rest of the coat around his left arm as a shield against the slashing blade of the Sheikh's jewelled dagger.

The Sheikh lunged at Jeff. Jeff caught the slashing blade on the coat wrapped around his arm, as he parried the lunge away he hit the Sheikh with his fist giving the Sheikh a bloody nose. The Sheikh backed away in shock, he did not expect to be attacked, as he felt he had the upper hand.

This made the Sheikh's eyes water from the blow, but it made him even angrier and he attacked with a new frenzy stabbing and slashing at Jeff.

As Jeff backed away from this latest onslaught, he crashed backwards into a pillar.

The Sheikh saw his opportunity and lunged forward at Jeff, screaming in Arabic.

As the Sheikh lunged forward Jeff caught the blade of the dagger in the coat wrapped around his arm, Jeff felt the blade bite into his arm, at the same time Jeff kicked out hard with his right foot at the Sheikh catching the Sheikh hard in the crotch.

The stunned look of shock and surprise on the Sheikh's face was a picture. The Sheikh went down gasping for air and curled up into a ball holding his crotch dropping the jewelled blade in the process.

"Tie him up so he can't escape this time," Jeff said to one of the men standing near that was still shocked at the knife fight he had just witnessed. The man looked confused as to where he was going to get a rope from.

Jeff saw his confusion and said, "use the tie-backs of the curtains, but this time tie him to a pillar and make sure he can't escape."

Derek came over to him holding the jewel-encrusted dagger the Sheikh had just used to good effect. Derek said, "yours now I believe?". As he handed Jeff the dagger, and added, "where did you learn to fight like that, I am impressed?"

I grew up in the rough part of Tooting South London during the Teddy boy days and there are something's you never forget, by the way, where were you? You were supposed to act as my bodyguard," he said smiling at the big man.

The big man looked hurt at first, then realized Jeff was joking, then a big grin came over his face and he bear-hugged Jeff and said, "you know I would die for you."

Jeff looked down at the dagger and said, "this will be a matching pair to the other one," as he said this, the coat he had wrapped around his arm dropped to the floor and there was a wound on his forearm where the blade of the jewel-encrusted dagger caught him.

"You're bleeding," Karen said, looking stunned and seeing her husband in a light she had never seen him in before, she had never seen him in an actual fight, and she was not sure it was a side of him she liked, as it had frightened her.

"It's only a scratch," Jeff said.

Karen grabbed a napkin from the table and wrapped it around his arm, and tied it tight, she said, "you frightened me, I have never seen you like that before, and it's not a side of you I like."

"It was me or him," he said defensively to Karen, "and don't forget he was armed with a knife," then being flippant he said, "he's ruined my tuxedo, my tailor will go mad over this."

Karen laughed at his remark more out of relief than humour, and then she fussed over him for a short while as the hub-bub of what had just happened died down.

As they were gathering themselves together, there was an almighty explosion and the ship shuddered, there was smoke starting to rise from the side of the cruise ship where the hull had been breached by the explosion.

What was a celebration had now turned in to a panicking mob of people screaming and wanting to know if they had been torpedoed.

Jeff grabbed a microphone from the staging area and asked people to calm down, he said, "you are on the safest part of the ship so stay where you are until we find out what has happened."

Just then the ship's Public Address system burst into life.

"This is your Captain speaking, as you know we were high-jacked by pirates, but that is all over now, there has been an explosion in one of the lower decks due to damage sustained we will be making for Nova Scotia in Canada where we will berth. The danger from the *NAT GAS 2* has passed as that is at least six miles away now thanks to the brave volunteers who sailed it away from us, we have sent out distress calls and help will arrive soon in the meanwhile please stay in the restaurant area as this is the safest part of the ship."

Just then a bedraggled John came into the restaurant and said, "it was Abdul, he set off an explosive device, I tried, but I could not stop him."

After what seemed an age John got to Jeff's side, he appeared battered and bruised.

"Where is Abdul now?", Jeff said.

Scattered all over the cargo hold, John said graphically

"I see you have been having fun," John said looking at the Sheikh tied up against the pillar still bent double in agony and groaning.

He showed John the dagger the Sheikh had attacked him with, and said, "now I have the matching pair."

John raised his eyebrows in surprise, "I can see. I will have to keep an eye on you if you show me any more sides of yourself, I did not know existed.

Jeff smiled.

As they talked about what happened, Jeff pointed out the NAT GAS 2 in the distance and told John how Mustafa had seen sense and helped take back the NAT GAS 2, free it from the *Baroness of the Sea* and sail towards Sable Island and the Atlantic Graveyard.

John said, "where is he now?"

Jeff said, pointing to the NAT GAS 2, "over there, making sure we are all safe."

"Rather him than me," John said.

Just then there was a rumbling sound coming from the direction of the NAT GAS 2 all eyes turned again in the direction of the giant gas ship as they could just see in the distance the side of the NAT GAS 2 peal apart as though someone had used a mighty can opener then the tanker was shrouded by a giant white gas cloud that looked like sea mist drifting and tumbling towards them, Jeff knew his greatest fears had been realized, and a catastrophe was playing out before his eyes that he had spoken of, and he had been ridiculed as being impossible to happen.

Then there was a deafening explosion emanating from the *NAT GAS 2* and the nightmare scenario unfolded as the white freezing cryogenically cold fog of boiling Liquid Natural Gas started flowing from the *NAT GAS 2* reacting with seawater causing Rapid Phase Transition explosions. Jeff knew his worst nightmare was about to unfold before his eyes and there was nothing he could do about it.

Mustafa's wife Asar looked horrified at the explosions coming from the NAT GAS 2 put her hands to her face and screamed out, "Mustafa!"

Jeff then could just make out the powerful Fast Lady in the distance, she was powering its way away from the unfolding nightmare.

Jeff pointed the Fast Lady out to Asar and said, "he might have made it," they watched as the Fast Lady turned and faced the massive deadly gas cloud emerging from an explosion on the *NAT GAS 2*, then everything seemed to happen in slow motion as the nightmare unfolded in front of their eyes.

The appalling cryogenically cold gas cloud was rapidly rolling towards them at a colossal rate.

In between the *Baroness of the Sea* and the expanding deadly gas cloud emanating from the crippled *NAT GAS 2* was the lone Fast Lady waiting as if in defiance.

Jeff could tell by the way the gas cloud of Methane was rolling towards them they were going to be in its direct path and there was nothing they could do about it.

It would only be a matter of a short while before the crippled *Baroness of the Sea* with all its passengers and crew were engulfed in the deadly cryogenically cold expanding Methane gas cloud, Jeff also knew that when that cloud was at the right mixture of gas and air, it would find an ignition source then it would create a disaster of biblical proportions and they were trapped in its path with no way to avoid the unfolding scenario.

All they could do is watch as the ever-expanding cloud of death rolled towards them from the crippled gas tanker, their only hope was if the wind suddenly changed direction and blew the deadly gas cloud in another direction but that was very unlikely.

In the distance, he could just make out that the Fast Lady had stopped and was now facing the expanding gas cloud that was approaching it.

Then there appeared a red star shell from a vary pistol arcing its way towards the expanding gas cloud that had been fired from the speed boat.

The star shell seemed to hang in the air above the gas cloud for ages, and then with a devastating concussion, the gas cloud ignited, firstly at the edges and then flashing back to the crippled gas ship almost instantly.

The searing heat of the ignited gas cloud spread out from the gas ship as the massive amount of released gas exploded into a fireball of horrendous temperature.

The concussion from the exploding gas that followed this ignition was like an invisible wave of raw power slamming against everything in its path.

Forward panoramic windows in the dining room on the *Baroness of the Sea* cracked with the concussion from the blast emanating from the now crippled *NAT GAS 2* and even at the distance, they were away from the giant gas ship they could feel the effects of the searing fireball of heat.

If the expanding gas cloud had been any closer to them or the person on the Fast Lady had ignited the gas cloud any later the *Baroness of the Sea* would have suffered more devastating damage from the heat sear of exploding gas than it did when the gas cloud exploded, it had been a very close run thing.

Jeff realized straight away, the person in the Fast Lady that had fired that star shell into the expanding gas cloud had sacrificed themselves so that those on board the *Baroness of the Sea* might stand a better chance of survival.

The people on board the Fast Lady's chances of survival was virtually zero, so Jeff sent out a silent prayer of thanks to them, thanking them for their sacrifice.

The events that started to unfold before him now was like something out of a disaster movie of biblical proportions.

There were further mighty explosions from the crippled *NAT GAS 2* as it was in its death throws.

The fireball that was engulfing the *NAT GAS 2* was hundreds of feet high and blotted out the horizon, it was as if a piece of the sun had landed in the sea and was boiling it in some vast cauldron.

The concussion on the seabed from the massive detonation of the exploding gas ship and the tidal wave that it was creating was being born from the devastation. It was like some giant invisible monster had woken up and was rising from the bowels of the sea in some sort of vengeance for being woken up from its sleep. The pressure built up and the giant tidal wave was born.

Jeff could see the horizon starting to tilt. At first, he thought it was an optical illusion, but as the pressure wave built up, the size of the massive Tsunami that was building up was unbelievable, it looked like a mountain of water heading their way and it was growing in size the closer it got.

He shouted out loud, "everyone better brace themselves for impact, you had better hold on to something firm when those waves hit, it looks like it will swamp this ship."

Jeff thanked God that the sea was relevantly calm but the tidal wave that was heading for the crippled *Baroness of the Sea* was swelling in the distance and the Captain was desperately trying to turn the crippled ship to head into the giant Tsunami wave that was heading for them.

To give them a better chance of survival, he needed to hit the giant wave head on and ride the wave and hopefully cutting through the wave with the bow of the ship, rather than letting the giant wave hit them broadside where it might roll the ship, and the ship would flounder.

To add to the desperate plight they were in, the device that had exploded in the cargo hold that killed Abdul outright was on the waterline. The explosion had pierced a hole in the cruise liner's inner and outer hull so every time the cruise ship rolled with the swell seawater poured into the hold, which then started flooding the decks below the waterline.

The Baroness of the Sea seemed to be getting heavier and more sluggish as the water coming in through the hole in the side of the ship made the Baroness of the Sea start to list.

The crippled Cruise Liner handled like an old sea cow instead of the slick beautiful luxury state of the art vessel that had been the pride of the fleet.

The innocent passengers and crew on the Baroness of the Sea had been thrown into the middle of what seemed to be a political nightmare. At first, it felt that it would end only in one way, their sacrifice. They were the pawns in a giant game of political chess they were being sacrificed so even more people did not die and political faces could be saved.

If they were to survive, it had been up to themselves to bind together, fight for their own survival against professional killers, there was not going to be any outside help, for the *Baroness of the Sea* and its passengers, they might be on a luxury ship but, it was a death ship with no hope of survival for the passengers as they had been counted as the victims of the fallout of the global policy of not giving in to terrorism.

What had started with the excitement of a luxury holiday, then the diversion of the participation in a mercy mission, now that mercy mission had turned into the worst nightmare imaginable, with their lives being forfeit, because they were in the wrong place at the wrong time.

The passengers and some of the crew were huddled into the restaurant and recreational areas on the upper decks except for the crew required in the engine room where some had all been until recently under guard by the fanatical pirates that had high-jacked the *Baroness of the Sea.*

The culmination of the scenario that was unfolding in front of Jeff was like something out of a bad dream.

The Captain of the Cruise ship told the passengers he had sent out an international "May Day" so help would be on its way soon. He then explained to the passengers via the Public Address system that he could not use the lifeboats yet as he felt they would be swamped by the tsunami type wave heading their way until they had outridden the tidal wave caused by the concussion of the explosion of the gas ship that was in the shallower water.

The wave was heading their way. He felt everybody stood a better chance in a bigger vessel, also he felt the wave would hit in the middle of launching the lifeboats and there would be more lives lost. He had hoped to keep passengers calm during this next crisis.

The Captain knew he could not outrun the wave and if he tried, it would swamp the ship from the stern, if the wave hit on either side it would probably roll the ship over the only chance he had was to head into the wave bow first with the engines at full power and try to ride the wave and cut through it.

Even in a relatively calm sea, the tidal wave looked big as it slowly made its way towards them swelling bigger as it got nearer.

Over the PA system, the 1st Officer was now instructing everyone on board that just before the wave hit, everyone should hold on very tight and brace themselves for the impact. He said he would sound the ship horn three times just before the wave hit.

Jeff could see the wall of water heading their way through the windows at the side and front of the ship it seemed to get bigger as it got nearer the bow of the ship was turning towards the wall of water slowly and was now pointing straight at the wave as it rushed towards them.

The ship's horn sounded at the first long blast. Jeff finished tying Karen to a pillar with Table clothes from the table he made sure she was facing the stern of the ship so any loose debris flying around would hit the pillar first and afford her a little protection and not pin her to the pillar. She also had a knife so she would be able to cut herself free afterwards.

It was the only protection he could find for them at short notice.

He strapped himself to the binding that held Karen and they both held onto one another and prayed as the second blast on the horn sounded.

He could feel the tilt of the ship as the third horn sounded.

It felt as if he was on a fairground ride and was being tilted backwards, as everything twisted out of kilter, he could hear the thundering sound of the huge wave as it slammed into the *Baroness of the Sea*.

Lots of things happened as if in slow motion.

The ship felt as if it was climbing a giant hill as the *Baroness of the Sea* rose up the giant wave like a surf board.

The water from the top of the wave crashed down onto the bow of the ship cascading the sea over the ship swamping the ship from bow to stern.

Tables and chairs were flung about like matchwood as was anything that was not nailed down, debris was flying around everywhere.

As the ship shuddered and ploughed through the crest of the wave, the engines could be heard above the sound of the crashing wave as the screws of the propeller rose out of the water.

It was then that Jeff felt a pain in his left arm and shoulder that was wrapped around Karen to protect her as something that was flying loose had hit him. He looked at terrified Karen to see she was unharmed he was relieved that whatever it was had only hit him and missed her.

As the Baroness of the Sea crested the wave and slammed back down into the sea the second wave hit just after that but this wave was not as powerful as the first.

After the fourth wave the Baroness of the Sea had turned slightly sideways and the Baroness of the Sea started to corkscrew and slowly settle at least they were still afloat but the crippled ship had been severely damaged even further from the swamping it had taken by the giant waves.

Jeff felt the pain that was coming from his arm and shoulder was made worse as they were being flung from one side of the pillar to the other that they were tied to, just like rag dolls, he felt as though he had been put through a tumble drier.

He knew that if he had not strapped himself to Karen, he would have been unable to protect her during the violent tossing about.

Jeff could see that the brave captain had headed the *Baroness of the Sea* to the shallows of the sandbars hoping to run the ship aground on the sand bar in doing so to beach the ship before it sank.

As the Baroness of the Sea settled down from lurching to just swaying, Jeff looked at a terrified Karen then they both thanked God they had survived the initial blast and concussion wave from the dying *NAT GAS 2*.

Now their troubles would really start as they would have to try to survive the inevitable shipwreck of the *Baroness of the Sea* as he believed the ship had taken more punishment than it was originally designed for.

Using his right hand to cut the strapping he had used to bind them safely together, Jeff freed himself and Karen and they staggered as the ship swayed. Jeff staggered into the pillar he had strapped the pair of them to in doing so landed on his injured shoulder which pained him greatly something hit him on the head hard and he passed out.

Jeff came to his head throbbed, his arm and shoulder were very sore. Karen was bending over him, he was covered in dust and a few bits of ceiling, she was asking him if he was alright as she wiped away the blood from the wound on his head.

"How long have I been out of it?", Jeff said to Karen.

"A few moments," she said, "you were hit on the head by falling debris, you got the worst of it when you shielded me."

Jeff sat up, his head was thumping but as it gradually cleared to a dull ache he could look at the damage done by the tidal waves that had hit the *Baroness of the Sea*. It looked as though someone had swung a wrecking ball through the restaurant area, there were people moaning and some women were crying some were silent just holding onto their pain.

As Jeff stood up the world spun for a while and the throbbing in his head came back then died away slowly. Derek was supporting him in case he fell, "thanks, big feller", Jeff said to him.

"We need to see to the injured," Jen said, then she added, "come on girls there's work to do," then turning to Jeff, Derek, and John said, "you three make yourself busy and find my Cyril," then she turned to Asar and said comfortingly, "we all hope Mustafa makes it."

"Where's the Sheikh?," Jeff said, "he's not where we left him, he must have broken free during all the chaos."

"Well, he didn't go far," John said, as he looked at the twisted body of the Sheikh lying in a heap with a broken piece of handrail sticking out of his chest. It looked like he had speared himself on its jagged point as the cruise ship was tossed around like a cork in a washing machine.

"Hey, you three! Go and find my Cyril," Jen said again, "and don't come back without him," then pointing to the Sheikh added, "he's not going to do anybody any more harm, so go!"

They rushed off to find where Cyril was like told off children trying to make amends for being naughty.

They took a deck each and looked about amongst the debris and the smashed sun loungers, and then they met up and decided to split up again and do the same on the other decks.

As they met up on one of the upper decks, "he's nowhere to be seen," said John, "I don't want to be the one to tell Jen we can't find him so we better keep on looking."

"Where can he be?", Derek said looking worried.

"The only place left he will be," Jeff said, "is in the bridge, we better go there and find out, if not he could have been swept overboard, and I don't want to be the one to tell Jen that."

They approached the bridge as they got there a voice said, "you're not allowed in there that's for crew members only", it came from a crew member holding a gun captured from guards that were pointing directly at Jeff's stomach.

On hearing the disturbance, the first officer came out of the bridge and asked what the fuss was about, on seeing Jeff, Derek, and John, he said, "you're very welcome sight for sore eyes."

The crew member said, "but sir you told me not to let anyone through and to shoot them if they did not obey."

"We will make an exception with these three," the first officer said, "we have them to thank for the retaking of our ship, by the way," the first officer said, "we have a friend of the captain's you should meet as he escorted them into the bridge.

Standing next to the Captain was Cyril.

Jeff let out a sigh of relief upon seeing his friend and said, "Jen sent us out to look for you when we couldn't find you, and we thought you might be feeding the fishes."

"The fish would have choked themselves, and then spat him out," Derek said, as he laughed with the relief of seeing his friend unharmed then he gave Cyril a massive bear hug, "Boy! Am I glad I don't have to tell Jen we lost you."

The captain said, "we are not out of the woods yet, the cruise ship is taking on water fast, I don't think we can make Nova Scotia with the hole we have in her side and the battering she has just taken. The only piece of land anywhere near here is Sable Island, and we are already within the area known as the Atlantic Ocean graveyard, so Sable Island is the only chance we have.

Then the Captain added, "I need to beach her before she sinks, it's our only chance to save as many people as possible. It's going to be rough on them but of the two options it will give the rescue services a better chance of helping us and they will be able to save more people."

"To add to our problems," the Captain added, "I have to avoid the burning *NAT GAS 2*. Luckily she has run aground on the far eastern tip of the treacherous sand bars."

"We also need to put a patch over the breach in our hull", the Captain said, "so that would give me a bit more time to cover the distance between us and the crippled NAT GAS 2, also make for the western end of the Island before this ship starts wallowing and sinks, it's going to be a close-run thing."

The first officer interjected and said, "the sandbar the burning *NAT GAS 2* has run aground on has to be avoided at all costs otherwise we will be going from the frying pan into the fire literately," then he added, "we need to be able to avoid the other sandbars and make it to the beach at the western end of Sable Island."

"I don't want to add to the problems," the first officer said, "but unless we get a patch on that breach in the hull we are not going to make the beach, and we will sink in the most awkward spot possible for a rescue attempt, so if we are to save as many people as possible we must make that beach and to make that beach we have to put a patch over that breach in the hull and it's not going to be easy putting a plaster over that wound."

"How do you put a plaster over that sort of wound in a ship?" Jeff said.

"We will use a massive canvas to slide it over the side of the ship above the hole, when we lower the canvas over the hull where the hole is, the pressure of the sea will suck the canvas towards the hole in the ship and hold the patch in place, and this will slow down the massive amount of water that is pouring into the ship every time the ship rolls towards that side of the ship, the more the ship is wallowing in the lower she settles in the water, once the hole in the side of the ship goes below the waterline the ship will go one way that's straight down. The hardest part is keeping the canvas out square so that it covers the whole of the breach in the first attempt. To do this we will need every able-bodied man to hold the canvas as we lower it as we don't have any cranes or jibs, we can use, as this is a passenger ship."

"I see the theory you are trying to put in place," Jeff said, "but that will be very dangerous for the men holding the canvas if it goes wrong, they could be dragged over the side as the sea takes hold of the canvas and sucks it into place."

Jeff thought for a minute and then said, "why not use the jibs from two of the lifeboats to hang the canvas from whilst the canvas is lowered in place, then you can use one of the lifeboats to take the ropes from the bottom end of the canvas and help get those ends of the ropes to the other side of the ship so the bottom of the patch can be held in place using the other side of the ship to secure the ropes from, by going around the front of the ship the lifeboat can slide the rope under the hull till it is in the right position.

Like keelhauling but with a large canvas.

"That's brilliant! We have nothing to lose by trying it," the Captain said, "see to it number one, take as many of the crew you need to get the job done, see they are wearing fire suits as well in case we get too close to the gas ship."

"We might be sacrificing two lifeboats in the short term but in the long term it might make all the difference between being able to beach this ship and losing her and I would hate to lose my ship or get any of my crew or passengers roasted alive in the attempt to save her."

The officers departed and went to find the massive canvas required, so they could put the patch in place. They knew it would be a race against time to get the job done and get to the beach in time before they sank.

"Now gentlemen," the Captain said, "I personally would like to thank you for all your help and co-operation in taking back my ship, I will be forever grateful as will my company.

Now how is everything in the restaurant area, it looks as though it took a battering, do you know what is the extent of the casualties?"

"I think it needs a fresh lick of paint," John said wryly.

"A lick of paint? You must be joking!" Derek said, "it looks like a wrecking ball has been swung around by a petulant giant."

"Jen is organising the injured and she is quite a formidable force," Jeff said, "and there is a lot of help from your first aiders."

John, then told the Captain his side of what happened, as to how he defused the explosives, and how Abdul had set fresh charges and what happened to Abdul when the explosives detonated.

Cyril told him his side of everything of how his team made sure the guards were put to sleep and how Mustafa turned out trumps and knocked out the last of the guards on deck five, then how Mustafa and his crew of volunteers had commandeered a lifeboat to take back the *NAT GAS 2* and the last he had seen of him was Mustafa disappearing into the gloom with the lifeboat, they presumed that they had somehow made it onto the *NAT GAS 2* because when they had heard shots fired coming from the bridge of the tanker and that was when he ordered the tow rope cut, he told them one of his men got a broken arm from the whiplash of the snapping rope, it was shortly after that he heard the signal of a blast on the gas tankers horn, and the gas ship veered away and sailed towards the eastern end of Sable Island.

The gas ship eventually run aground and it looked as though the explosives aboard the gas ship detonated, this released the deadly cargo of freezing Liquid Natural Gas which boiled out of the hull which seemed to cause other detonations, they saw a very light that ignited the gas cloud and *NAT GAS 2* blew up.

Cyril added, "that Mustafa was a very brave man he saved us all and I want that on record," then added, "without his change of heart and him helping us when he did, we would all have been part of that fireball we just witnessed."

Derek told the Captain how he understood Arabic and how he let them think he was a dummy and because they thought that, he was able to overhear what their plan was which gave them the advantage they needed.

Derek hung his head down when he told the Captain how he had to snap Jake's neck, "I did not know he was an Olympic Champion, I did not want to kill him but if I had let him go he would have killed Jeff, his neck snapped in the struggle."

Jeff told him about his part and how he was concerned for Mustafa, and said, "if he was on that speed boat then he would have been the one to ignite that gas cloud if he had not done that, that cloud would have reached us on this ship, and then ignited, and we would have been cinders."

"I will put out an alert for Mustafa, which is the least we can do," the Captain said, "if he is alive, they might pick him up in a search and rescue operation whilst they are helping us."

"In the meanwhile," the Captain said, "you had better go and let your wives know you are safe, by the sounds of it they are very busy with the injured and could do with some help."

Then he said, "I will need all my skill in saving this ship and that is going to be a close-run thing as we have to sail past that burning gas ship to get to a safe beach."

Then he added, "this area of the sea is going to be very busy as there is going to be the biggest air and sea rescue ever carried out."

"What about helping your crew with that canvas?" John said, "it looks like they could do with a hand."

"Leave that to my Number one and the crew," the Captain said, "They know how to carry out emergency drills and they are the best people to deal with the operation. You have done more than enough by helping to save my ship," the captain added, "it could not have been done without your daring."

Then he said, "you can best help by letting your wives know you are well and by helping with the injured if you can."

"My Medical Officer, the Nurses and all my First Aiders are going to be stretched to their limits until help arrives from the rescue squads that are on their way as we speak, then he said, to the crew member outside guarding the wheelhouse, if any of these four want to see me for any reason they are the only passengers that are to be allowed on the bridge."

"Now if you will excuse me, Gentlemen," The Captain said, "my crew have a plaster to put over a wound in my ship, I then have to make it to the western end of Sable Island, and then I have a gauntlet of sand bars to run, and to top it all I can't get too near that burning inferno of the *NAT GAS 2*, otherwise we get roasted alive before can beach the *Baroness of the Sea*, it is going to be a very close thing because if we keep going as we are without putting that plaster on our wound we will start wallowing and then we will sink too close to the burning *NAT GAS 2* for a rescue attempt."

He then added, "everyone will be safer in the restaurant area or in the inner areas of the ship as we get nearer the *NAT GAS 2* anyone exposed to it and out on the deck will get badly burned any of my crew out there will be wearing fire suits that will afford them some protection."

All four made their way back to the restaurant area much to the delight of Jen who just walked over to Cyril and hugged him as though she was not going to let him go, they all greeted their wives warmly, it was a sad sight that Mustafa's wife Asar stood alone but very proud, the four women quickly surrounded her and started to reassure her that Mustafa might still be alive and if he was he would be found by the rescue services.

The crew outside were making very good progress and fast work in getting the patch over the hole in the side of the Cruise Liner, they could hear the winches of the second lifeboat as it was being lowered with the end of a large sheet of canvas stretched out from stem to stern of the lifeboat.

The first lifeboat had already taken the ends of the ropes connected to the bottom of the canvas sheet they had gone around the bow of the *Baroness of the Sea* trailing the ropes behind them as the ropes tightened the rope slid under the hull, the ends of the ropes were passed up to the deck on the opposite side of the ship and connected to the lifeboat winch on that side.

As the second lifeboat was lowered, the winch on the other side of the ship lifted the ends of the ropes, therefore, the patch slid slowly down the side of the ship towards the gaping hole, it was guided into place by the second lifeboat as it was lowered.

As the canvas slipped over the hole in the side of the Baroness of the Sea there was a sucking noise as the pressure of the seawater that was flooding into the "Baroness of the Sea" dragged the canvas over the hole, that in turn covered the hole like a great big plaster, it was secured in place by ropes from both sides of the ship.

The Baroness of the Sea turned towards the burning NAT GAS 2that was stuck fast on the sandbanks at the far eastern end of Sable Island, the Captain knew he had to get the Baroness of the Sea passed the NAT GAS 2 it would be like running a gauntlet that was now a giant flaming beacon pouring out death and destruction for the unwary.

They had to sail as close to the inferno of the burning NAT GAS 2 as they dare, to save time and to avoid the hidden sandbars, they had to get passed it and then get as far away as possible from the burning inferno and to the other end of the Island before they started wallowing and then sank.

The canvas patch had afforded them some time as it slowed down the rate at which the sea was flooding into the

Baroness of the Sea, how much time they did not know, all they could do is pray the canvas patch held, and the pumps that were pumping out the water in the hold that was running at full capacity could afford them enough time to make landfall and safety.

The Captain could not put on too much speed he had to be very gentle with his crippled ship otherwise the canvas would be dragged from the hole and the sea would cascade into the hold of the ship and the *Baroness of the Sea* with its precious cargo would founder.

They had got to the point of no return, the captain knew he had to run the gauntlet of getting past the inferno of the burning gas tanker on one side and the deadly sandbanks on the other side.

The captain could not get to close to the sandbanks for fear of running aground in a slowly sinking ship on the other side of the ship he could see they were getting nearer the burning gas tanker.

The heat was intensifying as they drew level with the *NAT GAS 2* and for what seemed an eternity they could feel the heat seer of the burning gas as they slowly passed it.

The paint on the cruise ship started to bubble and peel away and smoke appeared from light flammable materials dotted about the decks as the heat seer intensified, wooden parts of the superstructure started to go brown as the searing heat scorched them.

For what seemed forever, slowly the *Baroness of the Sea* edged its way passed the crippled burning hulk that was the NAT GAS 2.

Jeff, Cyril, Derek, and John had rejoined their wives in the restaurant that was now serving as an emergency hospital; it was a hive of activity, there were a lot of injuries mainly broken bones and severe bruises, there were three elderly people that had had heart attacks but all three were being treated by first aiders as the Medical Officer was seeing to other badly injured passengers, the ships medical staff were stretched to breaking point everyone had been shaken up by the pounding the *Baroness of the Sea* had taken.

Jeff said to Karen, "Darling we are not out of the woods yet; we have to get past the burning *NAT GAS 2* so the Captain can beach the ship at the other end of the Island, and it is going to get awfully hot as we pass that burning gas ship."

Jeff went to the Medical Officer and said, "We have to move these people by the walls to the middle of the restaurant otherwise they might get severely burned when we pass the burning *NAT GAS 2*."

"We can't move all of them," the officer said, "some have very serious injuries, we are lucky none have died so far, some need urgent hospitalisation and medical help beyond what I can do for them.

"The only other way is to use the fire hoses and wet down that side of the ship as we sail past the burning gas ship," Jeff said, "and as a second thought remarked, that's if they are working?"

"The fire hoses are designed to work when everything around them has failed," the Medical Officer said, "if you want to put a water screen up covering that side of the ship, I will get the patients that can't be moved covered up so you don't drown them."

"Right, I need volunteers that are not injured," Jeff shouted, above the hub-bub of people talking and the moaning and crying of the injured passengers and crew.

We need to wet the side of this ship as we pass the burning gas ship otherwise the heat seer will burn everyone.

Cyril left Jen's side as she was organising medical supplies for those in pain, John left Rose tending a woman, Derek left Sandra helping splint a broken leg and they joined Jeff.

"What do you want us to do?" John said.

"Find a member of staff to show you where all the fire hoses are on this deck then form crews of men at least two to a hose, put the hoses on spray and dowse and soak the walls then as we pass the burning gas ship we make a water curtain of spray, we can't have any gaps in the water curtain so we need to work as a team."

There were a number of volunteers that helped form the firefighting crews some were still sporting bruises from the battering they had taken but they were determined to help in any way they could.

A crew member showed them where the wet risers were and explained how they worked, these are a system of fixed solid pipes that are full of pressurised water, these pipes cover the whole ship they have outlets at different staging points throughout the ship and are used to fight fires at any given point within the ship, so instead of trailing long lengths of firefighting hoses all over each deck you can fight a fire from any part of the ship using shorter lengths of hoses connected to the wet riser, these lengths of hoses are stored in a compartment behind a panel next to the wet riser.

They opened the panel and connected the length of the hose to the wet riser broke the seal and turned the valve Jeff felt the hose pressurise and was ready to deploy as soon as he turned the hose nozzle on.

The crews manned the hoses and started wetting down the outer side of the restaurant walls soaking the beautiful drapes.

As the gas ship came into view it started to get hotter in the room as the heat seer from the burning *NAT GAS 2* was blasting out heat

They formed a circle and within that circle, they sprayed the hoses outward towards the damaged windows forming a giant curtain of water cocooning everyone in the restaurant within it and behind the wall of water.

Steam was forming as the water curtain was boiled by the intense heat but the water curtain held as the hoses replaced the heated water that was turning to steam with the heat from the heat sear given out by the burning *NAT GAS 2* with cold water from the wet risers.

There was the noise of hissing steam as a cloud formed from the water curtain as it boiled off and blew all along with the ship and trailed behind the crippled *Baroness of the Sea* like a trailing fog.

It seemed to last forever but as the *Baroness of the Sea* slowly passed the inferno of the burning gas ship the room cooled down and Jeff ordered the hoses to be turned off.

"That was a close-run thing," John said, "where did you learn that trick from?"

"I used to be a fire manager of a building at one time and I had to go on a fire fighting course.

The heat seemed to ease off as they got further away from the crippled NAT GAS 2, all of a sudden there was an explosion that came from the bowels of the NAT GAS 2 and like a searing sunspot a gigantic flame erupted from the gas ship as it was in its death throes of fiery hell there was a mighty concussion that rocked the crippled *Baroness of the Sea* as a giant fireball exploded from the gas ship right where the cruise liner had just come from, boiling the sea that they had just sailed through and the concussion from the explosion sent a giant wave towards them chasing them down the coastline of Sable Island."

John looked in the direction of the *NAT GAS 2* then said, "Oh No! Not another tidal wave, get everyone to brace themselves for impact before that wave hits us."

The wave created from the concussion of the detonating gas also blew apart one of the giant gas domes, a giant fireball started to swell and tumble out behind them just where the passage they passed through was.

They knew if the Captain had left it any later to run the gauntlet of fire they would have been hit by that expanding fireball of intense heat and certain incineration.

It was now a race against time to reach the shoreline at the western end of Sable Island. They had to make the beach before they sank and, on the way, they had to avoid any sandbars that were dotted about on the coast of the island to give the rescue people the best chance of helping the passengers and crew to safety.

Sable Island looked bleak and windswept, the sand dunes that covered the island looked inhospitable, the sparse dwellings that dotted the island looked dated and the old ancient lighthouse looked tattered. ---------o-------

They were limping along the coastline of the island when they heard the roaring of the small tidal wave that had developed from the last concussion of the death throes of the *NAT GAS 2*, The wave was following them along the coast and was building and it was getting bigger as it approached them.

The Captain knew he could not manoeuvre the crippled *Baroness of the Sea* to face the wave before it hit them. He had to hope that it hit them in the stern, and they could outride it, he knew if it hit them in the side they would roll sideways and with the damage they had already received they could roll over completely.

It seemed ironic that they had fought so hard against impossible odds and come so far only to have their hopes dashed at the last moment.

The *Baroness of the Sea* started wallowing like an old sea scow in the heavy seas caused by the wave from the concussion of the explosion from the dying *NAT GAS 2* that was now lighting up the sky like a giant burning beacon.

The crippled cruise liner started to flounder as they neared the coast.

They had every faith in the Captains ability to handle his crippled ship, but they knew it was now a race against time and that timing was going to be crucial as the wave was bearing down on the *Baroness of the Sea* towards the stern of the vessel and there was no room for manoeuvring the big ship in the shallow waters all they could hope for was for the wave to lift them onto the sandbar near the beach that they were heading for.

The stern of the ship lifted as the swell of the wave hit them as it run down the whole length of the ship, the cruise liner gradually swung around facing the beach, there was a loud snapping sound like a rifle shot as the ropes holding the patch over the hole in the side of the ship parted and the patch was swept away with the force of the impact of the wave, the Baroness of the Sea seemed to founder, the second wave swept the cruise liner toward the sandbar not far from the beach at the western tip of Sable Island.

The last of the big waves swept along the ship with such a force it turned the bow of the ship to face the sandy shore and the sand dunes with one last effort the Captain swung the bow of the ship around and headed the cruise liner for the shallow waters, he shut off the mighty engines of the *Baroness of the Sea* and let the waves take her she was now at the mercy of the Atlantic graveyard the ship started to founder and he managed to beach the ship as the last wave washed over the *Baroness of the Sea* and forced it to a grinding halt up and onto the sandbar near the beach and the sand dunes.

As the sea boiled around them and slowly settled the cruise liner was held fast on the sandbar and there she settled, tilted slightly at a drunken angle and then with a grinding noise came to rest.

After an ordeal, the Baroness of the Sea was not built to go through but the fact that she had pulled through against all the odds was a testament to the builders who constructed her and her Captains skills in handling her and a few people who said "NO!"

The wave and the pounding sea withdrew from the *Baroness of the Sea* it was left high and dry stuck fast on the sandbar very close to the western tip of Sable Island shoreline and the Canadian territory of Halifax County.

Jeff looked out onto a bleak and desolate spit of barren land that was covered in sand dunes; they were at the end of a very long narrow stretch of land that was shaped like a very long sabre that was bravely and defiantly sticking out into the edge of the Atlantic curving away into the distant ocean defying the sea to do it's worse, on the high stretches of rough grassland there were horses' grazing looking quite unperturbed at the scene that was unfolding before them.

Jeff could see why the inhospitable coast of Sable Island was named the Atlantic Graveyard and why over many years 350 ships had foundered on her coast with the loss of hundreds of lives.

But this time this inhospitable coast, this Atlantic Graveyard, had been the saving grace of the souls aboard the *Baroness of the Sea* for without this stretch of coastline being strategically where she was, the *Baroness of the Sea* would have foundered and sank in the unforgiving seas of the Atlantic Ocean with the loss of many lives.

In the distance, the death throes of the dying gas tanker were like a burning beacon lighting the way to the destruction of the unwary mariner.

In the restaurant you could cut the atmosphere with a knife the silence was very eyrie as the people realized, they were stationary and safe, the deck tilted as the ship settled, then the silence was broken with the sobs and cheers of the injured.

They started treating the injured and tried to make them as comfortable as they could until help arrived.

As Michael and Valerie got to the American Canadian border they were met by Laurence, he had people take their travelling luggage put it in the back of a stretch limousine.

Michael greeted Laurence with a firm handshake, whilst Valerie just went in for the full hug and a kiss.

When Laurence looked at them both, he said

"On seeing you two together, it's about time you two became a serious item, you have been dancing around one another for years, everyone in the family knew you two belong with each other, except you two."

Valerie looked at Michael and said, "is it that obvious?"

Laurence said, "I should say so."

Then he said, "I've cleared you both through customs, so get in the car where we can talk, we have a lot to do, and a lot to catch up on, things have moved fast since we last spoke last night."

Their driver was heading fast to Nova Scotia on blues and twos.

Laurence looked at Michael and Joked, "we still use horses in the outback, and we still believe a Mounty will always get his man."

"It's only just before dawn now, what's the latest?" Valerie said, just as her phone rang, she answered it and listened, then commented O.K. keep me informed as soon as the situation changes.

She said to Laurence, "according to the American Atlantic fleet report, the sub has been found and sunk, by the Texas Ranger, an American Nuclear Sub, they don't think it had time to send out any messages. Apparently, they found it just before it came to the surface, as soon as the conning tower of the sub hit the surface the Texas Ranger fired on it, hitting it many times, rather than surrender the sub did an emergency dive, and a little while later it imploded with the loss of all hands.'

'Well', Laurence said, 'according to our satellite report just in, there is activity aboard both ships, the ships have parted and the *NAT GAS 2* is steering away from the *Baroness of the Sea* towards one end of Sable Island."

"The Texas Ranger has orders to fire on and sink the *NAT GAS 2* if she gets anywhere near Territorial Waters," Valerie said.

Just then there was a flash on the horizon followed by the concussion of a blast, then there was a flickering glow on the horizon

"Oh my God!" Valerie said, "that must be the Gas Ship exploding."

"Get to the nearest helicopter base," Laurence said, "and put a Helicopter on stand by.

"Also, get me the emergency co-ordinating group, we will have to get a massive search for any survivors underway."

They got to the helicopter base, the helicopter was ready for them the rotors were feathering ready for take-off.

Laurence herded them to the helicopter. They strapped themselves in and the rotors speeded up, the copter tilted forward and lifted off the ground.

They flew towards the islands. Valerie's phone rang again it was her office, the up-date came through, apparently, the *NAT GAS 2* was sailed away from the *Baroness of the Sea* it has now exploded and created a tsunami.

Unfortunately, there is a tidal wave is bearing down onto the *Baroness of the Sea* which looks like it has been crippled by an explosion on board her as there is smoke coming from amidships.

Laurence said, "they are going to need all the help we can get to them as soon as possible."

Laurence called out on his radio for all emergency services to form up at Sable Island, he wanted all hospitals on alert for disaster recovery, plus a back-up force to evacuate the injured, use small aircraft like a shuttle bus, by using the small runway to evacuate victims from Sable Island to hospitals in Nova Scotia.

Valerie ordered all the American ships in the vicinity to act as mobile hospitals, all helicopters to act as flying ambulances, and all medical staff to be flown to the crippled ship as soon as The *Baroness of the Sea* runs aground.

The world's biggest ever sea rescue began and swung into action like a well-oiled machine, even though they were from different countries, the American and Canadian medical staff worked side-by-side together.

Help arrived in the shape of throbbing helicopters that hovered over the stranded *Baroness of the Sea*, winch men and paramedics descended onto the sloping deck of the crippled cruise ship bringing much needed medical supplies and expertise in medical emergencies.

The paramedics quickly organized a triage system where the worst cases were evacuated first to the beach makeshift hospital that was being quickly erected on the nearby beach and then onto hospitals in Nova Scotia Canada.

Light aircraft were also brought in and the beach a little further down the coast was used as an emergency runway this was then used as air ferries for the injured to be transferred to Nova Scotia Canada.

The area was getting very busy with rescue ships from both Canada and America being used as staging vessels and the makeshift hospital that had been erected on the nearby beach.

The lifeboats from the *Baroness of the Sea* and the lifeboats from the other vessels that had responded to the May-Day that were in the area were used to ferry people to and from the cruise ship to the beach it was like the "D-day landings".

The helicopters in the sky around the area were like dragonflies hovering over a pond in the summer sweeping backwards and forwards on their urgent missions.

John later said that the logistical nightmare of moving so many people to safety was organized brilliantly.

Jeff, Karen, Derek and Sandra, Cyril and Jen, John and Rose, also Asar, Mustafa's wife were one of the last groups to leave the Cruise Liner, they were then transferred to the beach as the sun was going down, it was now getting dark.

They were tired as they had spent the day helping the injured, they themselves were checked out by a medic in the beach hospital.

They were flown in a private light aircraft to Nova Scotia in Canada, where they were met by members of the Canadian Mounted Police, who escorted them through a bevvy of reporters at the airport.

The reporters were told there would be a press conference in the morning after everyone had all rested, they were then taken by cars under escort by the Canadian Mounted Police and taken to a five-star hotel.

As they arrived at the hotel, they had to run the gauntlet of the press and dodge the crowds milling outside the hotel and they were chaperoned through all the reporters waiting outside the airport there were Canadian Mounted Police guarding the hotel where a very official reception committee was waiting for them in the foyer to greet them.

A man stepped forward and introduced himself as a special envoy of the Canadian Government and welcomed them to Canada he asked when they were rested could he be given a briefing so he could make a full report to his government of what had happened.

Then the Government envoy said, "I understand one of your party lost something very dear to them," he beckoned and from behind a pillar came to a very bedraggled Mustafa.

We only just found him a short while ago, he said.

Asar rushed into his arms crying as she ran to him, "I thought I had lost you!" she cried.

They all crowded around Mustafa telling him how pleased they were to see him.

"I must let you all rest you all look done in, we can get the details in the morning when we will also get the Captain's report, a meal has been laid on for you if you are hungry and then you must rest, you all have a busy tomorrow."

They were escorted to a private small restaurant area in the hotel where a light meal was laid on, they all wanted to know how Mustafa was and what happened after he left Cyril on the deck of the *Baroness of the Sea* and went aboard the NAT GAS 2.

Asar never let him go, she clung to his side like a limpet as they all listened intently to every word he had to say, gasping when he told them about the shooting in the wheelhouse of the *NAT GAS 2*, and looked apprehensive as he said about the escape by the Fast Lady.

When he told them about when he came to the realization that the gas cloud had to be ignited or it would have spread to cover the *Baroness of the Sea*, then he looked at Asar very lovingly and said he knew that she was on that ship and he felt he had to save her and everyone on board before the gas cloud ignited killing everyone.

He said he had the idea of using very pistol just as James Bond did in one of his movies, he then fired the star shell from the very pistol and dived into the water so the heat sear from the exploding gas swept over them, he said he did not expect the tidal wave that came from the crippled *NAT GAS 2*, he told them of his decision to try and outride the tidal waves, which he nearly did, he said it was the second one that caught them unprepared and swamped them, he felt that was when he lost the last two remainings volunteers. “I was in the water for quite some time before a helicopter found me and brought me here.”

“You’re safe with me now,” Asar said, “I thought I had lost you and I am not letting you out of my sight ever,” she clung to him like a limpet afraid to let him go in case he was not real and he suddenly disappeared.

Jeff turned to Mustafa and said, “now we know you are safe we can all get some sleep, we will see you in the morning for breakfast,” and they all went to their rooms for a well-earned rest.

As all ten of them had just finished breakfast in the same little private dining room in the hotel, they had all gone to the suite that had been set aside for them, it was then the Canadian Ambassador entered the room he had with him five men two he introduced as the American Ambassador Charles Watson, and the British Ambassador Edward Edwards and the other three men are our aides.

Ambassador Watson said, “We have had a short de-briefing with the Captain and his First Officer, we wanted to hear your side of what happened and we would like to hear the individual reports, it is so we can report to our various governments as to the whole political mess and what we do about it.

We need to work out which Middle Eastern country was responsible and how we might be able to retaliate against the Arab country that trained these terrorists and sent them out to attack America and Canada with this diabolical plot."

"What do you mean by the whole political mess?" Jeff retorted, "may I remind you we have just had to pull your political chestnuts out of the fire because you were going to do nothing about them."

"How can you say that?" Ambassador Watson said, "We carried out an act of aggression when we sank an old submarine, then we pulled your sorry arses out of the sea, then we put into operation the largest rescue exercise ever mounted in the full glare of the media, how can you say we did nothing."

"Apart from the sinking of the submarine which we told you was there, and was threatening to blow us all up, the rest is a political smokescreen to save your sorry arses, as you like to put it, and we also saved your political face."

"Gentlemen," the English ambassador interjected, "let's not start out on the wrong foot," then holding his arms out in an all-encompassing gesture, "you have all been through a terribly traumatic time, and the shock of what has happened is having its toll."

"Don't be so bloody condescending," Jeff said, "we were the ones that stopped you having the biggest disaster in history on your doorstep," then he pointed to Ambassador Watson and said, "if we had not done what we did, you would have blown us out of the water as we got near the American coastline killing all of us."

"How can you say that?" Ambassador Watson blustered.

"Quite easy," Jeff said, "I open my mouth and the words come out, so what are you going to do about it, have us all bumped off so you can go back to your political world of lies and dammed lies."

"Gentlemen," the Canadian Ambassador interjected, "we can't be seen to be at one another's throats in front of the media, you are all heroes, the press is waiting to see you, they are aware of the daring deeds you have done, and the impossible odds you have overcome, we just need to get the parts we played in this happy outcome, right!"

"Is this the royal we? Or is this a political we?" Jeff retorted, "We fought for our lives out there because we knew there would not be any help from any country, we were on our own, and if we had not taken back that ship when we did, you would have sent out orders to blow us out of the water before we got within your territorial waters."

Then he added, "now you as politicians want to claim the glory for sitting on your hands and doing nothing, just hoping a miracle would happen, let me tell you that miracle happened when ordinary people decided to fight back."

Jeff then addressed Ambassador Watson, "that man there, who is proud to be an Arab, and I am privileged to call a friend," Jeff said pointing to Mustafa, "saved everybody on board the *Baroness of the Sea*. He risked his own life by igniting that gas cloud before it reached the *Baroness of the Sea* because if that gas cloud had ignited any nearer then we would have been brown bread."

"What do you mean brown bread?" Ambassador Watson queried.

The British Ambassador interjected and said to the American Ambassador its cockney rhyming slang, "brown bread, means dead."

Then trying to placate the situation said to Jeff, "the British Prime Minister, warned me about your reputation of taking no prisoners when you are put out, he also told me that you are a reasonable man when common sense is brought to the table, I appeal to that common sense now as we need to have a dialogue and a way forward must be found."

John interjected, "what Jeff is trying to say, if he," pointing to Ambassador Watson, "stops keep rubbing him up the wrong way," then added, "is it was not some Middle Eastern terrorists that carried this plot out, it was the *Senate*."

"Who's the *Senate*?", the American and Canadian Ambassador's said together trying to look very puzzled.

"They were responsible for the Estuary incident in England a little while ago," the British ambassador said, "we thought we had eradicated them, but if what John tells us is true, they have come back to haunt us, but this time, they are operating globally and that has to concern all of us, big time."

"I was told the Estuary Incident was an industrial accident," the Canadian Ambassador interjected.

"It was, but it was orchestrated by the *Senate*," John said, "which is a very right-wing Nazi-type organisation bent on world domination, they try to use, divide and rule tactics, and undermine the established regime and take control, then they use a very right-wing military rule to control the people."

Then Jeff added, "who and what is behind the *Senate* we have yet to find out, going by what we have been told it looks like they have raised their heads again, this time they wanted to attack both your countries via the gas supply wells in the Arab States and also the terminals that store the Liquid Natural Gas in both your countries and cause decent between yourselves and the Arab states."

"They very nearly achieved that," John Added.

"This *Senate*, where are they based?" Ambassador Watson said.

"They do not seem to have a base in any one country that we know of, John replied, but they are seriously organized."

"Well they were nearly successful in Great Britain and now they have tried to attack America and by the sounds of it they were nearly successful this time as well if it had not been for you lot taking them on", Ambassador Watson added, "I would not like to have predicted the outcome."

There was a knock on the door and a scuffle by the doorway and Michael pushed his way into the room followed by two security guards with guns drawn pointing them at Michael.

"Michael!" Jeff said, "where the hell did you spring from?"

"Do you know this man?" One of the security guards said.

"Yes," Cyril, Derek and Jeff said together.

"I have been following your progress on the high seas," Michael blurted out, "I can't leave you lot for a minute without you getting up to mischief without me," Michael retorted.

"It's good to see you," Jeff said, "what have you been doing?"

"Having my holiday spoilt by mysterious phone calls," Michael added, "good job you did though my cousin said the American Submarine Texas Ranger took out the *Senate* submarine was going off the station when you called, it only just made it to the rendezvous point."

"Lucky it spotted the *Senate* sub in time on its undersea radar just as it was surfacing to signal the *Baroness of the Sea*."

"They managed to jam the signal the *Senate* was putting out, fire on her, then they tried to board her during that confrontation the *Senate* submarine tried to fire a torpedo at the American Submarine as she dived, the American submarine deployed her defence systems then returned the compliment, the *Senate* Sub sank with all hands, the captain of the American Submarine said it was strange that the *Senate* seemed to dive for the sea bed instead of surfacing and she imploded when she hit the sea bed, it was as if they decided to commit suicide rather than be caught."

"I was not told of this incident that happened in our territorial waters," The Canadian Ambassador said.

"You are being told now," came a commanding female voice from the doorway.

They all turned to see a stunningly beautiful brunet dressed in an American naval uniform had just entered the room.

Michael said, "may I introduce my cousin, she is the one we have to thank for stopping the *Senate* Sub from meeting the *Baroness of the Sea*, she is the one that convinced naval intelligence the Sub was a threat."

They all crowded around her thanking her for getting the military involved.

Karen introduced everyone to her then the girls seemed to take her under their wing, it was so obvious that Michael has taken quite a shine to his cousin.

Jeff said to Michael as the girls were talking together on the other side of the room, "Cyril said you were visiting a cousin in the Naval intelligence but I did not expect her to be that gorgeous and she has her head screwed on right."

"She is lovely," Michael said, "technically we are third cousins and we have had a soft spot for one another for many years, but her career has always come first, I was hoping with this visit I might change all that, at the moment it seems to be going very well."

Michael added, "she is here to get a report from you all as to what happened out there, by the sound of it you had lots of fun and all without me to keep an eye out for you," he joked.

"You covered our back," Jeff said, "and without you and your lovely cousin intervening when you did it would have turned out very differently."

Just as they were speaking there was a knock on the door and a man dressed in a high ranking Royal Mounted Police Uniform entered the room.

Michael responded by calling out, "Laurence, meet my friends!"

Laurence replied, "I did not expect to find you here yet and with Cousin Valerie, mind you, I can see you two are now inseparable."

"What are you doing here Laurence?" Michael said.

"To report to the Canadian Ambassador that we have put the Captain of the cruise liner under close arrest as instructed."

"You what!" Jeff said aggressively, "on what charge?"

"And who the hell are you?" Laurence interjected and said to Jeff, "to tell me what or not what to do as chief of police in my country."

"Ease off Laurence," Michael said, "I think we have some crossed wires here."

Michael explained to Laurence who was who and what happened as far as he knew, the details Jeff and the others could give later.

"Then why was I instructed to arrest the French Captain of the cruise liner?" Laurence said.

"Maybe, because he was French," Jeff said.

"What do you mean by that remark?" Laurence said.

"Well," Jeff said, "we are all British and Mustafa is an Arab, to arrest us would create an international incident and draw attention to the incident that someone wants to cover up, next they will be saying the Captain endangered his ship and the passengers."

"How did you know the charge the Captain was being held on?" Laurence said with disbelief.

"Who told you to arrest the Captain before he gave his statement to the press?" Jeff said.

Laurence looked at the Canadian Ambassador and said, "I had written orders from your office with your signature on it."

As all this was going on, there was another interruption at the door, this time it was an elderly Arab Sheikh with two bodyguards.

"What's going on?" Jeff said, "it's like Piccadilly Circus here."

Mustafa raised his eyes in recognition at the Sheikh and stepped forward, bowed and said, "welcome Sheikh Ali Ben Mustafa, may I introduce my friends."

Mustafa started introducing everyone but the Sheikh interrupted him and said in perfect English,

"I am here to bring to justice my son's killer. My son's death will be the cause for a holy war against the west that will have no end, and you failed to protect my son and brought shame and dishonour to your family."

Jeff could not contain his anger and shouted at the Sheikh, "who the hell do you think you are going off half-cocked and putting two and two together and making six."

"How dare you speak to the Sheikh in that manner the Sheikh's bodyguard interrupted," then pointing to Mustafa, "and you son, how could you not have tried to save the Sheikh's son, he was your friend as well as your charge."

Jeff squared off to the Sheikh's bodyguard then said, "he saved all of us if it was not for him, we would all have perished."

Then turning to the Sheikh Jeff said, "if you want to blame anyone for your son's death you had better look at the *Senate*."

"Who are the *Senate*?" the Sheikh said.

John interceded, and said, "we first came across them in the Estuary in England there they tried to destabilise the country."

"Sir William Waites had owned the LNG terminal in Estuary area. Jeff was an environmentalist who had campaigned against the lack of safety at the terminal for many years, the terminal had exploded in an accident when they cut too many corners in safety, the resulting domino effect on all the gas and oil industry in the estuary area had created total devastation all the way along the estuary it had put that part of the country back to the dark ages and financially crippled the country.

"Sir William Waites tried to cover up the incident and blame terrorists which he said Jeff was the leader, during the ensuing days, Sir William using his contacts in a right-wing organisation called the *Senate* tried to destabilise the Government and take control of the military and wanted to blame and attack the middle east.

Jeff had gone back to The Estuary and found the incriminating evidence of corruption that was the downfall of Sir William Waites who had set a professional killer named Wilson after Jeff, Wilson hunted Jeff down and tried to recover the incriminating evidence, Wilson was killed by myself as I am the Prime Minister's special agent this was during an attack on Jeff."

Then he added, "Jeff had taken a long time to heal after the injuries he had sustained from the attack by Sir William Waites' hit man Wilson, after the arrest of Sir William Waites' and his subsequent trial there was a massive shakeup in the Government."

"Remind me who are you again?" The Sheikh said to Jeff, with respect, when he was a lot calmer.

Mustafa interjected and said, "let me re-introduce everyone," as he got to the Canadian Ambassador the Sheikh said, "Ambassador Thomas Waits and I are acquainted, I had to ask him diplomatically to leave my country after I found him having secret talks with my brother-in-law, who

I suspected was trying to usurp me, but I could not prove it."

Jeff turned to Ambassador Waites and said, "are you any relation to Sir William Waites who was responsible for the Estuary incident?"

Ambassador Waites suddenly turned very vicious instantly and drew out a gun and pointed it at Jeff and the Sheikh who was standing next to Jeff.

"He was my brother," Ambassador Waits stated, then pointing to Jeff, "so it was you that was the cause of his downfall."

Laurence turned to Waites and said, "tell the truth, you are responsible for my friend Paul's death as well, did you have his plane shot down? I told you I would hunt you to extinction."

Waites was frightened, he started blustering, "He saw the *Senate* Submarine entering the submarine pen, we could not let anyone know about the sub, it was the key link in the plan, it took years to put that sub together in secret, I hid it with the rest of my collection so people would think it was part of my museum collection and not suspect it was a fully functioning working Submarine.

We had to launch early and lay off Sable Island because we could not let anyone know about the sub, it was always going to put torpedoes into the *NAT GAS 2*, then looking at Laurence said, as you tried to rescue any passengers on board the *Baroness of the Sea* in the confusion to cover the escape of the *Senate*'s agents."

The Sheikh said, "so you also colluded with my Brother-in-law to put the blame onto my country creating unrest between the western world and us, you will die for that as he reached for the ornate dagger in his silk sash.

Everything happened so fast, but Mustafa reacted like lightning and dived into the path of the gun as Ambassador Waits fired three shots at point-blank range taking the fusillade of shots fired from the gun with his body in doing so wrestled the gun from the Ambassadors grasp then collapsed into a heap.

Like a cornered rat the ambassador saw the determination on Laurence's face he knew the Mounty was going to get his man, the doorway was blocked by the guards he turned and ran for the balcony, followed by Laurence in close pursuit.

In his mad dash to escape the Ambassador tripped over a stool by the balcony door, the momentum of his flight sent him tumbling onto the balcony where he overbalanced and went over the edge of the balcony.

Laurence caught Waites flaying hand and held onto the Ambassador stopping from falling, as he was hanging there Waites said, "I don't want to die, save me, I will tell you everything. It was the *Senate* they made me do it, please," he screamed, "pull me up."

Then added, "I will give you all the money I got from them, I am sorry about your friend, but he got too close and had to die before he exposed us all."

On hearing that last statement Laurence realized there were more involved than Waites and he would not stand trial, he would hide behind his political status and somehow get away with it, Laurence looked at Waites hanging there, with an effort he could probably have pulled him back up.

Laurence mouthed the words "bye-bye," made it look as though he was trying to pull the Ambassador up, opened his hand and released his grip, and Waites fell screaming to the ground thirty stories below with a sickening thud.

"Damn he was too slippery for me," Laurence said, "get a medic in here now," Laurence shouted to the guards by the door seeing that Mustafa had been shot.

One of the Sheikhs bodyguards reacted and shouted out, "son! And fell down on his knees next to Mustafa.

The Sheikh said incredulously, "he stopped the bullet that was meant for me."

The medics arrived very quickly and they attended Mustafa's wounds miraculously he was only slightly wounded.

"We need to get him to the hospital," the medic said.

"He goes under police escort and I want a 24-hour guard set up around his bed, he sees no one except his wife unless I say so," then he said gently to Asar, "you go with your man he needs you." The Medic took Mustafa away on a stretcher with Asar beside him and the Sheikh's bodyguard looking on very anxiously.

"Seal this area and the Hotel now," ordered Laurence then said to the guards at the door, "no one is allowed in or out without my direct authority."

"But I have diplomatic schedules to keep," the American Ambassador Watson suddenly announced, you can't hold me as a prisoner."

"You are not a prisoner, but as chief of the Police I can do whatever I want to do to safeguard my country and its diplomatic guests," Laurence said.

Ambassador Watson blustered, "the President of the United States will hear of this, this is an outrage, I demand you let me out of this room now."

Valerie spoke up, "The President, will also get my report as well," she said to Ambassador Watson, why do you need to leave very suddenly? A little while ago we could not get you out of here with a tyre lever, now you suddenly have urgent business elsewhere, why?"

"This is a conspiracy involving your family," the Ambassador said accusingly, pointing to Valerie and Laurence, then added, "you two are cousins and so is he a member of your family, then pointing to Michael, said, "you're all in it together, you're part of this *Senate* he spoke of" pointing to John, and they are going to kill us all.

"What do you know about the *Senate* and us being killed?" Valerie said to the Ambassador very calmly.

"Now Waits is dead, the *Senate* is going to kill us all," the Ambassador said, agitatedly, looking towards the window and the balcony expectantly.

"When is this going to happen?" Valerie said, still being very calm as the man looked like he was about to have a nervous breakdown.

At any time now, he blustered getting even more agitated and frightened.

"How is this going to be achieved?" She said still being very soothingly calm, whilst the Ambassador was slowly becoming a gibbering wreck.

"Now, as Ambassador Waits will fail to give the safe signal because he is dead," Ambassador Watson said, then panicking said, struggling to get to the door said, "they have two rocket launchers trained on this hotel suite balcony from one of the two buildings opposite," then screaming, "they will kill us all, and I don't want to die."

"Hit the fire alarm and evacuate the hotel now," Laurence said to the men stationed by the door, he said, reacting to the revelations the American Ambassador had announced, and said sternly, "find those rocket launchers and find them now!"

Everybody scurried for the door of the hotel suite. Ambassador Watson was deliberately held back by Laurence till the last person was out of the hotel suite.

They all made it to the landing and headed for the lift as the fire alarm started wailing.

"Use the stairs," Laurence said, "it will afford us more cover and it will give us more protection if what he says is right.

They all just made it to the stairs and close the fire door behind them.

As the fire door of the emergency stairs closed behind them there was the crump of a concussion that shook them all of their feet and they all tumbled into a heap on top of one another on the stair landing.

Valerie fell into Michael's arms. He hugged her to himself protecting her with his body from any danger.

"Is everyone all right?" Laurence shouted above the fire claxon that was wailing loudly, "and where is Ambassador Watson?"

Ambassador Watson had taken advantage of the confusion and was just getting clear of the landing and trying to make a run for it, but he had to pass Derek before he could make his break for freedom.

Derek let the Ambassador, get almost past him when he clamped his huge hand onto the back of his neck and pushed downwards and side-ways, propelling the unfortunate Watson into the wall headfirst with a sickening thud, he head-butted the wall then he collapsed into a heap.

Valerie leaned forward and snapped a pair of handcuffs on the unfortunate American Ambassador as he lay in a heap unconscious.

Michael looked at Valerie saucily and said, "I did not know you carried them cuffs with you," she looked at him with love in her eyes and slapped him playfully knowing what he was implying.

Laurence looked at them both and said, "about time you two got together, you have taken enough time about it, all the family has known for years you two were made for each other, you have my blessing."

They made their way down the emergency stairs to the lobby of the hotel with Derek carrying the American ambassador across his broad shoulders.

As they came to the stairwell of the emergency stairs, they were met with a wall of sound from the emergency sirens of the police cars and ambulances and fire trucks.

Laurence directed them into a reception room at the side of the main lobby where he put guards on both doors, "this is for your safety and protection," he said to everyone, then he said to the guards, "no one comes in here without my say so, is that clear?"

"Yes, Sir!" was the reply, then he went out and started organising his staff into investigating who fired the rocket launchers.

They all found seats and sat down to wait until emergency services had done their jobs and it was made safe for them.

The Sheikh was the first to speak, he said to his bodyguard, "I can't believe that after failing to save my son, your son saves my life, he took the bullets that were meant for me."

Jeff interjected and said, "Sheikh Ali Ben Mustafa, you do Mustafa an injustice if you blame him for your son's death, and he tried on many occasions to try and talk him out of his course of action."

"In fact, Mustafa was not on board the Baroness of the Sea when your son died, he was trying to save him, and all the other passengers and crew," he went on to tell him how he had met Mustafa, and what transpired during the high-jack, of how Mustafa fired the vary pistol into the gas cloud to ignite it, in doing so put himself in danger to save the passengers aboard the Baroness of the Sea.

The Sheikh listened intently to what Jeff had to say and then remarked, "then my son died as a result of the tidal wave swamping the cruise liner when the *NAT GAS 2* exploded which was the ultimate doing of this group called the *Senate* which also just tried to kill us all with that rocket launcher, just so they can destabilise and take over the Middle Eastern Countries control the supply of Liquid Natural Gas for their own political ends. Well, I can assure you that is not going to happen, now we know they exist."

"Yes," Jeff said then added, "I am so sorry about your son."

"I am a father who loved his son, I am also the father of my people," the Sheikh said, "but maybe I indulged my son too much, but he was also led astray by this group called the *Senate* and that I will have investigated, as to who was behind it in my country.

"I have had my suspicions about my brother-in-law the Minister for Energy for a long time, and when I find out who else is involved, heads will roll, literally."

The Sheikh added, "I am in your debt for exposing this plot to me and the danger it posed to my country."

"Well at the moment," Jeff said, "not only you are going to be busy but it looks like America and Canada will be carrying out their investigations as well."

"In the meanwhile, you have had a spoilt holiday, and that can be rectified," the Sheikh said, "therefore I insist you and all your friends be my guests on board my seagoing yacht. It will be yours to command for as long as you want."

The Sheikh then looked humbled and said, "I have a very brave man to see, I have done Mustafa a great injustice and that needs to be rectified now, I now have a debt of gratitude to fulfil," he added, "with a person who has not only become your friend, he also fulfilled his family traditions with honour, his father will be proud of him, he will be honoured, you will be hearing from me."

The Sheikh added, "men like you are a rarity in my country, my debt to you and your friends will not be forgotten, now I must act fast to clip the wings of my brother-in-law," he bowed and left the room with his bodyguards.

Laurence was informed that the four people that fired the rocket launched died in a shootout with Royal Canadian Police, apparently, they were Arabs from the Sheikh's country, the last one to die confessed they were sent by the Sheikh's brother-in-law to assassinate the Sheikh.

When he came back into the room, Laurence did not tell them how they got the dying man to confess, he just told everyone it was now safe, and who the rocket launchers were, "the Sheikhs bodyguards had taken the bodies, it was said to reunite them to their country, but I have let the Sheikh know of our findings, and we can let him deal with it his way when he returns home."

Laurence looked at Jeff and added, "like you had a clear-out in your political system we will also do the same, we will have an internal investigation and root-out any of these people involved with the *Senate* no matter how high up the political chain they are."

John said, "look I have reports to write up, so the British Ambassador can make his reports to the British government, to add to what Laurence has just said, I think Valerie might be able to confirm through her contacts, the F.B.I. is also doing their own investigation just like Canada are doing, between our three countries and now the middle eastern countries, we might be able to purge our countries of this *Senate*."

"You still work for the Prime Minister in secret then?" Jeff said.

"After this little trip I will be resigning my commission," John replied.

"Well then," Jeff said, "you and your lovely wife Rose will need a holiday with us, on a luxury yacht, and if Valerie and Michael can make it, we can get some time together."

Jeff looked at Valerie and Michael, "what are the chances of you two joining us?"

Michael said, "That's up to Valerie. Her work is important, besides, look what happened the last time I left you lot all alone, looks like I can't leave you alone for five minutes and you get up to all sorts of mischief, not only did you cause trouble at home, but now you caused trouble in three more countries, it's obvious you can't be left alone."

They all laughed together.

Valerie said, "I have put my work in front of everything until now, not anymore, I do not know how you knew John, but It has just been confirmed the F.B.I. are carrying our an intense investigation into the *Senate*, heads are rolling as we speak, it will be months before I am required to give evidence at the investigation as to the small part I played."

Valerie added, "I am due a long leave and I think I should take it now," then looking at Michael with love in her eyes said, "I want to get to know you all a lot more, now I have finally found you, she hugged and kissed him longingly not caring who saw how much in love she was."

Jeff added, "I don't know about you, but I have never been on a posh sea-going yacht, it seems a shame to waste it, and it would keep us away from the media for a time."

They all agreed.

Epilogue

At a secret meeting in a safe house on the borders of Canada and America near Niagara Falls, two American Senators and two members of the Canadian Government met with their host, the invitation was worded in such a way that they could not refuse it, as they arrived they were shown into an ornate room.

Whilst they knew of each other politically, they had never met in person, they all had the same thing in common, they were all members of the *Senate*.

Politically the *Senate* had kept them in power, and that came with financial power as well, the one thing they all knew was, once in the *Senate*, you stayed in the *Senate*, or you watched as all you hold dear die horribly, before you died screaming, praying for death.

It was the first time they had seen their host, who was an immensely powerful ex-Russian mafia leader boss called Val Voss, he was a stocky man with a granite looking face and hard eyes.

After a light evening meal Val Voss led them into a meeting room, once inside the daily-swept room for any listening devices, he said, “please be seated Gentlemen, we have a lot to discuss, I called this special meeting to discuss our latest situation as to how the Waites brothers let the *Senate* down by being too greedy too soon, in doing so, they nearly exposed what we are trying to achieve.”

He added, “we have progressed a lot further than mere drug and human trafficking, and we are legitimate now,” then he added, “we almost control the oil and gas fields in Russia and its pipelines to the west, now that you in America and Canada are stockpiling all your gas and oil reserves, you are controlling the gas fields in the west.”

“By using up the middle eastern oil and gas, when that starts running out in twenty years’ time, it is then that we will be able to pool all our resources together, it is then we have the power to control all the gas and oil sources and hold the world to ransom, we already control the mineral, gold, diamond, oil and gas rights in a lot of the African Countries.”

He continued, “now because of the reliance still on fossil fuel, we need to look globally, as I have said before, he who controls the fuel lines controls the price of fuel, and in twenty years’ time we can demand any price we like and we will dominate the world.”

Val Voss added, “As you are all aware, the only other very large untapped major deposits of minerals, oil and gas in the world is in the Wendell sea area in the Antarctic, and the British were allocated that area under the agreement back in the 1960’s, when the Antarctic was divided up between nations.”

He added, "the best and only jumping-off point controlling the Wendell sea area, is the Falkland Islands.

We encouraged the Argentineans to invade the Falkland Islands in the first place when they invaded and took over the Falkland Islands with our help, it served two purposes.

One to take the political pressure off the Argentinian Government at home in Argentina, by creating an enemy, this time it was to be the British.

Two, with the Argentinian Government in control, we would have been able to control the massive mineral deposits, plus the oil and Liquid Natural Gas fields that are in the Wendell sea area, and in doing so we would be able to control the distribution of energy worldwide and therefore control the countries we want."

Voss added, "we did not expect the British to take back the Falkland Islands with force, we wanted a political settlement, and felt we had enough people in Whitehall to bring that about, as you know originally that is why we wanted to control the British government by using the Waites brothers so we could get control of the Wendell sea area, but that failed because the Waites brothers were incompetent and got greedy."

With a deathly cold look in his eyes Voss said, "I have sent a visitor to Ambassador Watson in prison by one of our friends, by now he has joined the two brothers, and with them dead, so our secret dies with them, only the people in this room now know of our plans for world domination by controlling the energy sources of the world."

Val Voss said, "now back to how we can redress our present situation, we need to keep a low profile and keep in the background and keep everything secret until we can manipulate the situation back to our advantage, we must keep a very low profile and ensure that what we are planning is kept so secret, they will think we have disappeared into the dark corners of politics.

With a little patience, we will be extraordinarily rich, very soon, so until we meet again gentlemen, I wish you good health and wealth, your usual bonuses are on the way, with a little bit extra, as you know this meeting never took place."

They all stood up shook hands and went on their way.

The seats that the American Ambassadors and the Canadian diplomats sat on were laced with a slow reaction poisonous virus once they sat on them, they would die of what would be deemed as natural causes within twenty-four to forty-eight hours.

As he left the room the Val Voss let out an evil chuckle, "they were the only ones left who knew my mother was Hitler's love child, and she was sent to a Russian prison camp, I was born from her being repeatedly raped in a prison in Siberia and she taught me how to hate with a vengeance, revenge is so sweet when it is served cold."

"Now is the time for laying low and covering my back," Voss thought, "in case the F.B.I., the Canadian Secret Service and Royal Canadian Mounted Police get together with the British M.I.6 and they get too close, the link with me died when they left the room, plus it is very satisfying to send out death, and I will enjoy the power of dealing out that revenge."

Val Voss chuckled sickly, "who would suspect that under the smoke screen of a right-wing Nazi group, named after an American Institution the *Senate*, was controlled by an ex-member of the Russian mafia?"

Lightning Source UK Ltd.
Milton Keynes UK
UKHW040636210421
382355UK00001B/53

9 780578 887210